HOW TO
DITCH
DEAD GUYS

ANN M. NOSER
AUTHOR OF *DEAD GIRL RUNNING*

A Division of **Whampa, LLC**

P.O. Box 2160

Reston, VA 20195

Tel/Fax: 800-998-2509

http://curiosityquills.com

Cover Art by Eugene Teplitsky

http://eugeneteplitsky.deviantart.com

ISBN 978-1-62007-169-4 (ebook)

ISBN 978-1-62007-177-9 (paperback)

This book is dedicated to Colleen (Schofield) Chmelik, who harassed me so much I had to write this sequel just to shut her up.

Thanks, buddy.

TABLE OF CONTENTS

Emma Roberts, 20, overeager college student and amateur witch
Objective: I've used witchcraft to raise the dead. I want to use it to solve Steve's murder, too.

Education:
a) Biology Major/Math Minor
b) 3.87 GPA at University of Wisconsin Eau Claire (72 credits completed)
c) Self-tutored, slightly over-confident Wiccan

Work Experience:
a) Campus Math Tutor
b) Conflict Resolution Manager (unpaid position) for five people I personally resurrected from the dead:
    1) Sam Metzger, 23, UW-Eau Claire pre-med student
        a) cause of death: suicidal drowning
        b) survived by: diabetic mother
    2) Jake Cunningham, 22, UW-LaCrosse frat boy
        a) cause of death: accidental drowning secondary to traumatic head injury
        b) survived by: parents and dialysis-dependent sister (Jake signed on to give her a kidney in life, but ended up giving both in death)
    3) Mike Carlson, 21, UW-Eau Claire sophomore
        a) cause of death: accidental drowning while inebriated
        b) survived by: an angry mother and bitter brother (who blame me for his death)
    4) Bernard Mundahl, 68, retired hospital manager
        a) cause of death: drowning secondary to heart attack
        b) survived by: Claire, the sweetest wife in the world and my

good friend (who knows and keeps all of my secrets, even if she doesn't approve)

5) Steven Lawrence, 22, UW-Eau Claire history major

    a) cause of death: drowning, foul play suspected, under police investigation

    b) survived by: parents; his girlfriend, Abby; and infant son, Stevie (Abby is such a good friend. I hate that, under Steve's direct orders, I've lied to her at least a million times)

PART ONE

ASHES TO ASHES

CHAPTER ONE

SECRETS

've never met anyone quite like you," Officer Walker mutters at my side, his facial expression hidden in the dark. "Disaster really *does* follow in your wake."

I view my parking job. The front half of the Lexus is buried in shrubbery. Maybe jumping the curb and off-roading down to the river wasn't such a good idea, but I had to get Mike back into the Chippewa River before he ran out of air. Now, I'm the one who can hardly breathe.

I'm left alone. Again. With all my secrets and a *Book of Shadows*.

I turn to Walker. "Yes, my life is a mess. Thanks very much for reminding me. However, I can admit that it took me three times to pass my driver's license test."

He chuckles, easing around my car to examine the mess I've made. "Remind me to never give you the keys to my truck."

"Whatever. Are you going to help me get my car out of here, or not? *Please* don't say we need to call a tow truck. I can't handle a whole bunch of questions right now. I just need to be left alone." I wring my hands. *Thank God Walker is here*—did I really just think that? Maybe I *don't* want to be left alone right now.

Walker snorts. "What's all this 'we' business? Why don't you just conjure up a witchy spell and fly it back to the parking lot?"

"Very funny." *But not a bad idea.*

After a great deal of effort, grunting, and swearing on his part, Officer Walker eases my car back up the hill and into the parking lot with the help of his truck and some heavy-duty chains. There are some things in life that witchcraft can't fix. Sometimes, witchcraft makes everything worse.

I sigh in relief. "You're a lifesaver. My dad would kill me if he knew about this." As if I care about a car. Over the past year, I've first resurrected—then lost—almost every friend I had. Except Walker, I guess. But is he really my friend? My ears buzz, as if I'm floating outside my own head. I can't believe I'm hanging out in an empty campus parking lot with a police officer in the middle of the night.

"Yeah. I'm a real hero." He hands me my keys. "Don't panic or anything, but you won't hear from me for a few days. Tomorrow I'm heading to Chicago to check out a hunch about Steve's murder. I'll call you when I get back."

"Okay." I clench the keys until the sharp edges threaten to cut my fingers. I need to feel something, even if it's pain. Otherwise, I'll go numb like always, and be half awake, half alive.

He grabs my shoulder, giving me a little shake. "You're going to be fine, Emma. Don't worry. You're stronger than you think."

I straighten my back, faking confidence I don't feel. "Of course. Get going already. What do I need you for?" *Please don't leave me alone. I don't trust myself.*

"Okay, then. Now, go home and get some sleep. You can call me if you need anything." He opens the door to his truck. "And pray for good news on my return."

"Good luck." I wave as he exits the lot. Guess he's not a mind reader. And I'm still no good at telling people when I need their help.

His truck disappears around the corner. The temporary calm I felt in Walker's presence deserts me. Although I spent a good portion of the last year running away from him, things have improved since he discovered my secrets—except for the fact that he eats all the food in my apartment every time he comes over. But Walker also has his good points—like showing up when I need him most.

Like right now, after Mike sank into the river for the *second* time. From the deserted parking lot, I stare down at the flowing waters sparkling in the moonlight and wonder what happens next. I shiver then wrap my arms around myself.

The first time Mike Carlson disappeared into the Chippewa River, I had been swimming beside him. He drowned under my watch on his twenty-first birthday. Although I was the only one who made it out alive, a part of me died that night and sank into the depths alongside him. Wishing I'd died instead, I resorted to witchcraft to resurrect him and inadvertently raised Sam, Jake, Bernard, and Steve as well.

Would I really never see any of them again?

An image of Steve's beaten and broken body being dumped into the rolling waters floods my mind. Earlier this spring, I performed a séance at the site of his murder. It's hard to believe only a month has gone by since then—so much has happened. Walker *has* to find the murderers. We need to finish the job Steve started. Otherwise nothing was worth it and nothing makes sense.

Snippets of Steve's murder scene flash through my mind as I get in the car, unsure I should even be driving. My hands shake the entire drive home. Once I get inside my apartment, I wander the quiet rooms. The place feels so empty without the souls I raised from the river. How can I live without them?

Although the beauty of the Chippewa River drew me to study at the University of Wisconsin-Eau Claire, now we are enemies. I'll never forgive the raging waters for stealing away almost everyone I care about.

My vacant apartment is too lonely to bear. I'm drawn to their room, longing for evidence that they once lived here. The book Bernard never finished rests on the bedside table, along with Steve's work schedule, and a few of Mike's candy bars. My legs tremble. There's got to be more than this empty silence. It can't end like this.

I open their bedroom closet, my chest aching. Empty hangers crash to the floor as I grab their shirts, jeans, and socks, and shove them into cardboard boxes. Mike, Bernard, and Steve won't need them anymore. I blink back tears and tape the seams shut. Then I back away and retreat to my room, head spinning.

Jake's Doors shirt sits folded in the center of my bed, but I didn't put it there.

My breath catches in my throat.

The *Book of Shadows* is taunting me again. This time about the one I miss most—Jake. Everything about that annoying frat boy haunts me. His teasing laugh. His cocky smile. The truth about his dying sister, which he didn't tell me until the last day we spent together.

Let go! You're not coming with me! Jake screamed while being dragged feet first across the snow-encrusted yard.

I lost my grip on his jacket a moment before he disappeared from my life into a gaping whirlpool of ice.

Gone forever.

I press his favorite shirt to my face and inhale deeply. The lingering scent of Jake's sporty aftershave hits me. For a moment, I can almost feel his kiss.

But then the scent fades.

I sink to my knees.

Jake is gone. They are all gone.

I fought so hard, but the river won after all.

I only hope I get a fair chance to fight back.

CHAPTER TWO

SMILE! YOU JUST MET A PAGAN

The next day, the apartment seems as barren as my empty heart. I drive over to Claire's house for company. Since she also lost her husband, Bernard, twice to the waters, I'm sure she'll know what to say to make me feel better. Or at least I'll have company feeling worse.

Claire answers the door, not one white hair of her chin-length bob out of place. "Emma, what a nice surprise. Abby's still at work, but you're welcome to come in. I'm warming up a bottle for the baby."

I step inside, glancing around. "Maybe it's a good thing Abby's not here yet. We need to talk. Mike's *gone*." My voice cracks on the last word.

"What?" Claire's eyes widen. "I thought he'd be here until the next full moon."

"Yeah. I did, too, because that's when they separated from the host body." I hide my shaking hands in my pockets. "But last night he couldn't breathe. He begged me to take him back to the river. Then he left. For good."

"I'm so sorry, Emma." She tries to pull me into a hug.

I step back, blinking against the tears and mentally forcing my stomach to settle. "Please don't. If I break down now, I won't be able to hold myself together around Abby. There's so much I've never told her."

Claire sighs. "I wish Steve would've told her the truth. I hate lying to her all the time."

"I know. And how are we going to explain Mike's disappearance?" My shoulders slump. No matter how much I trust my friend Abby, Steve insisted on keeping his identity secret, even after his son was born.

Claire tests the bottled milk on her wrist. "Even though I love the company, I think Steve's master plan was a tad unfair. At least I got to spend a night with Bernard before the river took him away again." She picks Abby's infant son out of his bouncy seat, and cuddles him in her lap. "Did Mike ever talk to Kevin?"

"No. He wanted to, at the end. But it was too late." I cringe. I'd forgotten about Kevin. Now, Mike would never get a chance to fix things with his older brother.

"That's a shame." Claire wipes a trail of milk off baby Stevie's chin.

I nod, trying to remain calm. I hate crying in front of people, and I've no intention of blubbering in Claire's sparkling clean kitchen.

Claire continues, "Steve fixed everything else. He got Bernard and me back together and gave me a second chance at raising a child. I owe him a lot for what he did for me… for all of us. I want his murderer to pay for what happened."

"Don't worry," I say, possibly trying to assure myself. "Walker will find him. With my help." I resist the urge to check my phone. Walker couldn't have called yet.

Claire raises an eyebrow. "What have you got up your sleeve now?"

I avoid her gaze, glancing out the kitchen window at the flowers in the back yard. "Not sure yet. I guess I'll find out." Good question. What *did* Walker have planned for me?

She exhales loudly. "I don't like the sound of this. Steve warned me you have 'an inadequate sense of self-preservation.' Don't do anything crazy."

Before I launch into more promises I can't keep, a familiar car pulls into the driveway.

"We can't talk about this now, because Abby's here." I cross the kitchen to peer out the side door, relieved to have an excuse to change the subject.

Abby exits the car and pulls a cell phone out of her pocket. She paces back and forth in the driveway, the phone pressed to her ear. Soon the back screen door opens and she enters.

"Good." Claire grabs the milk out of the fridge. "You're just in time for dinner, and little Stevie's done with his bottle, so you can actually eat a meal when it's warm, for a change."

Abby scowls at me, gesturing with her phone. "Our jerk landlord won't let me out of my contract. Now, I have to sublet. This sucks."

"Bummer." I feel responsible since I encouraged her to take the apartment below mine last semester. "Do you want me to put up signs on campus?" That's me. Always helpful, trying to fix everything, even though some things can't be fixed.

"Would you? That would be great." She hurries to the sink to wash her hands. "Now I need a big hug from a little boy."

Claire hands over Stevie. "I haven't burped him yet."

Abby positions him over her shoulder, gently patting his back. "I better sublet fast. I need the money."

A wave of guilt washes over me for lying to her about so many things. "I could post the notice on campus tomorrow if you write it up tonight."

Claire sets plates and silverware on the table. "Emma, I bet you can't wait until the school year is over."

I shrug. "Yeah. Sort of, but I'm taking six credits this summer, too."

"You're crazy." Abby shakes her head. "Why don't you get a part-time job instead and have fun this summer? Why be so hard core?"

"No. I need to keep up with my studies. I can't sit around doing nothing." Or I'll go crazy for sure. My foot taps the floor. I can't look Abby in the eye because I'm afraid she'll ask about Mike, and I've no idea how to explain his sudden disappearance.

"Go ahead and slave away if you want to, but it's a waste of good weather." Abby shifts side to side, cradling her son in her arms. "Once you become a doctor or lawyer or whatever your big brain decides to do, you'll wish you'd listened to me, because you'll never get summer vacation again."

"You're probably right." I smile at my friend, wishing I could tell her the truth. But I promised Steve I wouldn't. It takes a lot for me to break my promises, no matter how much they suffocate me.

Bernie, Claire's big orange cat named after her dead husband, struts into the kitchen. His purr fills the room. I give him three pats on the head, which is all he ever wants. Besides food. Lots and lots of food.

"I can put my name and number on the ad," I offer, figuring that doing favors makes up for the lies. "That way you won't have to drive all the way over to show the place."

Abby grins. "That would be awesome! You're the best. And, don't worry, I'm sure whoever moves in there won't be as much trouble for you as I was."

The next morning I head to the Student Center to post Abby's sublet notice. Halfway across the bridge, I check my phone messages. Nothing from Walker yet. It's too soon, of course, but I want to hear about Chicago. I call his number and it goes straight to voice mail. I sigh and hang up.

In the Student Center, the hallway in front of the want-ads board is crowded with students. I drop my backpack on the floor with a *thud* and dig for the flier Abby wrote up the night before. Five seconds after I post the advertisement, a young Asian woman with stylish choppy hair jabs a black fingernail at the price on the ad.

"There's a rent I can afford." Bright green letters scream from her black T-shirt: *Smile! You just met a pagan.* "You're looking to sublet?"

"Yes. I mean my friend is." I try not to stare at her shirt.

She snaps her gum. "Is it far from campus?"

"No. It's only a ten minute walk." I can't help but gawk at the word "pagan." Why does she have to be so obvious?

"Which side of the river is it on?" She stuffs a handful of other phone number slips into her pocket.

My vision clouds and I have to place a hand against the wall to keep me upright. Instead of the student center, I see Pagan Girl standing on the bridge, surrounded by flaming candles. After all, she looks a lot more like a witch than I do. I blink enough times to dispel the image, then glance down the hallway, heart racing and ready to run.

"Oh, I see the address right here." She points again. "It's just off Water Street."

"Yup." Why won't she go away?

"Okay. I'm interested." She rips off a phone number slip. "Your friend's name is Emma?"

"No, that's me." Why did I offer to do this?

"Well, Emma. Nice to meet ya." She thrusts out her hand, her wrist tinkling with crystal jewelry. "My name's Phoebe."

I shake her hand, again staring at the word "pagan" on her shirt. Why does this word make me so uncomfortable? I don't have any right to disapprove. Phoebe obviously *wants* people to know she's a witch. I don't. And somehow it feels like *her* shirt exposes *my* secret.

"Well, it's going to rain soon. I better hurry. Call ya later!" Phoebe skips away, her black hair glistening under the hallway lights.

"Then I'll be sure not to answer my phone," I mutter so low she can't hear, hoisting my heavy backpack and heading for my next class in the Science Hall. I gaze overhead at a blue sky laced with marshmallow clouds. "And I don't think it's going to rain."

After my three-hour Organic Chemistry lab, I race home through a downpour. I glance down as I cross over the bridge. Heavy drops pelt the racing river.

A pale face stares up from the depths, then another and another.

A flurry of jumbled voices call out my name, begging for help.

I narrow my eyes, tired of the river mocking me. Slapping the railing in disgust, I turn away from the rushing waters to discover candles lining the bridge, their flames blurred by the rainstorm. The rain soaks my hair and clothing. A voice penetrates the wind.

I turn toward it.

Phoebe chants in the center of the bridge, her arms raised, the rain soaking the green letters of her black T-shirt.

I shake my head to dispel the vision, and the bridge reverts to normal.

I'm just seeing things. Again.

And it's all that Smiling Pagan's fault.

CHAPTER THREE

LOVE THY NEIGHBOR

The first person to check out Abby's apartment is Carl the Cyclist. He practically knocks me over with the 500-speed bike he insists on riding through the front door of the building. As he introduces himself, I'm blinded by his zebra print Lycra shorts. So disgusting.

I avert my gaze. "Hi. I'm Emma. You can park your planet-saver over by the mail slots. Or leave it outside with all the other bikes."

He exhales sharply. "Hold on a minute. This bike probably costs more than your car. Are you sure it's safe out here in the hallway?"

I roll my eyes, already hot and cross from spending the last two hours cleaning Abby's apartment. "You can lock it if you want, but I have a Lexus in the parking lot. No one's ever touched it."

"I drive a hybrid." His nostrils flare. "Everyone should."

Thirsty from cleaning, I take a long swig of diet root beer to avoid spurting out a hostile retort.

Carl points at the can. "Did you know that every sip you take of that soda acidifies your blood, decreases lung capacity, and kills your metabolism?"

"But it tastes so *good.*" Leveling my gaze at him, I guzzle the rest of the can.

Carl scowls. "You're killing yourself right now."

I clench my jaw and move toward the apartment. *Trust me, buddy, I've done much more dangerous things than this.*

"Whew." Carl fans himself. "I just got off work and really worked up a sweat getting here on time."

I swing open the door. "Here's the place. See what you think."

Carl pauses in the doorway. "I hope you don't use any of those cancer-causing anti-perspirants." He grasps my arm with a moist hand. "Natural deodorant rocks are much safer and work just as well."

I take a deep breath, trying not to tell him to stop touching me. That's when I get a big whiff. Apparently, his deodorant rock isn't as effective as he thinks.

The next contestant in the Great Apartment Search is Tremulous Alice. She nibbles her nails nonstop.

Great. Nail bits. Now I have to vacuum again.

"Are there mice?" She grimaces.

"No."

"How about bed bugs? Fleas? Did smokers live here? Are there gangs in the parking lot? Does anyone walk big dogs past the front door?"

"I don't think so." *My blood pressure is rising. I just know it.*

She frowns, hands on hips. "You're not sure?"

I pause, pretending to think. "Not about the dogs."

She doesn't call back.

Two more weeks pass without word from Walker. I leave several unanswered messages, worried something bad happened to him. I don't want to call the station, because I don't want to draw attention to myself. Where is he? I feel like I'm at the start of a race where the starting gun never goes off. That is, except for the running part. I don't do that. Jake did. Oh, Jake.

April warms as it comes to an end. Abby panics that no one will sublet her apartment for the summer and she'll be stuck paying the full rent. My birthday passes quietly. My parents stop by for a quick visit with presents. For once, I'm not terrified they'll find something strange in my apartment.

Life has become monotonous. It would be stupid to admit that I'm bored. I should simply be grateful things are quiet, but life is so dull now. I feel myself fading into a shadow of what I could be.

One otherwise silent day, my phone rings.

"Hi. It's Phoebe. Remember me?"

"Yes." I mean no. Anyone but her. Carl didn't smell that bad and Alice would never leave the apartment if I growled like a rabid dog when I got my mail.

"Hey, listen... is that sublet still available?" Phoebe asks.

I tense, clenching the phone. Is that chanting I hear in the background? Or am I being paranoid?

The next day, Phoebe appears at the front door. This time, her bright green T-shirt proclaims: *Salem Witch Trials—I was framed!*

"Hey, I remember you!" She grins. "You're Emma—that girl with the *humongous* backpack."

She's right. My backpack practically weighs as much as I do. But why does she have to be so super-observant and have such a good memory? She's trouble. Gotta get rid of her.

"Here's the apartment." I open the door and flick on the lights. "We just finished bug-bombing it yesterday. It stunk pretty bad in here at first." I inhale dramatically. "Oh, good. The smell is gone now. That's a relief."

Phoebe sweeps into the room and spins around in a circle. "I'll put the couch right here and the bookshelf over there. Oh, this will be *perfect* for my monthly Wiccan meetings. Hey, Emma, you should come sometime. We're always looking for new members."

She obviously missed the news bulletin about the bug bombs. I'll have to try harder. "Do you have any pepper spray? There are some tough-looking guys who walk big dogs past here at night."

"That's awesome—I love dogs!" Phoebe skips into the kitchen. "This place is *so* clean—much cleaner than all the others I looked at, but they had guys living there, and guys are pigs."

Dang it. I did too good of a job. Too bad I'm such a go-getter about every stupid thing on the planet. Right now, I hate myself. Or, at the very least, am highly annoyed.

She pops into the bed and bath, then returns to the kitchen. "I'll take it. When can I move in? Is next week okay? I'm *really* getting tired of my roommate. She's way too uptight."

Crap! No, wait—it'll be okay. At least Abby has a renter now. It's only for the summer, Abby needs the money, and it's not like Phoebe is going to force me to wear one of her stupid shirts.

Probably not, anyway.

I slide open the silverware drawer, forcing a smile. "Here's the contract. Fill it out and mail it to this address. Once you're approved, I'll give you the keys."

"Where do you live? Wait. Let me Guess." She raises a finger to point overhead. "Directly upstairs from this apartment?"

Her accuracy is uncanny. I consider lying, but figure she'd find out. "Yes, upstairs in apartment six."

"I thought so." My newest neighbor grins, grabs the contract, and waltzes out the door, her black hair gleaming in the sun.

I'm going to have to stay away from that girl. She'll see right through me, and I can't have that.

My plans to stay away from Phoebe dissolve at the sight of a long trail of shabby cardboard boxes leading from the front door of the apartment building all the way to her rusty Volkswagen van. I grab an armful of packages and knock on her half-open door. A hint of incense tickles my nose.

"Come in," she calls. "Oh, Emma, it's so nice of you to help. Sorry about all my stuff out there. I'm super slow about moving. It takes me *forever* to decide where to put everything. What do you think? I thought I'd start with the wall hangings."

She points at a Celtic pentacle tapestry. The image both repels and intrigues me. Fighting the urge to be drawn into her world, I back away and bump into a rickety bookshelf. Colored candles and witchcraft books tumble to the floor.

"Oh no! I'm so sorry." Scrambling around on my hands and knees to gather the fallen volumes, I pause, catching my breath as I recognize a few familiar titles. My own witchcraft books remain hidden in an unmarked box under the bed. The only two people left in town who know about my "gift" are Claire and Officer Walker, and that's how I'd like to keep it. Except Walker's still not in town. Where is he?

Incense clogs my throat. I can't breathe. I've got to get out of here. She can't know about me. I can't trust her; she's way too obvious. I make a beeline for the door, close to hyperventilating. "Sorry to drop and run, but I've got a zillion things to do. Have fun unpacking. See ya."

Phoebe raises a pierced eyebrow. "You bet. I know where you live now."

I escape into the hallway to catch my breath and check my mail. A letter from Jake's younger sister, Laura, waits in the mail slot. Desperate for a lifeline, I rip it open with shaking hands then pause, worried she'll have bad news. What if her kidneys—Jake's kidneys actually—have started to fail? What if she's sick again? Her news that she's been accepted here at UW-Eau Claire puts a smile on my face.

My smile fades as I read about her dog.

We're taking Nani into the vet tomorrow. She won't eat anything. I thought at first she was depressed about Jake, but when she started peeing all over the house, I knew something was wrong. I hope there's something they can do for her. I don't want to lose her, too.

I unlock my apartment door and nudge it open with my foot. The answering machine light blinks, but I finish Laura's letter first.

Then I hit play.

"Emma, it's Officer Walker. There's been another murder, and I need your help."

CHAPTER FOUR

THE STRANGLING

I call Walker right away, heart in my throat. My words come out in a rush. "Hey, did you figure out who killed Steve?"

He groans. "No, I'm afraid not. Plus, now I'm way behind at work. Listen, Emma, I called because I need your help with a *different* murder case, okay? Be ready to perform a séance in ten—no, make that five minutes."

"What?" My head spins with both excitement and dread. "I can't get ready that fast. I haven't researched the murder, I don't have my supplies organized, and I'm not centered at all."

He sighs. "Come on, Emma. This is important. And don't worry about it—you're a natural. Just grab your stuff and let's go."

I need a moment. "It's not that easy—"

"I'm getting in the truck right now. No more excuses. You promised you'd help, remember?"

"Fine, then." I hang up with a scowl. "I make the stupidest promises sometimes."

I race around gathering candles, parchment, and my *Book of Shadows*. I hate being rushed. It makes me sweat in an uncomfortable, non-athletic way.

Seven minutes later, Walker honks in the parking lot, peering up at my apartment through his windshield.

"I've got everything, right? Yes." I glance around the living room before dashing out the door.

Officer Walker gets out of his truck wearing jeans, a navy striped polo, and his ever-present cowboy boots. "Can we take your car?" He stretches from side to side in the parking lot. "I just drove back from Chicago, and your Lexus will blend into the victim's neighborhood better."

I shake a finger at him. "Promise you won't question my driving skills *or* choice in music."

He raises a dark eyebrow. "Try to remember that your car is *not* an off-road vehicle, okay?"

"You're so funny, I almost laughed." I open the massive Coach purse Mom gave me last Christmas. Three candles fall out as I dig for my car keys.

Walker bends down to pick them up.

"I didn't know you were such a gentleman." I shove them back into the purse, beep open the locks, and climb inside.

"And I didn't know you wore such hip outfits." He nods at my sporty attire. "Your mom must've picked that one out."

"Yes, Mr. Smarty. I got it for my birthday. While you were gone in Chicago and didn't keep me posted about anything, I might add." I pull out of the parking spot. "I don't usually like the clothes she chooses for me, but this fabric feels like butter. It's so comfortable."

"Then a happy belated birthday to you, and thanks for driving." He points to the left. "Go down Clairemont, then head south on 53 past Oakwood Mall. They've put the house on the market, so there's no time to waste."

"Okay. Got it. But before you tell me any more about *this* murder, I want to hear all about Chicago." I tap on the steering wheel as we speed away from campus.

He sighs and shakes his head. "The whole thing was a wash. Couldn't find even a trace of the gang I suspected. It's like they went underground, disappeared. The last six to eight months there's been zero criminal activity attributed to them in the area. It's like they knew

I was coming. I swear—every time I think I've found a lead, it's another dead end."

"Well, that sucks." Acid pools in my stomach. What if we never find out who killed Steve?

He exhales slowly. "Yes. It does."

I square my shoulders. Time to think positive. "Don't worry. You'll figure it out. Hey, maybe after we're done with this case, I could help you with Steve's murder again." Because that's what I really care about.

He taps his fingers on his jeans. "That's a good idea. I'll get the steel rod out of evidence storage."

Ugh, that awful bent rod. I hate that thing. "Good. Then it's a date."

He holds up a hand of protest. "Wait a minute—"

I smile at the grimace on his face. "Relax, Old Man, I'm just kidding. You're at least *twenty* years older than me."

"More like ten," he grumbles. "And don't let your rich mama hear you talking about dating a thirty-something, black cop from Eau Claire, Wisconsin."

I have to laugh. "Trust me, she'd rather I be dating you than doing what we're *really* up to."

He glances over, eyes wary.

"Mom can't ever know that I'm a witch. She'd have a heart attack."

He chuckles. "Then maybe you should consider majoring in something besides spell-casting."

"I can't even think about her finding out." Because I'd rather die than deal with her disappointment. "Let's focus on your murder case instead."

"Okay. Listen up. There have been several murders in the state this year, but the M.O. for two of them was the same. Both Eva Garcia and Jennifer Pearson were wealthy, middle-aged women strangled at night in their own master suite. Jewelry and electronic equipment were stolen from the premises, perhaps to use burglary as a cover for the murder, because all attempts to identify the attacker by tracing serial numbers and searching Internet sales have failed."

I focus on driving, but my mind is racing. "What about fingerprints or other evidence?"

"I just love it when you watch cop shows," Walker says dryly. "The murderer left no clues. Otherwise, I wouldn't be asking for your help."

"So you want me to do a revealing spell right in the house?"

"Yes. In Eva Garcia's bathroom, to be exact. Like you did for Steve's murder. So I can view the details of the crime."

I shiver, remembering the van, the spray-painted Smiley Face, and the gang that bludgeoned Steve to death before discarding his body in the river. Like watching a horror film where I knew the victim personally, but couldn't do anything to stop the worst from happening right in front of my eyes.

"I didn't have time to write a new spell, so I brought the old one. What if it doesn't work?" I haven't done any witchcraft in a long time. What if I do something wrong?

"Why wouldn't it work? It did last time."

My shoulders tense. "I've only done this once before, remember? It's not like I'm a professional witch, or something."

"Are there professional witches? Maybe I should hire one." He chuckles at his own joke, like always. "Just give it a try, Emma. That's all I ask. Since they've put the house on the market, this might be my last chance to view the crime scene."

"I'm surprised you got clearance for this."

He stares out the window, whistling. "Take the *next* left, okay?"

I pause at a stop sign. "You *do* have permission, right?"

He avoids my direct gaze. "I don't need permission."

"Why not?" I'm not taking my foot off the brake until he answers.

"Because I have the keys." He twirls them on his finger.

"Whatever you say." I ease off the brake. "You're the cop. I can't get in trouble if I'm with you, right?"

"That's right." He nods in time to the music on the radio.

"So, tell me more about the case. You said Eva was killed in the bathroom?"

"Actually, the victim's body was discovered in her bed, but forensics suggests that she was killed in the bathroom. I don't want to divulge any more details. I wouldn't want to influence whatever images your voodoo can show us."

My eyes narrow. "It's not voodoo." It's better than that.

"Whatever you want to call it, I'm cool with it." He points at a stone front McMansion. "Pull in here."

I park in the driveway next to a red and white "for sale" sign in the yard. I step out of the car and feel a sudden chill in the air.

"Brrr." Goosebumps cover my arms as my gaze catches on the long white curtains swaying in a closed window on the second floor.

Walker gives me an odd look. "How can you be cold? It's blazing hot today."

I point at the swinging drapes. "Is that the master bedroom?"

The instant Walker looks up, the curtains stand still.

"Yes." He glances back at me. "How did you know?"

"Are you *sure* no one else is here?" The hairs stand up on the back of my neck.

"Shouldn't be." Walker focuses on the set of keys as he strolls toward the front door, leaving me behind to stare at the bedroom window.

My heart stutters as the shadow of a head passes behind the curtain then disappears.

I rush after Walker, grabbing his arm as he reaches the front stoop. "Someone's up there. I swear to God."

"No way." He unlocks the door. "We're alone. Trust me."

A black moth flutters out the open doorway. It lands on my shoulder, and I brush it away. Walker steps inside.

The second I cross the threshold, a low voice growls in my ear, "*Get out.*"

I grab Walker's shirt. "Did you hear that?"

"Hey, stop messing up my shirt." He smoothes the creases as I release my grip. "What's wrong with you?"

My heart beats erratically. "That creepy man's voice... Didn't you hear it?"

"No." He starts up the stairs. "There's nobody else here, Emma. Don't act so paranoid."

Obediently, I follow him, listening intently to every sound. Once we enter the master suite, I drop my heavy purse on the floor. Still wary, I construct a Magic Ring of candles in the bathroom. I light each candle in succession. The little flames flicker timidly in the brightness pouring through the skylight above. The parchment paper crinkles in my sweaty hands.

"I'm ready." I take a deep breath.

Officer Walker leans against the glossy black and white tiled wall of the bathroom. "Go ahead. I'm watching."

My body warms as I read the familiar words:

"Reveal to me
The treachery.
Expose the crime
From back in time.
Bring forth, bring down
Let truth be found.
Draw back the veil
That hides the tale.
Make known the fear
That once lived here."

We wait.

And wait.

And wait.

Walker clears his throat. "Why isn't anything happening?"

"I don't know." I check that all the candles are still lit.

"What did you do wrong?"

I glare at him, then jump at a sudden sing-song voice from below.

"Hellll-ooo! Is somebody up there?"

"What the Hell?" Walker storms out of the master suite, leaving me alone.

The second he disappears, the bathroom door slams shut behind him.

The temperature inside the room plummets.

I glance up and watch an oily black film ooze down to cover the skylight.

The room darkens. It's like I'm standing in a cave.

Candles flicker and crackle to life as if startled awake.

The shower behind me starts to drip. I spin around and squint through the wavy glass. My fingers stick to the frosty handle when I open the shower door. Thick, scarlet blood oozes down the walls and pools on the tiled shower floor.

A ceramic cup spins counter-clockwise on the sink across the room. It twirls faster and faster, scratching on the enamel. The matching soap dish hovers in the air for a moment, then shoots straight toward my head.

I duck just in time as the dish smashes into the wall over my head and fractures into pieces.

A firm pressure chokes my throat, closing off my air supply. I claw at my neck but there's nothing to grab, nothing to pull away.

I try to scream for Walker, but my throat has snapped shut. I collapse onto the slippery tiles.

Black mist surrounds me, pushing in from all sides.

Gasping for air, I writhe upon the cold tile floor, choking on the smoky air.

From the shower, a golden snake approaches, undulating across the tiles.

The mist disperses with a flick of its tail.

His unblinking black eyes stare into mine.

The bathroom door swings back open, and Walker bursts into the room. "The stupid realtor is here—can you believe it?"

The pressure on my throat ceases immediately. I heave, gulping big breaths, then start to choke and cough, my lungs and ribs spasming.

"What are you doing on the floor?" Walker asks, gawking down at me.

I struggle to get into a sitting position then collapse against the tile wall, panting as if I've been kicked in the stomach. The room is silent, except for my gasps for air. The cup freezes in place and the soap dish sits innocently next to it. The shower walls shine as if scrubbed clean. The skylight is clear again, letting in the summer sunshine.

Even the snake has disappeared.

Like magic.

What the Hell just happened?

"Emma, you're shaking!" He grabs my arm to steady me. "What's wrong? Are you okay?"

I open my mouth to explain but a chilling voice interrupts.

"Don't say a word. I'm watching you," a male, but not quite human, voice warns.

"I'm just cold," I lie. "Doesn't it feel chilly in here to you?"

"No, it feels fine. The rich like to over-air-condition everything. Listen, we better get out of here, or that realtor is going to have my ass on a china plate."

"Okay." Trembling from head to foot, I stumble around the room extinguishing the filthy black smoke rising from the candles. "Where am I going to put these? They're still hot."

Walker watches me work without comment.

"Why aren't you helping?" I ask, shivering uncontrollably. "You said we had to hurry."

"The smoke is following you." His dark eyes scan the room. "Did you turn on a fan or something?"

"No, but that's a good idea." I flip on the bathroom ventilation and the lingering smoke trails vanish. "What are you going to tell the realtor?"

"I haven't figured that out yet." He hurries through Eva's bedroom.

I follow, warm candles soothing my cold hands. As we cross the bedroom, a large empty spot on the wall catches my eye. It doesn't look right. Something's out of place. Or perhaps missing is the better word.

I stop and point. "What used to be there?"

Walker pauses. "I don't know. Why?"

"Hold on. Give me a minute to focus." I glance around the rest of the room, which seems normal. Then I turn back to the open wall. For a moment, a black shiny surface covers the space. Then it disappears again. "Eva died because somebody wanted whatever used to hang there."

Walker steps closer, staring at the empty spot on the wall. "I don't remember any paintings or artwork listed as missing, but I'll look into it." He turns back to me. "Okay. Now we better go."

We descend the stairs as I hide the warm candles behind my back. An over-accessorized woman tenses as we approach. She forces a smile, showing far too many teeth.

"May I speak with the two of you *privately* for a moment?" she asks, fake-sugar-sweet and grips both our arms to escort us out of her clients' earshot. Her metal bracelets clank together as she hurries us into the next room.

"What are you doing here?" she demands. "I'll never be able to sell this house if you police-folk keep sniffing around. I thought you were done here. It's been months already."

I look to Walker for help, but he avoids my gaze. I guess it's up to me.

I clear my throat and shake off the fact that I'm still freezing to death. "I have an idea." Before the realtor can protest, I stride back toward the lofty foyer. With my costly bag and buttery-soft athletic attire, I know I can pull this off.

"Isn't it lovely here?" I grin with perfect teeth at the potential customers, thankful for my years of braces. "I always adored this house. Such a spacious kitchen."

They eye me suspiciously. Perhaps they've spotted the candles behind my back.

"I'll intrude no longer," I continue airily. "Just wanted to check on my favorite cousin's house. Be sure to take in the wonderful view from the breakfast nook." I head for the front door, walking backward so they can't see what's hidden in my hands.

Walker chuckles as we head for the car.

"What's so funny?" I dig in my purse for the keys.

"Didn't you notice the family photos? Eva Garcia was a Brazilian supermodel."

"So?"

"You claimed she was your cousin, and as my momma would say 'Honey, you're as white as a ghost.'"

I make a face. "Maybe I'm adopted."

"I would believe that. You don't look much like your mom." He smirks. "She's hot. You look like your dad with a ponytail stuck on the back of your head like a hippie."

"Very funny. The only reason I'm not kicking you right now is because the realtor is still watching us through the window."

He turns to give her a half-wave. She *doesn't* smile back, which makes him laugh even harder. "Just kidding, Emma. Sorry I made you drive all the way out here for nothing."

Why didn't Walker see the bloody shower and the spinning cup? Now that we're outside the spooky house maybe I can explain...

"Hey, Walker—" I begin, and my internal organs turns to ice.

An invisible hand crushes my throat as the inhuman voice warns: *"Keep quiet or he'll get hurt. You'll watch it happen. And it will be all your fault."*

Gulping air, I crumple against the door of the Lexus.

"Emma, are you okay?" He whacks me a good one across my back.

"Ouch!" I choke and cough on hands and knees. "Was that really necessary?"

"You tell me. You're the one acting bizarre." Walker stands up. "What happened to you in there? You look awful."

"Nothing," I say. I thought lying to Walker was over, but here I go again.

"Are you sure?" he asks, leaning in like a protective mother hen.

"Yes." I wave him away. "Just give me some breathing room already."

"Fine." He reaches out a hand. "Then give me the keys. I'm driving."

"Good idea." I pass over the keys, which jangle together noisily in my trembling hand.

"Seriously. What's wrong with you?" He throws me a you're-one-strange-chick look. "Did you choke on your gum or something?"

"No." I stand, bracing my hand on the Lexus. "I wasn't chewing gum, but that doesn't matter. I trip when there's no bump in the sidewalk, too." The automatic excuse flies out of my mouth.

"Uh-huh." Walker watches me a moment, apparently not convinced. "Let's get you home."

"Yes. Please." Take me home where I'll be safe.

Back in my apartment, I pace like a caged animal. I decide a jog might clear my head (that's what Jake would do, anyway) and head outside. Naturally unathletic, I run in short spurts and pant-walk the rest of the way to the bridge over the Chippewa River. Gripping the railing, I peer down as if one of the dead souls I resurrected might climb up and explain why my magic didn't work today.

Every spell I performed last year worked perfectly. Well, maybe not perfectly, but close enough. In trying to bring Mike back from the dead, I brought four other spirits along with him. But my early spring thaw and the séance at Steve's murder site had both been quite effective.

Have I lost control of my powers?

As the sun sinks toward the horizon, I trudge home. Back in the apartment, I strip off my running clothes, yank out my ponytail, and drop the elastic into my Grandma's bowl on my dresser.

"Oh, crap!" I hit my head with my hand. "No wonder the spell didn't work. I forgot to bring Grandma's bowl along. Man, I'm an idiot."

I jump into the shower, relieved to have figured out what went wrong. Toweling off after, I notice a strange smell, like a pan burning. Black smoke pours into the bathroom. An unseen force knocks me over, slamming my head onto the tiled floor.

A golden snake with dark shining eyes slithers out of the shower to slide across my wet skin and enfold me in its embrace. My legs jerk uncontrollably, feet slipping and sliding on the tile floor.

I whimper as the snake twists around my arm, scales cold as ice. His black eyes stare into mine, like the first time, but only for a moment before the scaled head dives down to impale my wrist with icy teeth. I try to scream, but the snake wraps tight around my neck, choking off my breath.

I fight to breathe, coughing on the putrid air.

The snake releases his hold, and I claw at the blackness. Desperate for water, I drag myself to the sink. An inhuman screech fills the room and bounces off the walls. A shrieking face with crooked front teeth appears in the steam-coated mirror, then morphs into the Smiley Face spray-painted at the site of Steve's murder.

I back away, choking on what feels like ash stuck in my throat.

The bite wound burns. Above the pierced skin, a metal snake-shaped bracelet encircles my wrist. I shiver at the golden image of a snake consuming its own tail.

What the Hell is this, a hallucination?

The smoke and the bracelet vanish, but two bite marks remain on the tender flesh of my inner wrist. I raise a hand to my tender, already bruising throat.

The truth becomes clear.

This time around, I won't just watch what happened.

I'll live it.

CHAPTER FIVE

WHERE THERE'S SMOKE

stagger to the kitchen, brush off a dark moth resting on the phone, and dial Walker's number. When he picks up, I don't even bother saying hello. "I saw who killed Eva."

"Wha...?" His voice is muffled, like I interrupted him mid-sandwich.

"I... had a vision," I explain. What else would you call it? I swat at the same moth, now fluttering over my head. How did it get in here?

"Okay." He swallows and his voice clears. "I'll be right there."

I glance around my apartment and tremble. "Please hurry."

"I'll bring you to the station to sort through mug shots."

"Okay." I nod, even though he can't see me. Right now, I'd do just about anything to get out of my apartment. I don't want to be alone. Shaking, I force myself back into the bathroom, slip on my glasses, and face the mirror. The attacker's image and the Smiley Face have disappeared. A filmy shadow hovers near my reflection in the mirror, faint as cobwebs. I narrow my eyes to focus, and the ghostly image disappears.

Only the bruises remain. Ugly maroon blossoms cover my shoulders, upper chest, and neck. I hurry into the bedroom, dig out a turtleneck from last winter, and flinch in pain while pulling it over my head.

Time for a disguise.

Once we reach the police station, it doesn't take me long to identify the murderer. The slight parting of his slim lips reveals the tell-tale crooked teeth. His computer image swirls with smoke.

"That's him!" I exclaim, suppressing a cough.

Walker leans over my shoulder. The smoke dissipates the second he glances at the screen.

He lets out a low whistle. "That's strange."

"What's strange?" I hack and sputter all over the place. How unhygienic. How come only I can see and choke on the smoke?

"He's got the same snake tattoo as the gang I went to investigate. Looks like he likes to go by the name of 'Shadow.' What the heck's he doing all the way up here?"

"Well... I haven't told you everything yet..." I pause, waiting for the creepy voice to interrupt with a warning, but it doesn't. "I think this creep killed both Eva *and* Steve."

Walker's eyes widen. "Too bad this guy's blood wasn't in the van. I'll need evidence to prove their murders are connected."

"Trust me. They are. I saw a Smiley Face in the vision—just like the one they painted on the tree after they threw Steve in the river."

Walker scratches his head. "Okay. I'll keep pushing the gang theory for Steve. As far as Eva's death is concerned, this rules out the ex-husband. He's been the prime suspect until now."

I shake my head. "He didn't have anything to do with it. It was this guy with the crooked teeth."

"Okay, I believe you, but I gotta *find* this guy before I can do anything about it. And that won't be easy. He probably disappeared along with the others." Walker scribbles on a scrap of paper and slips it into his pocket. "Don't worry. I'll handle it. Come on, I owe you dinner."

I stand up too quickly, then stifle a flinch of pain. "Let's go. I'm hungry. You know how we college students love free food." I smile, trying to keep the mood and my voice light. I have to keep Walker from asking too many questions.

Walker frowns as we drive off in his truck. "I don't understand why *I* couldn't see the vision this time. It wasn't that way with Steve."

I stare at him. Wait. Doesn't he believe me? Maybe I should try again to tell him the whole truth.

When I open my mouth to explain, something sticks tight in my throat, like a cork in a bottle. My mouth opens and shuts like a fish while I struggle to speak. Walker's too deep in thought to notice. After a few more futile attempts, I slouch back in the car seat, defeated.

At the restaurant, I can barely keep my eyes open. My words begin to slur.

"I better get you home," Walker says. "You look beat."

I nod and wince. I'm beat all right, in more ways than one.

Walker drives in silence. As we approach my apartment, I hesitate. Will the horrors return, or am I safe now that the killer has been identified? The cops can take over now, right? I almost ask Walker to come inside, but chicken out. After all, I don't want to give him the wrong idea.

After a thorough search of my apartment, I dress for bed. I get under the covers, then fling them off. Crossing the room to my witchcraft supplies, I grab my *Book of Shadows*. Maybe this will protect me. I slip my book under my pillow, drop into bed, and close my eyes, resting a hand on the soft cover.

After tossing and turning all night, I wake up exhausted. I swear every dead person I ever saw in the past visited my crazy dreams last night. Except for the five I raised. I'd love to see them again and maybe Elsie, the Laura Ingalls lookalike from my childhood. But I guess no one chooses their own dreams, which is a shame.

My bruises ache even worse than the night before. After choking down double the recommended dose of ibuprofen, I lounge around watching chick flicks. Even pointing the remote hurts. I'm going to move as little as possible today. No more running, that's for sure.

An eager pounding on my apartment door interrupts my plans to vegetate. Crap. Who could that be? Stifling a groan, I gimp over and crack open the door.

"Hi, Emma." Phoebe bounces in the hallway. "I'm glad you're home."

"What's up?" I clutch a blanket around me. Go away. You're too dang perky.

"Tonight I'm hosting our monthly Wicca meeting. Why don't you join us? It's a wonderful, life-affirming experience and *such* a healthy lifestyle."

I consider my injuries. Wicca is a healthy lifestyle, you say? Healthy, my butt.

"All I ask is an hour of your time." Phoebe's grin makes me feel like she's selling me a used car. With purple flowers painted on it.

I sigh. Where does she get all this energy?

She points downstairs. "It's conveniently located."

"So is my television." I glance toward it longingly.

"Please, Emma. Just give it a chance."

"Fine," I grumble, to make her go away.

"Great! See you soon." She grins and scoots away too fast for me to change my mind.

My last ibuprofen dose wanes as I join the eager spiritualists. Phoebe's black dress matches her glossy hair. She lights a ring of candles on a low table. There are only three other girls in attendance, all a little too over the top with their joy at my presence. They must be eager to add more members to their meager monthly meetings. They make every attempt to include me in their discussions about witchcraft books they read, websites they visited, and spells they performed. I tune out their talk about love spells, but perk up when they discuss ways to decrease menstrual cramping.

"Hey," I interrupt. "Do any of those spells really work?"

They all stare at me as if I have three heads, all of them unattractive. Apparently, that was the wrong thing to say.

"Does the incense bother you?" a pretty blonde asks.

"Or do you have asthma?" questions a red head.

Phoebe narrows her eyes. "Did you say you couldn't breathe?"

"What?" I shake my head, wincing at the sharp flash of pain in my neck. What are they talking about? "No. The candles are fine."

"Maybe we misheard you," Phoebe offers.

The others gawk for a moment, then turn back to their conversation. Even though she defended me, Phoebe's gaze keeps flicking back in my direction.

I glance at the clock, begging time to move faster. I never should have agreed to attend this stupid meeting. All these wanna-be witches don't know what they're talking about. Heck, I'm probably the only one here who has actually contacted the dead. Voices murmur in my head, getting louder, making it difficult to focus. I search for an escape, but am surrounded by eager wiccans and lit candles. Tufts of smoke curl off and sail in my direction. The spirits are coming for me, and I've no idea how to fight them.

"What's that noise?" a woman whispers in my ear. I turn to look, but no one's there.

Phoebe sets down her glass. "What did you say, Emma?"

"Nothing. I didn't say anything." I start to sweat. Did I bring a ghost with me to this meeting? I glance around, praying hard that a snake doesn't pop its head out of Phoebe's bowl of organic hors d'oeuvres.

"Is somebody out there?" My heart begins to race.

"Did I set the alarm?" I feel Eva's panic, the fear rising in her throat.

"Somebody's in the bedroom!" I'm going to die, just like Eva did.

The soda in my hand sloshes onto the floor.

"What should I do? Where can I hide?"

Phoebe's apartment disappears and I'm back in Eva's bathroom with nowhere to hide and no weapon for protection. I grab a can of hairspray and spin around to face him with my finger on the button, nailing the intruder in the eyes. He screams in anger; his arms flail to cover his face. I race past him out the door, but he grabs my shoulder, and slams me to the floor.

"I can't breathe. I can't breathe. I can't..." I gasp for air, choking, coughing.

The vision clears.

I'm back with the Wiccans.

Wide-eyed and open-mouthed, Phoebe and the others stand over me as a huge black moth hovers over my gaping mouth.

I scramble to my feet. "Sorry, I think the incense *is* getting to me." I flee the party, stumbling over collapsed cardboard boxes in an effort to escape.

Somehow Phoebe reaches the door before I do. She thrusts a plastic bag filled with dried herbs in my hands. "It's rosemary." She arches a pierced eyebrow. "To encourage peaceful dreams."

"Thanks." I grab the parcel before pushing past her. How does she know about my nightmares? I hurry upstairs to my apartment, breathing hard and rubbing my sore neck. The answering machine blinks as I sprint to the cupboard for more ibuprofen to calm the fire inside.

My cell phone rings.

"Leave me alone!" I growl before swallowing the pills without water. My throat constricts. I groan in pain then grab the phone. "What do you want?"

"Hey, Emma. I'm calling to congratulate you." I can almost see Walker smirk.

"What for?"

"I heard that the realtor sold Eva's house to the couple."

"Good for her." I rub my neck, wincing.

"They really liked *the view*." Walker chuckles. "You must've convinced them. Hey, maybe you've found a new profession. Your mom would like that."

"Not interested." I grab the countertop with my jittery hands, sweat beading on my forehead. "What about the killer? Any luck finding him?" Because then maybe these visions would stop.

"No. After murdering Eva last summer, the 'Shadow' disappeared along with his gang down in Chicago."

My hands tremor and my heart quivers. "What are you going to do about that?"

"Don't know... but at least I discovered what used to hang in that empty space on the wall in her bedroom."

"You did? What was it?" Maybe this will help me.

"Her Brazilian relatives reported that a black obsidian mirror used to hang there." He pauses. "Does that mean anything to you?"

"Obsidian." I recall my witchcraft research. "It's a shiny, black stone that's supposed to ward off evil spirits."

"I guess it didn't work very well for Eva." Walker sounds sad.

"No. It didn't." I shiver, rubbing my arms with my hands. "I wish you could've found the killer."

"Me, too."

"I'm sorry I'm not more help." What a ridiculous thing to say. Guilt is my main emotion sometimes. That and fear.

"Hey, at least you tried. I still owe you. How about dinner?"

"Where are we going?" I ask, even though the only place I want to be is unconscious on my couch. That is, if the spirits will leave me alone.

"How about my place tomorrow night? Seven o'clock sharp."

His place? That's weird. "Can you cook?"

"Don't worry, oh Queen of the Noodle Casserole. I'm a gourmet chef."

"That's funny." I gaze at the ibuprofen bottle in my hand, wishing it were something stronger and more effective. "Then why are you always eating my food?"

He hangs up, laughing.

I turn down the hallway to the bathroom. Gritting my teeth, I push in the door. The cup spins on the counter, and a black moth flutters on the mirror.

I turn right around, grab my keys, and flee the apartment.

Ten minutes later, I pull into Claire's driveway. Abby sits on a blanket in the backyard, holding her baby. She waves me over, but for a few minutes I can't do anything but sit and breathe. I finger the fabric of my turtleneck, tensing when I come close to the bruises.

I can do this. I can be normal around regular people. Regular as in non-dead, non-scary people, that is.

Finally, I get out of the car, legs shaking only a touch. Nobody else would probably notice. I force myself to smile as I approach.

"Hey there, Emma," Abby calls out. "I didn't know you were coming over tonight."

"Sorry I didn't call first." I enter the back garden. "Hope you don't mind me barging in on you."

"Of course not. I'm glad to see you. " Abby glances toward my car. "Where's Sam-Jake hiding out these days? I haven't heard from him in weeks."

"Um… he went home for the summer."

"That's odd. Why'd he leave without saying good-bye? It's kind of rude, actually."

I swallow. My befuddled mind can't come up with a good lie, so I go with the first thing that flies out of my mouth. "He said his grandma was sick."

The screen door squeaks. Claire pauses on the top step with two glasses of lemonade in her hands, her face unreadable.

"Really?" Abby glances up. "I thought his mom had cancer. At least that's what Claire said."

"No. That's Mi—" I raise my hand to my mouth, realizing my mistake.

"Abby, don't you think—" Claire speaks at the same time.

Abby interrupts. "It's too bad Sam's whole family is sick. I should send him a card. Maybe two cards. Do you have his address?"

Claire and I exchange glances.

"Never mind." Abby shakes her head. "I'm not stupid. I know when I'm being lied to. And if neither of you are willing to trust me, I'll figure it out on my own."

"It's not that I don't trust you—" Tears spring to my eyes. The last thing I want is to hurt Abby. She's been hurt enough as it is.

Abby levels me with a stare. "It sure feels that way."

"I already explained it to her." Claire sets down the lemonade on a small metal table. "We're not free to tell any more than we have already."

Abby glares at both of us in turn. "That's not much of an explanation, if you ask me."

"But we made a promise," I try to explain. Steve wouldn't even like the fact that we're having this conversation, but I can't tell Abby that, either.

Abby cocks her head to the side. "Because breaking promises is a big no-no, but lying to me repeatedly doesn't bother either of you?"

Claire catches my eye. Abby has a point. Maybe it's time. I open my mouth, ready to forget Steve's directions and tell Abby everything when I notice a young girl in a gingham dress, standing in the garden behind Abby.

"Emma, what are you staring at?" Abby turns to look. "There's nothing there. What is it? What's wrong with you?"

The young girl raises a finger to her lips. She speaks without moving her mouth. Her words echo in my head, *Keep quiet or they'll get hurt.*

I shiver, as if my blood has frozen within my veins.

Claire grabs my arm. "Emma, you're pale as a ghost. Are you okay?"

Her touch burns. My throat closes, but not before I get out the name "Elsie."

"Who's Elsie?" Abby asks as the sky darkens.

My legs melt beneath me and I collapse.

"She's obviously not getting enough sleep." Claire's voice floats above me.

"Are you sure that's it?" Abby asks, her voice suspicious. "That was bizarre. What on earth did she see out there?"

"She didn't see anything." Claire's voice again, cutting through the darkness. "There was nothing there."

"I thought she was going to have a seizure. Shouldn't we take her to the hospital?"

I want to argue, to get up, and demand to be left alone. I don't want to see any doctors. But I can't move. Is this what dying feels like? Maybe it would be nice to be done, to rest.

No, not that. I'm not finished.

There's more I can do.

Except I'm so tired now. I'll fight later.

"No. Let her sleep here on the couch tonight." Claire tucks a blanket around my shivering shoulders. "Poor dear. I'll keep an eye on her, Abby. Don't you worry."

CHAPTER SIX

WALKER ALWAYS APPRECIATES HIS MOMMA

The clock reads 6:40 when I wake up the next day. I stumble into Claire's kitchen. She's alone feeding Stevie.

"Wow. I slept a long time." I rub my face. "It's already morning."

Claire frowns. "Emma, it's already *evening*. Around noon, Abby tried to convince me to call 9-1-1 before she headed off for work, but I held her off."

"Thank goodness." I plop down at the kitchen table, glancing at the clock again. "It's almost 7 p.m.? I'm going to be late." I jump up and grab a glass of water, careful not to stumble. I'm not sure I trust my feet yet.

"For what?" Claire asks.

"I gotta go to Walker's." I down the whole glass, even though swallowing still hurts.

"He can wait." She pushes a chair toward me. "You sit down right now and tell me what's going on."

"There's no time." I grab my car keys and race to the car.

"What's your hurry?" she yells as the screen door slams behind me. "You shouldn't be driving!"

I shove the key in the ignition and pause. What is my hurry? I don't even know. But I've got to go. I can't sit still. I rev the engine and pull out of the drive. Fifteen minutes later, I arrive on Walker's doorstep.

As I approach the front door, I glance down at my rumpled, slept-in clothes. I attempt to smooth my hair, not that I'm worried what Walker thinks of my appearance. I ring the doorbell twice before he answers.

"Emma?" Walker opens the door with a puzzled expression on his face. "What are you doing here?"

"It's 7 o'clock. Don't you remember inviting me to dinner?" My neck and shoulders pick this exact moment to spasm. I should've taken more ibuprofen.

"And who's this?" A plump woman barges into the doorway. Even though she barely stands five feet tall, her attitude towers over both of us.

"Mom, I'd like you to meet someone," Walker mumbles, a sheepish expression on his face. "This is Emma Roberts. She's... uh... interested in police work."

"Is she, now?" Mother Walker puts her hands on her ample hips.

My forehead throbs. I am so not up for this.

"Why don't you come in?" Her words are a command, not a question.

What can I do but obey?

"*Charlie* didn't mention he was having an extra guest for dinner tonight." She sighs dramatically. "I guess his mother and sisters aren't enough company for him anymore."

Walker crosses the living room with long strides and flops into a chair at the kitchen table. "Sorry, Mom, I forgot."

I wait for Walker to apologize to me, too; but his mouth stays shut and he avoids eye contact. That's real nice of him. Plus, his place looks like *That 70s Show*. This is so not cool. The carpet is green. The walls have patterned orange wallpaper. And all the trim is dark and narrow. Walker wears cowboy boots and drives a truck, but lives like this? It's so weird.

"I'll get you a plate." Mother Walker grabs my shoulder and directs me into a chair at the dinner table, igniting another surge of pain from the bruises concealed by my turtleneck.

I glance across the table at Walker's two teenaged sisters. Their wide eyes take in the scene. Their hands stifle giggles.

"Would you like a glass of wine, Emma?" Mother Walker pauses before adding, "That is, if you're old enough."

"No, thanks. I just turned twenty," I mumble, knowing full well this is the wrong answer.

The look she gives her son could freeze fire.

"Charlie has always dated the most *beautiful* women." His mother's gaze settles on my bed-head and slept-in wardrobe. She turns to her son. "What ever happened to that lovely Jasmine girl?"

Walker focuses on the table. "Uh... It didn't work out."

"Why not?" She slides a plate of food in front of me, but I'm completely distracted by Walker's embarrassment. I've never seen him this awkward before.

"We... didn't have anything in common," Walker mumbles.

"What are you talking about?" Mother Walker crosses her arms. "You had lots in common!"

He brushes imaginary crumbs from the table.

Mother Walker turns to me. "Emma, what do your parents do for a living?"

The worst question ever! "Uh... my father started the Roberts Hardware store..."

"I bet you've never had to work a day in your life. Had everything handed to you on a silver platter, eh?"

I shove a forkful of roast in my mouth. "Dinner is great." Actually, I can't taste a thing. Walker is going to pay for this. And I have an on-campus tutoring job, by the way, lady.

Mother Walker glances out the window. "That's a nice car you've got parked outside."

"Thanks." Swallowing hurts so much my eyes water. I grab the glass of milk off the table.

"Was that a high school graduation present?" she asks.

I swallow hard. "Unfortunately."

"Unfortunately? Don't you even appreciate what your parents do for you? My son always appreciates his momma."

I spend the rest of the meal listening to Mother Walker's ideas of what type of woman is good enough for her son, and by that I mean definitely not me. Every time I try to tell her she needn't bother worrying, because I've no interest in her glorious son, Walker glares at me with eyes that could silence a storm. I push the last five peas around the plate until Mother Walker's pursed lips accuse me of insulting her cooking. I shovel the cold peas in my mouth, wincing in agony.

"Since you ate your veggies, you can have dessert." She removes my empty plate.

"Thanks, but I can't eat another bite," I protest, basically because it hurts so much to swallow. Plus, I've most likely lost my appetite for the rest of my life.

"Why? Are you on a diet?" She studies my waistline. "Real men like curves, not sticks."

"Listen—" I feel like I'm fighting my own mother. Walker's mom doesn't even know me, but she sure knows all the right buttons to push.

"Emma, how about I walk you out to your car?" Walker grabs my arm and steers me toward the front door.

We head down the driveway in icy silence. I keep waiting for him to apologize, to admit that he made a mistake.

When we reach my car, he pauses. "Can you help me early tomorrow morning with another case?"

I spin around. "You have some nerve, asking for a favor after what you just put me through." Good grief! He's not even going to apologize?

He shrugs. "Mom can be a little overprotective."

"That's not the word I'd choose." I beep the unlock button twice for emphasis.

"Really? Then what word would you choose for *your* mother?" Walker opens the car door for me. "As I recall, the first time she saw me at your place, she acted the same way."

"Actually, it's not your mom's fault. It's *your* fault. Why'd you invite me over when your family was here, anyway?"

"I'm sorry. I honestly forgot they were coming up today." He clears his throat. "Plus, we were fighting before you even got here. Her friends keep setting me up on dates, and Mom's pissed it never works out.

She's got grandchildren fever or something."

"Fine. But why didn't you tell her that we're *not* dating?"

"What else am I going to tell her? That I'm just using you for your witchcraft abilities?"

Glancing back up at the window, I see her spying on us. "I don't know, but if you stay out here talking to me any longer, she's going to chuck a casserole dish at my head. And I bet she has good aim."

Walker chuckles.

"You think the stupidest things are funny." I grumble, easing into my car. I'm not sure who bugs me more—Walker's dysfunctional family or the shower snake waiting for me at home.

CHAPTER SEVEN

A SECOND STRANGLING

Walker calls early the next morning, as promised.
"I'm waiting in your parking lot. Where are you?"

"What? Already?" I moan. After a long night spent staring at the ceiling, waiting to be terrorized again and startling at any little sound, I only slept for what seemed like two minutes before Walker's call. Ugh.

"Are you gonna hurry up, or what?" he asks.

"Grrr. Sometimes I hate you." I hang up on his laughter.

Again, my ragged reflection stares back at me from the bathroom mirror. I dig in my closet for another turtleneck to cover the bruises, and hurry downstairs. My cumbersome bag bounces off my sore hip.

I slide into the passenger's seat. "What's the rush? Didn't this murder happen months ago?"

"Yes, which makes the family all the more desperate for answers." He turns on the engine. The radio blares, I jump, and he turns down the volume. "They've been waiting since March."

"What's her name again?" I ask, buckling my seat belt carefully to avoid any pain.

Walker digs in his pocket and pulls out a key. "Mrs. Jennifer Pearson."

"Where did it happen?" I ask, dreading the answer. I shouldn't have agreed to this, but how can I explain why I can't help Walker when those voices won't let me tell him the truth?

He hands me the house key, then pulls out of the parking lot. "In her bedroom, but this time the house isn't for sale. We don't have to worry about any interruptions."

The key glimmers in my hand. I stare at it awhile then break away to gaze out the window. The houses slip by. One, two, three... it's like counting sheep with attached three-car garages. Safe at last, I fall asleep until Walker parks in the driveway of another monstrous gray McMansion. I yawn and stretch.

"College students... you never get enough sleep." He shakes a finger at me. "You must party too much."

"Yeah, that's me. I'm a real party animal." I give him a thumbs up sign. "Listen, I forgot a few steps last time. I'll need to gather some supplies."

"What kind of supplies? You won't find any witchcraft candles hidden in their cupboards. You can trust me on that."

"That's not what I'm talking about. I only need some rocks and flowers and stuff." This time I need to do the spell right—for my own protection.

"Go for it."

Wincing, I haul my bag of tricks toward the front steps. I pause to grab a handful of landscaping rocks and drop them into my purse. Once inside the house, I crane my ears for any strange voices, but hear only silence. A vase of fresh flowers rests on a table near the front entry. I nick a bud and pocket it as I ascend the stairs.

A slight tremble in my hands, I arrange candles around the bedroom and master bath. This time, I brought Grandma's wooden bowl. I can't believe I forgot it before. But it's Walker's fault—he rushed me. Perhaps using it—along with being more careful—will protect me. I made a mistake last time. I didn't do the spell correctly. I'm not losing control.

I glance toward the nearest sunny window to find a black moth plastered on the glass. My heart stutters. "Walker... is there any way we could do this tonight instead?"

He barely glances up as he texts into his phone. "Why? Is there something else you'd rather be doing right now?"

"Yes—sleeping, but that's not what I meant." I glance around, seeking something to comfort and protect me, but I know it's a lost cause. "I think things might go better if we did this under the moon... a full moon, preferably."

Walker stops typing. "Did you have a full moon when you did Steve's spell?"

I think back. "No. One night after. So almost full." I wait, wishing he'd abort this mission at least for the moment.

"Just try it." He starts texting again. "If it doesn't work, we'll come back again during a full moon."

"Okay. Fine." I grit my teeth, prepared for the worst. My stomach clenches.

I fill Grandma's wooden bowl with sink water, place it at my feet, take a shaky breath, and begin to chant:

"I call upon the elements of Air..."

I peel apart the bud, cradling the petals in one hand.

"Water..."

I sprinkle petals over and around Grandma's bowl in the center of the Magic Ring.

"Earth..."

Within the Magic Ring, I build a small pentagram of rocks.

"And Fire... Watch over me!"

The flames sputter and take hold as I light the candles.

"Guard and guide me during these rites.

Protect me during this... day as I call upon the... Sun."

I pause. "Are you sure we can't do this tonight?"

Walker spreads his hands wide, exasperated. "Don't worry. It worked last time, didn't it? Have some faith in yourself."

He doesn't know what he's asking.

My shoulders tense as I continue the ritual, dreading the outcome.

"Let us see

The treachery.

Expose the crime
From back in time.
Bring forth, bring down
Let truth be found.
Draw back the veil
That hides the tale.
Show us the fear
That once lived here."

Silently, I add, *Jennifer, please protect me. I'm trying to help you.*

Walker frowns, disappointed that the vision doesn't roll forth like a home movie. "Well, hopefully this will be like last time, and you'll call me later with your report." He turns away and puts his phone to his ear.

I watch for any signs of movement, but this time nothing dances on the sink.

"Maybe." Too bad he doesn't know what he's wishing for.

I settle into a cross-legged position to watch the candles burn down, then blow them out and gather them up after they are halfway melted. As I reach for the ones encircling the bed, the edge of the comforter lurches toward my outstretched hand. A thin trail of dark smoke curls out from underneath the fabric.

I gasp and draw back. My heart starts to pound so loudly I swear Walker should be able to hear it.

"Yes, Mom, I'll be home soon." Walker speaks into his phone across the room, his back to me.

There must be a cat under the bed or something. I grab the comforter, but when I lift the heavy fabric, there's nothing but a fat mattress and solid wooden frame. A chill penetrates my bones.

A high-pitched hum fills the air, but Walker doesn't seem to notice.

"Let's get out of here." I grab the rest of my supplies in a rush.

"Is something wrong, Emma? You're shivering again. Why are you always cold? Is there something wrong with your thyroid gland? Maybe you should go to the doctor."

"I'm fine," I lie, dashing down the stairs. "But thanks for asking about my hormones."

Walker trails behind me, texting again. "I'm afraid Mom isn't pleased that I'm working on my day off. She called to remind me that brunch is getting cold."

"Momma's boy." I mask my words with a cough, as we reach the front door.

He sighs. "And she's not pleased that I don't want to quit my job."

"What?" I swing around. "Why would you quit?" What would I do without him? I've lost everyone else.

Walker clears his throat. "Mom's under the impression that my job here was meant to be temporary, to get a few years experience in before moving on. She wants me to work in Milwaukee or Madison, somewhere closer to home."

Forcing myself to be fair, I don't ask him to stay. "Well, what do *you* want?"

"Right now, I'm too busy working on these cases with you to think about anything else." Walker gestures at my bag of witchcraft goods. "Especially Steve's. I don't want to leave town before we put his murderers in jail. But I can't exactly tell Mom that."

The breath I was holding releases. "So, what did you say to her?"

Walker busies himself with opening the front door. "I... uh... told her I'm your grief counselor and can't leave you now."

I halt in place as he hurries out the door. "What?"

He turns back. "You know. About Mike. And because I know what you're going through since my friend Billy drowned when we were kids, remember?"

"Yeah, of course I remember." Now I feel bad, reminding him of that. "But I don't like looking pathetic, or having people feel sorry for me."

He rolls his eyes. "That's not the worst thing in the world that could happen to you."

"I'm aware of that."

"But that excuse didn't work out too well. Mom envisions us sitting around, wallowing in grief and guilt, and doesn't think this is healthy for either of us. She's determined that I leave town. And soon."

I pause on the front step. Maybe she has a point. It would be nice not to feel guilty all the time. But Walker leaving won't fix me.

"Sorry I'm always telling you about our arguments, but I guess you're used to that, right?"

"Huh?" I shake off my train of thought.

He shrugs. "Steve told me you always fight with your mom."

"I do not," I huff. "Mom and I get along fine." *Thanks a lot, Steve. Mind your own business.*

Walker raises his brows. "I'm sure you do, because you're such an easy person to get along with."

I glare at him as we approach his truck. "You always think you know so much about me."

"I do know a lot about you." He smirks.

Not this time, he doesn't. I brace myself. He needs to know what's going on with me. "Listen, Walker, I *have* to tell you something. It's import—"

A dark cloud catches my eye. But it's not a rain cloud; it's a clustering of black moths headed our way. They swarm my head, catch in my hair, and flutter against my ears.

I scream, my knees buckling beneath me.

A downpour drenches me. I'm soaked, still fighting off the moths.

I scramble, flinging my arms to knock down the flying insects until there are none left.

My vision clears. Walker comes back into focus, two water bottles in hand. I lean against his vehicle, legs shaking. Water drips from my hair.

I glance down. My shirt clings to my chest.

"Hey, this isn't a wet T-shirt contest!" I unstick the shirt from my skin.

"What the Hell is wrong with you?" Walker gawks at me like I've lost my mind, which is a good possibility. "I thought you were having a seizure or something. Are you epileptic? Because you should've told me."

"No." I attempt to squeeze the water out of my shirt.

"Are you sick?" He tosses the empty water bottles in the back of his truck.

"No." *Not physically, anyway. Maybe mentally.*

"Are you trying to hide something from me again?" Walker narrows his eyes. "I thought you were done with all that. I'll find out anyway, so I wish you'd just spit it out."

I only wish I could.

I focus on breathing, because that's the only thing I'm capable of at the moment.

"What is it, Emma?" He comes closer, inspecting me like some bug on a pin. "Tell me."

My throat constricts each time I try to talk. There's no use. I can't tell him, even though I'm dying to. I wish he would figure it out on his own, because this time I guess he'll have to.

Walker takes my arm, his touch a lot more gentle than I'd expect. "Come on. I'll take you home. Or I can take you to the doctor—"

"No! No doctor!" I can finally speak, but say nothing of significance. "I'm just having trouble sleeping."

Walker stares at me, suspicious. "I believe it. You look like Hell."

He doesn't know the half of it. I only wish he did.

I wave half-heartedly as he pulls away from my apartment parking lot. Staring at the building, an unexpected wave of homesickness hits me. I dig out my phone and call my parents, but have to leave a message. I force my voice to be chipper as I invite them to visit later this month. The bruises should be gone by then. As I slip the phone back in my pocket, something slithers across the sidewalk in front of me. I jump back with a shriek.

Oh, grow up! It's just a harmless garter snake.

I shake off my fears and head inside, checking my empty mail slot before I hike upstairs. Heart racing, I cross the threshold, my right hand in a fist. I creep through each room, straining my ears in the silence. I scan the walls for errant moths, the space under closed doors for curls of smoke, and find nothing out of place.

What if I'm making all this up? Is that possible?

I change and go for a walk to calm my nerves, pausing near the edge of the river to stare at the spot where Mike and I entered the waters that stole him away. I miss him, and all the other souls I accidentally summoned along with him.

Especially Jake. If he were still here, he'd fix everything. He'd force me to tell him what's wrong. Somehow I'd get past the choking and coughing, and tell him the truth.

But no, the river took them all away.

None of them can help me now.

CHAPTER EIGHT

A DATE FROM HELL

Back at the apartment, I jump at every sound. After a quick shower, I lie on top of the bed, resting my wet head on the pillow.

Much later, I wake under a dark forested canopy. At first, I'm not sure where I am or even *who* I am.

One certain fear pounds in my head: *He's going to kill me!*

But who is he?

I'm no longer Emma Roberts. I'm Jennifer Pearson and I'm in trouble, big time. I roll to one side, scramble off the ground, and push through the underbrush. Branches whip my legs and face, but their repeated stings hurt far less than my black eye and bruised ribs. If only I could move faster, but a shooting pain in my groin hampers my gait.

I'm almost there, I tell myself. *God, if you get me out of this, I swear I'll never cheat on my husband again.*

The trees thin as I near the parking lot. Fumbling in my pockets for the keys, I sob in relief.

Out of nowhere, he attacks from the side and knocks me down. I scramble to get off the ground, but he kicks me full in the stomach. Screaming obscenities, bloody spit flying from his mouth, he strikes me over and over. I'm swimming in pain, struggling not to pass out.

Then he kneels on top of me, and rips at my torn shirt. He's going to kill me! Hands shaking, I jab him in the eyes with my car keys.

He screams and falls away.

Sticky blood stains my fingers.

I lurch off the ground and lunge for the car. My hands quiver so much it's hard to get the key in the lock. But I get inside and the engine roars to life.

I made it!

He charges toward my car, his feet slipping on the pavement.

I hit the automatic locks three times, then speed off, tires squealing.

Why didn't I run him over while I had the chance?

Breathing hurts. Every part of my body aches. I glance in the rearview mirror. I'm half-dressed, covered with blood, and beaten. How will I explain this to my husband? Will he ever forgive me?

Too scared to go to the hospital or call the police, I drive home, stash my ripped blouse in the bottom of the neighbors' outdoor garbage can, and shower. I can't stop the cut on my lip from bleeding. Trembling, I dig out my long flannel pajamas. I have to cover up some of these bruises.

The garage door opens as I comb through my wet hair.

Footfalls sound on the stairs.

What am I going to tell my husband? I brace myself, finally ready to tell him the truth.

We'll get counseling. We'll figure this out.

I turn to face him.

But my husband isn't home.

The wrong guy darkens the doorway, backlit by the hall light.

Blood spattered across his face, the bastard comes for me.

I'm frozen in place. I can't do a thing to stop him.

My screams echo in my head. Everything careens to black and painful.

Then only the black remains.

CHAPTER NINE

NO MORE

An invisible force pins me down on the bed.

I flail, kicking the sheets onto the floor.

Get off me! I can't breathe!

The pressure on my neck eases. I clutch my burning throat. Why is this happening? Why'd I ever tell Walker I'd do this?

I stumble to the bathroom and examine myself in the mirror. I look like a bruised banana. Raised red and purple splotches cover both cheekbones. Two fingernails have ripped off, their ragged edges catching in my hair and on my clothing. My puffy right eye droops half shut. I need something stronger than wimpy ibuprofen, but consulting a doctor in my current state would raise a lot of unwanted questions and send me straight to social services.

This is getting way too dangerous.

Mike was right. I should have listened to him and gotten rid of the *Book of Shadows* ages ago.

The phone rings. I wince as I grab it with my injured hand, then limp to the nearest chair.

"Emma, it's Walker." His voice calms me, even though he's nowhere near. "Do you have any news?"

The second I open my mouth to tell Walker the truth, a wave of nausea hits me. I cover my mouth and gag.

"Did you have another vision last night?" he presses.

"Give me a minute." Now, I want to slap him. After all, it's *his* fault I hurt so much, whether he knows it or not. Finally, I regain control. "Yes, I... saw what happened."

"Was it the same guy?" He sounds hopeful.

I'm sweating profusely across my forehead and in the back of my knees. "No. Jennifer was cheating on her husband with the guy that killed her."

"What?" he spurts out.

I detect a hint of doubt in his voice, which really pisses me off. "There was no forced entry."

"That's right." He sounds impressed. "How did you know that?"

"He came in through the garage. I heard him."

"Okay.... But how did he get the key?"

How dare he challenge me? I've gone through Hell to get him this information. "Maybe she gave it to him," I growl. "I don't know. You figure that part out. It's your job."

"You're telling me that some dude the victim was *dating* murdered her?"

"Yes!" I croak, my throat scratched raw. "Why don't you believe me?"

"Calm down. What's wrong with you this morning? I *do* believe you. I just expected a different answer."

I scowl, which hurts so I stop. "Sorry to disappoint."

Walker pauses. "What did he look like?"

"I don't know..." I search my fuzzy brain. "Dark hair... blue eyes... and I'll bet he fake bakes."

Walker sighs. "Seriously, Emma? I'm supposed to investigate tanning salons?"

Why can't I remember more details? I should've checked out his car in the parking lot, for starters. "Maybe he went on a cruise or a trip or something. Nobody is naturally that tan in March in Wisconsin. Oh, and this guy had straight teeth."

"You sure have a thing about teeth."

"What can I say, Walker? I wore braces for years. I *always* notice people's teeth. Oh, and one more thing—Jennifer jabbed him super hard in the eye with her keys."

"Interesting."

I hear tapping in the background. Isn't he going to say something about the eye injury? "How about checking the hospital ER records for a guy with a bloody eye?"

"I'll look into it." It sounds like a dismissal.

Anger bubbles up like a volcano inside me. "What? No more questions? Isn't that what I'm here for? To be your psychic guide?"

Walker clears his throat before speaking. "I'm not sure what I did to piss you off."

"Then you're not as smart as your mommy thinks you are," I spit out.

He exhales. "Nobody's as smart as their mom thinks they are."

The line goes quiet for another long second. I hear the grumbling of spirit voices inside my head, but ignore them, focusing on Walker instead. I wish he'd figure it out. Because something or someone inside of me won't let me tell him.

And I'm afraid we're both gonna get hurt. Or killed.

He clears his throat. "Will you *please* come down to the station to look through mug shots?"

"Uh... I can't." I shudder. I can't go anywhere looking like this.

"Why not? I promise free food if you come. And I do appreciate your help. You know that, right?"

"I'll have to take a rain check. I have the flu." I hurry to the bathroom and flush the toilet as evidence.

"Oh." Walker sounds disgusted. "Do you think it's the twenty-four hour kind?"

"Um... probably more of the one-hundred-twenty-four hour kind." I groan and run water in the sink.

"Okay, then, call me when you're feeling better... and use my cell number. I don't want Mom to answer. She's on my case enough as it is."

"Okay. Cell phone. Got it." I glance at my beat up reflection. "And one more thing, Walker. I can't work with you on these murder cases anymore."

"Why not? You've been a big help already."

I stare at my extensive bruises, up and down my arms and legs. What can I tell him? What am I "allowed" to tell him, I wonder. Gotta try something. "I'm getting too freaked out by all these visions."

"Okay, then, we'll focus on reworking the spell for Steve. I think you're right about that. I probably missed something important."

My stomach lurches. Oh, no. Not that. "I don't know if I can even do that."

"Why not? You've already seen it once. You already know what's going to happen."

"Well..." Seeing it I can handle. Living through that crow bar smashing down on my head is another thing altogether.

"This was your idea, remember?" he reminds me.

"Yeah, I know." Damn it. What am I going to do?

"We both owe it to Steve, don't you think?" he wheedles.

Crap. Now I feel guilty, on top of everything else. But then again, I'm Catholic. I pretty much feel guilty about everything, anyway. I try to drum up my courage. When I worked this spell for Steve last spring, no one entered my mind or attacked my body, so maybe I'll be safe this time.

"Okay. I'll do it. But only under the moon." I whisper, my fingers tenderly probing my black eyes.

"Good! We'll figure this out together."

I doubt it. So far Walker hasn't figured out diddly-squat.

CHAPTER TEN

PRISONER IN MY OWN HOME

A **voice calls out my name. "Emma? Are you in there?"**

"Walker? Is that you?" My words squeak like a mouse. I blink and glance around the room. Is it day or night?

"Emma? Are you okay in there?" His muffled words float in from the hallway.

"No. I'm not okay. I think I've gone insane." Oh, wait. He can't hear me.

"Emma—let me in!" The door shakes with his pounding fists, or else he's kicking it. I can't tell.

Shuddering with sudden chill, I shuffle to the apartment door and lean against it, panting in effort. Just walking the length of the apartment winds me.

I whisper through the thick wooden door, "What do you want?"

"So you *are* in there."

"Where do you think I'd go, feeling like this?" I blink hard, trying not to collapse to the floor. My legs are so weak.

"To be honest, I wasn't sure you were telling me the truth."

"Really?" Maybe he *is* finally catching on. I peer at him through the peephole.

He taps on the doorframe. "I brought you some stuff."

"What kind of stuff?" Presents always excite me, even if the rest of my life has turned to crap.

"Uh... Mom said that if you had the flu, I should bring you some 7UP, applesauce, saltines, bread, and butter."

"That was nice of her." And unexpected.

"Then she asked if I'd gotten you pregnant." Walker fidgets in the hallway. He can't stand still. He paces back and forth in the hallway, leans on the doorframe a moment, then back to pacing. I've never seen him this uncomfortable before.

All because his mother thinks he got me pregnant. How far from the truth can she be? "You've got to be kidding me. She asked you that?"

"More like an accusation. A series of accusations, actually, accompanied by a baseball bat." Walker wipes a hand across his face.

"A bat? Is she crazy? Maybe it runs in the family." I'm starting to like Walker's mother. She's much better at torturing him than I am. I should ask for pointers.

He shrugs. "Mom said I'd pay closer attention if she was holding a weapon."

I lean against the doorframe, my feet tingling like they fell asleep. "That's probably true."

"So, can I come in?"

I will my hand to reach for the doorknob, but it hangs limply down by my side.

A cold voice inside my head warns, *Don't let him in.*

I glance back into the apartment, but no one is there watching. At least no one I can see. "No, I think I'm still contagious." I fake a cough.

"I doubt that. You've been sick for days. I called at least ten times, but you never answered."

"Really? I never even heard the phone." I've been unconscious for days? This is worse than I thought.

"That's what got Mom suspicious. I kept checking my phone for messages."

I need to stall him while I figure out what to do. "How long is she staying?"

Walker clears his throat. "She originally planned to leave two days ago, but now she's staying a bit longer. My sisters are on summer vacation, anyway."

Through the peephole, I watch him shift from side to side. I wish he'd break down the door and get me out of here. But even then I wouldn't be safe. I know that now. These voices will stay with me, wherever I go.

They're getting stronger.

And I'm getting weaker.

Walker clears his throat. "If there's nothing more I can do, I'll head out. Your 'care package' is right by the door."

"Okay. Thanks." My already weakened shoulders slump further. "And thank your mother for me, too."

"I'll be sure to." His steps retreat down the hallway.

Careful to remain hidden from view, I creep into the living room and peer out the window to watch him leave.

A door slams downstairs, followed by a voice yelling, "Wait!"

Phoebe rushes out of her apartment, grabs Walker's arm in the parking lot, and points toward my window.

I growl and back away.

"Get away from me, witch." The words fly out of my mouth, but the deep voice isn't mine.

I'm not in control anymore.

Maybe I never was.

I turn away from the window, then sneak into the hallway to nab Mother Walker's presumed pregnancy supplies before Phoebe comes upstairs to force her inept Wicca spells on me.

My phone rings. Who is it now? I explore the package and let the machine get it. After all, I haven't eaten for days.

"Emma, pick up. I know you're there," Walker speaks through my answering machine. "I just got done talking to you."

I snatch up the phone. "What do you want?"

"Your weird neighbor, Phoebe, practically assaulted me. Why is she so suspicious of you?"

My eyes narrow. "What do you mean?"

"She said you freaked out on her last week, and now you're holed up in your apartment like a conspiracy theorist."

What do I say? "Did you tell her that I'm sick?"

"Yeah, but..."

"But what?"

"She *claims* she can hear you screaming." I can sense Walker squirming through the phone. "She even considered calling the police."

Thank goodness she didn't. Anyone but Walker would've slapped me into an insane asylum. "Are you sure she didn't confuse retching for screaming?"

He sighs. "They don't sound anywhere near the same, Emma, and you know it. What's going on? I'm starting to worry."

My mind races for something intelligent to say. The voices argue and grumble inside me. Somebody is crying. Someone else is praying, I think, but I can't be sure. None of the voices make any sense. Nothing is clear. I can only make out half the words—unless they're talking to me.

Then it's clear. And terrifying.

"Are the visions giving you nightmares?" Walker's voice is gentle, for a change. "Or have you always been this crazy?"

I approach the window again, so I can see his face. "Yes." *The worst nightmares I've ever had.*

Walker stares back up at me. "Which one are you saying 'yes' to? The nightmares or the crazy?"

"I don't know." I place a hand on the glass. "Maybe both."

He sighs. "I'm sorry. You're right. I won't ask you to do this any more... that is, after we resolve Steve's case. I didn't realize it affected you this much. Uh... does Phoebe know you're a witch?"

I flinch. "No, and I'd like to keep it that way. At least, I hope she doesn't know. Why?"

Walker covers his mouth over the phone, as if for privacy. "Well, when I told her I brought you a get-well-soon package, she said she's gonna gather some candles and other crap to fix your current illness."

That's all I need—more witchcraft. Wait a minute… maybe Phoebe's right. Maybe I could reverse this…

"Goodbye, Walker, and thanks for the warning." I slam down the phone, filled with a sense of relief. Phoebe's a genius! Why didn't I think of a Healing Ceremony before? I'm such an idiot. All I have to do is work some spells to dispel bad spirits, and I'll be safe again!

Panting hard, I shove all the furniture in my living room against the walls to clear space for a Sacred Circle. I close every shade tight against the sunlight. I dump my purse on the floor and grab red, turquoise, and black candles. Placing them along the perimeter of my Sacred Circle, I alternate the colors. I knock over everything in my spice cabinet in pursuit of the salt and sage. Carefully, I pour a trail around the candles.

I light each candle, repeating the words over and over:

"Black candle of death, banish those who haunt me.

Red candle of fire, protect me from your flame.

Turquoise candle of healing, restore me to health."

I hunch cross-legged in the middle of the ring. For a moment, the air feels peaceful—until the smoke twirling off a red candle floats straight toward me. I cough as more trails of thin, gray smoke dance around me, clouding my view. The cup squeaks in the bathroom, spinning faster and faster. There's an ominous thick drip from the shower.

A hissing noise spits from under the couch. Two oval yellow eyes glow there in the shadows. I tremble as a huge golden snake approaches, the great length of its body waving in serpentine fashion. It pauses at the edge of my Sacred Circle, its long pink tongue flickering in and out.

My heart hammers in my ears as black smoke pours from the bathroom into the living room. Choking on the smell and my fear, I jump to my feet and flee the Circle, lunge for the front door, and ram right into someone standing in the hallway.

"Help me, please!"

CHAPTER ELEVEN

EVIDENCE

Are you insane?" Walker storms through the apartment, blowing out all the candles. "You're gonna burn down the whole building!"

"No... I..." I tremble outside the Circle, trying my best not to hyperventilate.

"And your shower's running full blast!" He ducks into the bathroom and turns it off. "Ever heard of water conservation?"

I hesitate before following him into the smokeless bathroom. No dripping blood. No spinning objects. Everything has returned to normal. We both look into the mirror at the same time. The formidable dark circles beneath my eyes hide the residual bruises.

"What's going on?" Walker gestures at the living room. "It looks like you're performing an Exorcism out there."

My eyes widen.

Exorcism—that's an even better idea.

Walker grabs my arm and yanks me toward the door. "You're coming with me. I know how secretive you are, and this is getting way too weird, even for you. What you need is fresh air and real food."

"That sounds good." I let him lead me to his truck. "What made you come back?"

"Your voice didn't sound right. Of course, I drove all the way home before I decided to come back, and freaked out my mom all over again." Walker moans. "She's never going to leave now."

I sink into the passenger seat, safe for the moment. At least I hope so.

"Where do you want to eat?" he asks.

"Anywhere your momma isn't. I don't think she should see me like this."

"Agreed." Walker pulls out of the parking lot. "You do look awful."

"Yes. Thanks for that." I stare out the window as tidy houses flash past. All those people living their quiet lives, never wondering if something in the night will creep up and kill them. Why can't I be like them? I have to fix this mess I made. But how?

I turn to face Walker. "After we eat, I'd like to look at those mug shots again."

He pauses. "Are you sure? We could do it tomorrow."

"No. I want to get this guy." One way or another.

Two hours, two burgers with fries, and several cups of coffee later (for Walker, not me—gross, I hate coffee), I give up.

I slap my hands on the table. "The murderer's not in here, and no matter how many times you slip a different picture of *this* guy in the mix, I'm still gonna say no."

Walker chuckles. "You caught that, hey?"

I roll my eyes. "Yes. I'm not stupid. Who is he, anyway?"

"Jennifer's husband, and the prime suspect… until you came along." Walker taps his foot.

"I told you already—she was cheating on her husband with the guy who killed her. *Try* to believe me, okay, Walker?"

"I know that, but like *you* said, there was no forced entry, and only her husband had the key." Walker closes his laptop and gathers his things. "Unless she left it unlocked."

"But she didn't." I shake my head. "Somebody else had a key."

Walker drums the desk with his fingers. "Plus, there's an attractive life insurance policy on her."

"It's not him. I know it." I bite my lip, pausing to think. "I don't understand how none of her girlfriends knew she was having an affair."

"Well, at the time I didn't *know* to ask them that particular question, but I'm not sure they would have told me if I had." Walker files away folders in the cabinet near his desk.

I tug on his shirt. "But I'm a girl."

"Thank you for that news bulletin."

What an idiot he is sometimes. Apparently, I have to spell it out for him. "Do you think they'd tell *me?*"

Walker locks the cabinet. "I realize you've had great success in the past crashing funerals and weddings, but this is official police work."

"You need to pursue this angle. Girls talk. You know, a real heart to heart. Jennifer was their friend. I'm sure they're devastated, but maybe they knew she was cheating and didn't want to tell you—a guy—about it because they didn't want to 'speak ill of the dead' or whatever."

"I'll think about it." Walker drains his coffee cup.

I stretch, scanning the police station. "In the meantime, we should search Carson Park for clues. That's where the attack started."

"You sound like Velma on *Scooby Doo.* Are you sure you're up for this?" Walker frowns at me like I'm crazy. Maybe he's right.

"Yes." I sure as Hell don't want to go home until I figure out how to exorcize my demons.

Walker's truck rolls up the steep drive into Carson Park and nears the playground as the sun begins to set.

"Pull in here." I point to a corner spot. "This is where she parked."

Walker obeys. I shiver as my arms turn to ice, despite the summer heat. I jump out of the car and my heart begins to race.

At the edge of the blacktop, I pause. "Here's where he knocked her over, and she stabbed him with her keys."

Walker kneels down to study the spot as I rush past swings and slides.

Pausing at the tree line, I reach out for guidance. "Help me, Jennifer!" I call out.

"Ah... you're talking to her now?" Walker's heavy boots snap a twig behind me, making me jump. "That's new for you, right?"

"Shhhh. Be quiet. I hear something." Pushing branches out of my way, I ease into the woods. The fading orange sun glints through the gaps in the dense greenery.

"Please don't," Jennifer pleads with someone deep in the woods.

I glance back at Walker. His face is blank, questioning. It's obvious he can't hear her.

"You asked for it, baby," the murderer growls.

Jennifer's screams agitate the leaves. She's close by. The underbrush catches my hair and shirt as I rush toward the sound of her agony.

"I'm coming, Jennifer," I call out. "I'll help you."

"Does talking to her help?" Walker asks, and I ignore him.

Her perfume tickles my nose—then I'm after the scent like a bloodhound.

Heart pounding, I push through the branches.

Just a little further. I'm almost there. She's just a few steps away.

I halt, sweating in my hot pink turtleneck. Walker runs into me from behind.

"Watch out." I spread my arms to stop him.

Walker leans over my shoulder. "Holy sh—"

"Don't say that. I'll tell your mother."

"Emma, I'm loving you right now." Walker whips out his phone, then pauses. "Don't tell her that, either."

I don't respond. I'm too busy staring at the ground before us, at the remains of Jennifer's clothing, bloodied and torn.

CHAPTER TWELVE

ARREST WARRANT

Walker's hurried phone call rallies the troops. Police vehicles crowd the playground parking lot. Headlights reflect off shiny yellow security banners stretched across the bushes. Uniforms march into the woods. Flashlight beams bounce through the trees. Everyone barks orders at each other and stares warily at me.

"How did she know about this?" one cop asks Walker.

I can't make out his reply.

After that, I hide in Walker's Ford, away from the questioning looks. Maybe I should walk home. But it's late and I'm so tired...

I wake hours later, stomach growling. I scrounge around in the glove compartment, hoping for a granola or candy bar. No such luck. A woman's scream draws my eyes back to the edge of the woods. Again the murderer stands over her, kicking her in the chest and abdomen.

"You're not going anywhere, bitch!" Is that angry voice coming from outside the truck or inside my head? My stomach twists and quivers. Gripping the armrest, I close my eyes, trying to block out the vision.

"Don't turn away. Help me. Look closer." Jennifer's plea forces me to open my eyes.

I lean forward until my head touches the windshield. She races past unseeing policemen into the parking lot, jumps in her car, slams the door, and jams the keys in the ignition slot.

CLICK.

The truck door opens right next to me.

I shriek and flatten myself against the seat, bracing for the attack.

Walker jumps. "Emma! You just about gave me a heart attack!"

My eyes widen. "Oh, thank goodness! It's just you."

"Who'd you think it was?"

I pause, my heart still banging in my throat. "No one. Can we go home now?"

"Not quite." Walker grins like he's the smartest man on the planet.

I groan. "Why not? What are you up to?"

"I have a hunch." Walker's eyes light with excitement. "You're coming with me."

"Right now? I haven't showered, or eaten, or anything."

"Sorry, but I need to question Jennifer's best friend again before news of this gets out. She's either hiding something, or maybe she doesn't even know yet..."

Fifteen minutes later, the sun bursts over the horizon. We pull up to a large two-story house with a cupola.

"Here we are." Walker gets out of the car and gestures for me to follow. "Come on."

I trail him up the front steps. He rings the doorbell. Twice, which is kind of rude this early in the morning.

"Are you sure they're even awake?" I yawn as a sleepy looking woman wearing a silky turquoise bathrobe opens the door.

"Officer Walker?" She cocks her pretty blonde head, giving him an uncertain smile.

"Mrs. Hudson, I'm sorry to intrude at this hour, but there's a new development in Jennifer's case. I have a few urgent questions to ask."

"Of course." She waves us in. "I'd do anything to help find Jennifer's murderer. And, as I told you before, please call me Naomi." She tightens her robe and directs us into the living room.

My tired feet drag across the plush carpet. Overstuffed couches laden with pillows in warm fall colors surround us. Everything seems too big, like I've reverted back to a small child. Why did Walker bring me here?

"Make yourselves comfortable." She eyes me quizzically.

"Thank you," I reply, feeling like a toddler as I sink between two enormous cushions.

Walker gestures in my direction. "This is Emma Roberts. She's been job-shadowing and helping us with the case."

Naomi smiles as if I'm a girl scout and she's buying cookies. "You both look so tired."

"That's part of the job," Walker says. "We just pulled an all-nighter."

Naomi shakes a perfectly manicured finger at him. "Don't work her too hard. You should let her get more rest."

For a moment, my mother's face flashes before me instead of Naomi's. I blink, and everything returns to normal.

Naomi stifles a delicate yawn. "Excuse me! Would you like some coffee?"

"I would," Walker replies.

"Nothing for me," I say.

"I'll be right back." Naomi leaves the room.

While she prepares coffee, I glance around. The furniture is well made, the décor tasteful. Two grade school photos hang above the gas fireplace—a boy and a girl.

Soon Naomi returns. "Here you go." She hands Walker a mug and turns to me. "I brought you some juice, in case you're thirstier than you think."

"Thanks." I swallow the refreshing drink. My throat doesn't burn so much anymore, which is a relief.

The metallic ticking of a clock fills the empty silence as we all stare at each other.

"Naomi." Walker clears his throat. "I need to ask you a difficult question. Did Jennifer tell you she was having an affair?"

Her eyes fly open. "What? That's impossible. She wouldn't... or at least she would have told me about it if she did."

The front door slams.

"You're not going anywhere, bitch!" the killer's voice rings in my head.

I stiffen, put a hand to my head, and turn to find Walker watching my reaction.

"Richard, we're in the living room," Naomi calls out. "He runs every single morning before work."

"What's going on in here?" Behind us floats the voice from my nightmares. But this time it's crossed into the day, in real time.

Right now. In this very room.

The bottle slides from my trembling hands, spilling juice all over the carpet.

"Oh, dear! Let me get a towel!" Naomi rushes to the kitchen, explaining over her shoulder. "The police are here asking a few more questions about Jennifer."

I whirl around, knowing I'll find the demon from my nightmare.

Here in the daylight.

Where he can hurt me. Again.

My heartbeats flail then calm. Because now I can hurt him, too.

"How's your eye?" I ask.

"My eye is fine," Richard replies quickly. Too quickly.

Naomi hurries back with two hand towels. "Oh, dear. Did you ask about his eye? He sure is a sight, isn't he?"

She kneels down and dabs the carpet. "But it looks much better than before. Silly Richard, driving right into a bee in his convertible. You wouldn't believe how bruised and swollen it got. I told him to go see a doctor, but you know men."

"I'm so sorry," I apologize to Naomi, not taking my eyes off her husband. She probably thinks I'm referring to the spilled drink. But I'm apologizing for ruining her life, for exposing Richard as the monster he is. Poor woman. She'll soon discover she's married to a murderer.

"Don't worry about it," Naomi says. "You're just tired, working all those hours."

Walker stands up, clearing his throat. "Mr. Hudson, I think we'd better ask the rest of our questions down at the station."

"What are you talking about?" The rest of his face flushes purple-red to match his eye.

I cross my arms. "I think you know."

"Oh, my God," Naomi whimpers, grabbing the couch arm to brace herself. "What's going on?"

"I didn't do anything!" Richard yells.

"Listen, buddy, we can do this the easy way... or the hard way." Walker takes out a set of handcuffs.

Richard stares at the handcuffs for a long moment. He swallows hard, then turns and rushes out the front door. Walker dashes after him, two seconds behind.

"What's going on?" Naomi's voice cracks.

I turn back to face her.

Naomi gapes at me, her complexion draining to white. "Jennifer? Is that you?"

What? I glance down at my hands. Long red fingernails and the mother-load of a diamond wedding ring on the left hand. My hands aren't mine, not anymore.

"Oh, my God." Naomi collapses onto the sofa. "Jennifer, you've come back from the dead to tell me something, haven't you? It's like a movie. This can't be real... can it?"

"Richard killed me." Jennifer's voice and Jennifer's words. She's using my body and making it hers. "It's true. And I'm so sorry... for everything. Your husband is a murderer and I'm a terrible friend."

"No! It can't be! Get away from me!" Naomi scrambles to the far end of the couch. "Get out of my house! You're lying! This can't be happening." She collapses to the floor with a sob. "Please. Get out before the kids see you."

I flee outside and find Walker on the phone. "Mid-forties, dark hair, Caucasian, fake-baker." He winks at me.

I lean against his truck as the world starts to spin. Trees and cars fly by.

"Emma, what's going on?" Walker sounds small and far away. He grabs my arm and holds me up.

A kaleidoscope of images flood my brain: Jennifer running through the woods, Richard knocking her to the ground, Naomi calling me Jennifer, and the flashing yellow lines in the road.

I refocus on Walker's face. "Richard's headed for the park."

His eyes widen. "What?"

I finally feel in control. "Trust me. I can see what he sees."

Walker pauses only a moment before speaking into his phone again. "Watch out. He's headed your way. I'll be there as soon as I can."

He shoves his cell into a pocket and nods at the car. "Come on. Let's go."

My knees buckle. "I feel so dizzy." So much for being in control.

"Whoa." Walker eases me onto the passenger seat. "Don't worry. I got ya."

"Thanks." I can't see Walker's car, there are too many visions in my head. I'm blind to everything but Richard. When will this stop?

"Is this what happens every time?" Walker asks.

I shudder. "Sort of." Only it gets worse. Way worse.

"No wonder you don't want to do this anymore." Walker hops in and slams his door shut.

We speed to the park. Finally, my sight clears. Richard stands in the middle of a crowd, arms flailing, a crazed look upon his face.

Walker touches my shoulder. "I want you to stay in the car. Got it?"

Not gonna happen. I throw open the car door and stumble into the parking lot.

Everything is blurry.

"Get back in the car, Emma!" Walker yells.

I stagger forward. "I can't let him hurt anyone else."

Richard glares across the parking lot at me. "Jennifer! You're such a whore. You deserved it."

The images crowd my mind again, leaving me woozy but

determined. Richard's ugly, screaming face. Jennifer's torn clothes. Her pain rips through me. I keep moving toward him, egged on by an inner force. My legs jerk forward without any thought of my own.

I'm not myself.

I'm Jennifer's puppet.

"You bitch! You're supposed to be dead, damn it!" Richard lurches toward me, his breathing loud and ragged.

I tense, but remain still.

He's so close I can see the color of his eyes.

And yet I refuse to move.

A single gunshot echoes across the park.

Richard falls at my feet. The ground darkens below his chest. Dark red. Oozing.

Blood. I don't like blood.

I cover my mouth, trying not to gag. Guess I'll never be a doctor.

Colored sparkles dance across my vision.

"Emma. Can you hear me?"

I strain to focus on the face of a female police officer. Oh great, I passed out in public. How embarrassing.

"What happened?" I sit up too fast in the damp grass, and feel dizzy.

"The ambulance took Mr. Hudson away," she says. "But don't worry about him. Are you okay? You're white as a ghost."

Ha. Ghost. That's almost funny. "Too much excitement."

"Walker asked me to drive you home." She smiles kindly. "He said he'd call to check on you later."

I glance at my trembling hands. Once again, they look familiar: short nails, unpolished, and no jewelry whatsoever.

I shudder. Even my hands looked like Jennifer's. This is going too far. If Richard and Naomi can see Jennifer within me, it's high time to learn the fine art of exorcism.

I knew I was raised Catholic for a reason.

Not sure whether to be relieved or afraid to be home, my hands clench as we pull into the parking lot of my apartment building.

"Thanks for the ride." Once again, I feel like a small child. When do I get to be an adult?

"Now get some rest." The concerned policewoman pats my shoulder. "You need it."

"I will. Don't worry." I step onto the sidewalk near my apartment building, pausing to check for snakes. None. Thank goodness. I head inside and up the stairs. My stride slows as I approach my apartment door. I reach for the handle, then drop my hand to my side.

You can do this.

I take a big breath, unlock the door, and rush inside, heart pounding. The living room looks innocent enough. Everything sits in its proper place, as if there had never been a disturbance. All right, so far so good. No funny noises or billowing smoke. I flick on all the lights, yank open every shade, and flip on the computer.

After grabbing a snack, I settle down to conduct a web search on "exorcism." Several warnings caution that only a priest designated by the local bishop should perform them. This doesn't bother me. I'm not a very good listener. But the admonition that demons can take possession of a person simply because they read *Harry Potter* or ask a Magic 8 ball a question make me angry.

You've got to be kidding me. Why is *Harry Potter* so bad when *The Lion, the Witch, and the Wardrobe* is considered Christian Lit? Both of them are great, as far as I'm concerned. I modify my search to find more pleasant (and practical) websites, take a few notes, but eventually give up. In some ways, Internet surfing sucks. There are too many psychos out there and so much mis-information.

I slump in the chair, wondering what to do next. The bright blue sky out the window beckons to me. Maybe sunlight can kill demons like it kills bacteria. I grab my backpack, shove in writing supplies and a few water bottles, then venture outside. Hearing a commotion in the stairwell below, I peer over the railing and spot Phoebe dragging a chair out onto the lawn. I'm not in the mood for her nosy questions. I turn down the hall toward the back staircase instead.

Once I get outside, my feet bring me straight to the edge of the Chippewa River. I can't stay away. Part of me needs to stare deep into the depths.

"You are both my torment and my comfort," I tell the rushing waters as I plop down on a large rock. There's got to be an answer. Even though those exorcism websites *claim* to be religious, they leave me feeling dirty, as if I somehow *asked* for this to happen. I'm only trying to help those murder victims. What's wrong with that?

Sunlight glints off the swirling water. I will the soothing flow of the river to calm me. It doesn't. Maybe I'm not really possessed by evil spirits. Maybe I'm over-tired. That's it. After all, it's so peaceful out here next to the water. I lean back on the warm rock, closing my eyes.

A squeaking noise begins. I'm not even in my bathroom, and the sound can reach me. I still hear the echoing *drip-drip-drip* of the blood in the shower even though I sit outdoors a mile away.

My cheeks flush and my stomach burns. This is too much. I've had enough.

I open my eyes, and spot a dark form floating along the bike path. A cloud in the shape of a cloaked man approaches as the world around grows silent.

I sit up. Everything stops. I don't even breathe.

The wind stills in the grasses.

The rushing water pauses in its hurry.

A hot flash of pain sears my eyes. I can't see! I fall off the rock to the ground, rubbing desperately at my eyes, the tears flowing.

Everything is black. The sky. The world. My heart.

By the time my tears clear, the swooping dark shape has disappeared.

I tremble, huddled on the dirt, glancing around in search of my tormentors.

Who am I fooling? I need serious help.

CHAPTER THIRTEEN

GET ME TO THE CHURCH IN TIME

Once my heart rate slows to normal, I make a decision. I hurry home, rush past Phoebe's thankfully empty lawn chair, and jump into my car. That's it. I'm going to church.

I head to the one where Mike's funeral was held last fall, determined to procure the necessary supplies listed on the Internet for an exorcism: holy water, rosaries, and the like. In addition, I'll check out any religious books they have lying around. Too bad there's nothing in my *Book of Shadows* on exorcism.

As I drive to the church, I pass a park. People in tank tops and shorts throw Frisbees or absorb a year's worth of Vitamin D while lounging on beach towels, eating ice cream. Why can't I do that? I'm pasty-white. I could use a tan. Why does my life have to be so crazy? How did an innocent crush on a cute boy cause me so much trouble?

Although part of me realizes I need divine intervention, I fear running into any priests. I don't want to have to explain how I let these spirits in. Surely, I can get rid of them on my own with the right combination of spells and religious paraphernalia.

I pull into the parking lot. Everything looks just as I remember. The majestic building towers over me once again. Last time, I left this place in tears. I hope it brings me better luck this time around.

I hurry up the gray stone stairs, and pause to read a posted sign. *The front door shall remain unlocked during daylight hours.* But when I pull on it, the door doesn't budge. I rattle the metal handles. What's the deal? The sign says it's supposed to be unlocked.

A young, dark-haired priest approaches behind me and easily opens the troublesome door.

"Oh, thanks." Stupid demons, they don't want me to get inside.

"Is there something I can help you with?" His voice is kind, but I can't meet his gaze.

"No, thank you." I rush past him, noting a box of colorful plastic rosaries for sale. I'll come back for them later. No need to arouse suspicion.

I enter the sanctuary, pausing to glance up at the balcony. There hang the red velvet curtains I hid behind almost a year ago. The accusations of Mike's distraught mother still curdle my stomach, but I block them out.

From the corner of my eye, I spot the young priest hovering inside the church doors. Busy-body. He's as nosy as Phoebe. I step to the side and dip my hand in the holy water, trying to look normal, then gasp when my fingers burn. Crap! Way to blend in. I shake the blessed water off my hand, trying not to cry out. I hope the two people kneeling in the church pews can't hear me. I slip into a back pew next to the stained glass windows, lower my head, and wait for the priest to leave his watchful post.

Kneeling, I scan the surroundings. There's got to be a church library here somewhere. Once the priest is out of sight, I stand, hoping to avoid any further confrontation. I soon discover what I'm after—a small corner room filled with faded leather-bound books. Scanning the titles, I pull volume after volume off the shelf. The smell of old paper and glue comforts me.

Pausing at a row of gold embossed Bibles, I reach for the fattest one. In a wave, the whole row of books flattens itself against the light blue wall, avoiding my grasp.

"I don't think so." I use both hands to yank a gigantic Bible off the shelf.

It shivers within my grasp. Feeling guilty, as if I've trapped a small kitten in my hand instead of a book, I glance around the small library. A movement outside draws my attention toward the windows. The wind has picked up. Caught in a tree branch, a plastic grocery bag flings about as if struggling to get away. But it can't escape. It just flaps in vain. I know how that feels.

Settling down next to my stacks of books, I grab my notebook and pen and copy anything that might help:

Mark 16.15-18

In my name shall they cast out devils; they shall speak with new tongues; they shall take up serpents; and if they drink any deadly thing, it shall not hurt them; they shall lay hands on the sick, and they shall recover.

Luke 11.14-22

And he was casting out a devil, and it was dumb. And it came to pass, when the devil was gone out, the dumb spake; and the people wondered. But some of them said, He casteth out devils through Beelzebub the chief of the devils.

General Information:

-Demons enter through a person's senses

-Magic and communion with dead spirits opens a person up to a possession.

-Needed supplies: holy water, blessed oil, crucifix.

-Dribble holy water in laundry of an afflicted person.

Exorcism Chant: I cast you out, unclean spirit, along with every Satanic power of the enemy, every specter from Hell, and all your fell companions...

After copying the entire exorcism chant into my notebook, I glance at the piles of books scattered across the table. I need to collect my supplies before that priest comes back. I grab my bag and duck out of the tiny library. Soon I discover a miniature pink-tiled bathroom that smells like old lady soap. There's barely enough room to turn around as I empty the water bottles from my backpack into the sink.

Treading slowly on the dark carpet to make as little noise as possible, I sneak over to the holy water font at the back of the church. I fill the bottles, peeking into the empty sanctuary, dreading discovery. My hands tremble as I will the third bottle to fill faster. A few drops splash on my fingers. Ouch! That burns! Then I creep to the table by the front doors, slip a twenty dollar bill in the donation box, and drop a handful of plastic rosaries in my bag.

Now I've got my supplies, and that priest is nowhere to be seen. Time to head home. I reach into my pocket for the car keys. Empty. Must have left them in the library. I rush back into the small study.

There stands the tall priest, looking down at the books I pulled from the shelves, and, in my hurry, forgot to put away.

"Interesting reading." The priest's hand rests on an open church text.

I stare at the floor without answering.

He approaches. "Why are you researching exorcisms?"

I clear my throat. "Research for a college paper."

"A summer class?" He's trying to make this easy on me, but there's no making this easy. That's for sure.

My right hand trembles. Voices grumble inside my head. This time, oddly enough, they sound like old ladies. The really crabby kind who yell at you for stepping on their grass.

"Run! Now!"

"Get away from here!"

"Stay away from him!"

"Do you need assistance with your research? I'm the diocese-appointed exorcist. The bishop in LaCrosse thought I should be placed here in Eau Claire near the campus. When college students become interested in the occult, it can lead them into trouble."

"Really?" I squeak, my limbs turning cold and numb.

The priest chuckles. "Although there are those who still believe that Satanism started in Whitehall, Wisconsin."

"We'll kill him, right here, in front of you," warns the chorus of crabby old lady voices. "Unless you leave. Now."

I grab my keys off the table. "Thanks for your help, but I'm in a hurry."

He taps the table with his fingers. "But I haven't helped you yet, have I?"

The keys clink in my shaking hands. I take a deep breath and will my hands to still. Goosebumps riddle my skin. Eyes rooted to the floor, I stand speechless before his black attire.

"You can't look me in the eye, can you?" he asks.

I try but can't do it. "You're right. Why is that?"

"You're a wounded soul." His voice is kind, inviting.

I inch toward the door. "I'm sorry." For so many things.

"When you're ready to come back, ask for me. My name is Father Joe."

I rush out the door and tear down the front steps, the old ladies calling after me, *"You won't be coming back. We won't let you."*

CHAPTER FOURTEEN

SPEED

My heart races as I peel out of the church parking lot and hurry home. As I crest the top of State Street Hill, I tap on the brake to slow my acceleration.

It doesn't respond.

I pump the brake. It collapses to the floor.

I scream as the car accelerates down the hill. My hand slams on the horn as I whip past rows of old houses. Cars swerve out of the way, honking in protest as I tug the emergency brake. Please let the Hibbard Hall parking lot be empty. Please. Please. Please.

As I near the lot at the bottom of the hill, I see that the lot is vacant. My tires screech as I yank on the steering wheel.

Rocketing into the lot, I circle until the car slows to a crawl. I turn off the engine with shaking hands. Throwing the door open, I stumble out of my car and collapse on the pavement, chest heaving. What just happened? Did the demons or that exorcist priest do this to me? So much for the Lexus's high safety rating!

I grab my phone and call Walker. "Can you come look at my car? Something's wrong with the brakes."

"Where *are* you?"

"On campus," I choke out the words. "In the parking lot by

Hibbard Hall."

"Of all the women drivers in the world, you are the absolute worst. I'll be right there."

Dizzy with fear, I stand up and lean against my car. The empty lot slowly stops spinning. A tree right in front my car comes into focus. A red Smiley Face has been painted on it. The open mouth leers at me.

My stomach heaves. I'm going to be sick. I gag, kneeling down and putting my head on the ground to keep from fainting. A movement to the side catches my eye. What is that? Do I even want to know?

I force myself to turn toward the scraping sound. Far across the parking lot, a massive black snake undulates across the warm tar, headed right for me.

I want to run but am frozen in place.

It nears, hissing and spitting as it approaches.

I can't move. "You're *not* real! This is *not* happening! I'm going to close my eyes and when I open them again you'll be *gone*."

A fear niggles in my brain that shutting one's eyes against a demonic reptilian attacker may not be the wisest course of action, but when I open my eyes again, the snake—and the Smiley Face—are both gone.

A moth settles on my arm. I brush it away.

Am I going insane? How does one know for sure? I wish I had some answers. I wish I had someone to help me besides Walker.

My favorite police officer arrives ten minutes later, checks out my car, then shakes his head. "There's nothing wrong with it."

I cross my arms. "Tell that to all the people I almost ran into as I plowed down State Street Hill!"

"Did the brakes fail last month, too, when you annihilated the bushes near the parking lot by the Fine Arts building?"

"Very funny. You know I did that on purpose to help Mike get back into the river."

He shrugs, wiping his hands on a rag. "Maybe you slammed on the gas pedal instead of the brake."

I punch his arm. "Do you really think I'm that stupid?"

He throws up his hands defensively. "Listen. I grew up with two sisters and a single mom. I know better than to call any *female* stupid."

I cross my arms. "Can you at least escort me back home, in case it happens again?" *I need you to keep me safe.*

"Yeah. I'll drive in front of you, but try not to run into me, okay?"

I nod. "Good idea."

As we get back into our respective cars, Walker hollers, "And what's with all the rosaries? Is that a fashion statement, like Madonna back in the eighties, or a 'born again' thing?" He slams his door shut, not waiting for an answer.

I glance over at the passenger seat. The contents of my bag spilled onto the floor during my near accident. I scoop everything back inside, then trail Walker across the parking lot and out into the street at an elderly pace. After we both park near the apartment, he rolls down his window.

"I should arrest you for going too slow. You drive like an arthritic bingo junkie with bad cataracts."

"I just wanted to get home safely."

He smirks. "You're welcome."

Stupid Walker. He would make me grovel. "Yes, thank you, kind sir," I reply sarcastically as I get out of my possessed car.

"No problem." He grins wider. "Actually, I'm in the best of moods today. Jennifer's case is wrapping up nicely, and I have a hot date for this weekend."

I frown. "Does she have to meet your momma, too?"

"No, she took my sisters back home." He laughs, then narrows his eyes playfully. "Don't tell me you're jealous."

"What?" My cheeks flush, which embarrasses me. I'm so not jealous. It's my mother who thinks he's handsome—not me. "Don't be ridiculous."

"It's not my fault I'm this good looking."

"Well, I'm *not* jealous!" Okay, I am a little envious, but only because he's sane and I'm totally losing it.

He shakes a finger at me. "Better have a mechanic check your brakes tomorrow. In case there is something wrong with your *fancy* car."

"Ugh. Nothing makes me feel more stupid than talking to auto mechanics." I grimace as he pulls away, laughing.

"Lovers' quarrel?" Phoebe's voice comes from behind me.

Grrr. Her again. Why can't she mind her own business? I spin around to face her. "Walker? No way. We're not dating. I don't even like him that way."

"Hmm. I don't believe you. He's a fine-looking man." She lounges on a chair in the front yard, completely in the shade of a row of evergreen trees. Her large sunglasses pair well with her fifties-style swimsuit.

"What are you doing, Phoebe?" I ask. She looks ridiculous. "It's not like you can tan in the shade."

"I'm not tanning. I'm perfect just the way I am. This is called research." She gestures at the pile of Wiccan books at her feet. "I'm determined to figure you out."

"Good luck with that, because *I* can't even figure myself out." I step inside and check my empty mailbox in the foyer. No letter from Laura. I head upstairs to my apartment. When I open the door, the air inside is heavy and cool. And it's supposed to be summer.

"I've had *enough* of this," I announce to my inner demons as I unpack my supplies. "You're not welcome here. It's time for you to go."

I cross over to the living room windows and glance down. Phoebe stares up from her nosy post.

"Stop watching me," I mutter through clenched teeth and yank the shades shut.

After digging through my dresser drawers, I add a Bible and a small wooden cross to the collection of rosaries.

I sit cross-legged on the floor and encircle myself with a dozen white candles.

"White for purity."

Even before I reach the first wick with a lit match, every candle bursts into flame.

Huh. That's different.

I clear my throat and continue.

"Lit to guide my way."

I string rosaries around my neck, wincing as electric shocks prickle my skin. I grasp one of my water bottles filled with holy water.

"Bottoms up!" I close my eyes, bracing myself before swallowing. As the holy water trickles down my throat, my neck and chest burn as if I'm chugging a bottle of fierce whiskey.

"There, that should weaken you, unwelcome spirits!" I feel empowered, alive, almost aflame.

"You can do it!" Jake's voice.

My eyes fly open. He's sitting on my couch, smiling, both hands held in the thumbs up position.

"Jake," I breathe the word, heart racing for once from pleasure, not fear or pain.

"I don't think this is such a good idea." Mike appears beside Jake on the couch, shaking his head.

"No shocker there," I mutter.

"Just be *careful,*" Bernard shows up next, wringing his hands.

"I will." It's so good to see them, but it's not clear if they can really see me or if I'm imagining the whole thing.

The last to arrive is Steve, pacing back and forth, and checking his watch. "How long is this going to take?" he asks. "I've got an important meeting in ten minutes."

"When did you turn into such a jerk?" I scowl. "I need your help."

No answer from the Dead Guys. It's like they're talking to each other, not me.

"Come on," I beg on my knees. "I need you, *now.*"

The images fade from view, Jake last of all to go.

"No!" I collapse, my head in my arms. "I want you to stay! Why won't you stay?"

Through my tears, I hear a hissing from under the couch.

Not again. If I have to do this myself, I will.

Ignoring the snake's bile-yellow eyes, I read aloud from the Bible. The holy book shivers in my grasp while I recite passages to banish demons.

The windows creak and the shades flutter.

A great snake, perhaps the largest one yet, slides across the room toward me.

Once it reaches my Magic Circle, it raises its head up to the ceiling and towers over me.

The Bible falls from my grasp.

"Our Father, who art in Heaven... Holy Mary, Mother of... Where there is darkness, let me bring light..." mumbled bits of prayers fall from my lips.

My mind breaks into little pieces, and I can't put any of them back together.

The shower drips.

The bathroom cup spins. The refrigerator shudders.

Curtains flail.

The snake flicks its tongue.

Furniture whirls around the room.

"Nothing shall enter the Circle!"

I stand on shaky legs, arms outstretched, to recite the exorcism chant.

"I cast you out, unclean spirit, along with every Satanic power of the enemy, every specter from Hell, and all your fell companions..."

Everything pauses for a moment. The furniture halts mid-air.

The curtains cease their fluttering movements and hang still.

The room seems to hold its breath before releasing a puff of air.

Silence. For only a moment.

Everything comes flying toward the Magic Circle, with an ear-piercing shriek.

The snake's giant mouth opens wide, aiming straight for my head.

Black smoke spills out from under the couch.

My notebook flutters helplessly in this spirit wind.

The floor shakes below me.

A swarm of black moths swirls around my head, catching in my hair.

A sharp pain slices into my neck.

I'm dead. Or I'm dying. And I'm not sure which is worse.

CHAPTER FIFTEEN

TEMPTING FATE

What's that nasty smell? Why's it so dark in here? Something's on top of me—what is it? Weak sunlight filters through the shades as my eyes focus. There's a huge crow on my chest, black eyes glassy as marbles.

I scream and shove the stiff bird away. The dead body thumps to the floor, its tongue hanging out of a gaping beak.

Ugh. I've got to get that rotten thing out of here. I dash to the kitchen for a plastic garbage bag. When I return, the crow has disappeared. What the Hell? Where is it?

Even the smell is gone.

I yank aside the shades and crank open the windows, disrupting the black moths hovering there. The sun hangs low on the horizon. How long was I passed out? After making a thorough search for the missing bird in my apartment, I head into the bathroom. As I remove the rosaries, I realize that they don't prickle my skin any longer.

I stare at the quiet sink. Then turn to examine the shower.

No blood.

No voices.

I dig out another water bottle filled with holy water and gulp it down.

No pain.

"I'm free! I did it!" After a happy dance, I change clothes and go for a walk down by the river. The sky fills with the sounds of rustling grasses, croaking frogs, and distant traffic. The night is so peaceful. My bruises don't hurt much anymore. Soon I won't even need these stifling turtlenecks.

The ring of the cell phone interrupts my quiet, self-congratulatory reverie.

"Emma, where've you been?" Walker asks. "I left you three messages."

"Oh, sorry. I didn't check them."

"I want you to work Steve's spell tonight. It's a full moon. Are you ready?"

My chest fills with dark, cold fear. I almost drop the phone.

"Emma? Are you still there?"

I can barely breathe, much less talk. "Yeah," I finally mumble.

"Well, can you do it?" He sounds impatient.

I shift the phone to the other ear. "Walker, I'm not so sure about this."

"I know these spells are getting scary for you, but this one's important."

"I know." But I don't need any more trouble.

"It's the *last* time. I swear." I visualize Walker crossing his heart.

"Give me a minute." I focus on the moonlight sparkling on the water. I need to decide right away, but it's like I've split into two people, each one fighting with the other. This time, neither of them is from the spirit world. They're both just me: Brave Emma and Cowardly Emma.

I wish I could tell Walker the truth, but those words are trapped down deep inside.

I really don't know if I can handle any more of this.

But it's only one more. And now I know how to get rid of any unwelcome visitors: a simple exorcism—or maybe not so simple.

I sigh. "All right, Walker. I'll do it."

"Great. I'll pick you up in ten minutes." He hangs up.

I sink to my knees. Oh, God, I'm so afraid.

As the full moon rises, Walker drives us to the site of Steve's murder. He parks his truck a discreet distance away. He jumps out, but I linger inside, heart sinking to my knees.

"Come on, let's go." He carries the bent metal rod in his hands, the one that was used to kill Steve almost a year ago.

"Okay." My shoulders slump.

The truck door creaks as I get out. We travel the rest of the dirt road on foot, the beams from our flashlights bouncing ahead of us. My flashlight illuminates the tree branded with the menacing Smiley Face symbol. Chills shake my body, even though the air temps are in the eighties.

No matter what happens, this is the right thing to do. I owe Steve this much.

My hands tremble as I line the road leading up to the desecrated tree with candles and incense bowls. I light the white petition crosses first, then the red and black cats. Last of all, I hold the lit match to the black-winged devil holding court under the branded tree.

Just before I reach the wick of the devil candle, it lights itself.

Then its wax eye winks at me.

I flinch, dropping the lit match to the ground. Tears spring to my eyes as I snuff the flames out with my shoe. I'm caught in a trap I built myself.

"Are you ready yet?" Walker asks, tapping his hands on his jeans.

"Almost." My voice wavers. "You can position the weapon now."

He places the rod in the middle of the dirt road. I fill Grandma's wooden bowl with river water and set it at my feet. When I open the *Book of Shadows* to find my spell, the night wind whispers words I can't understand.

What are they saying? I can't quite hear them. Are they talking to me?

I shake my head to help gain focus. Instead my mind fills with images.

Steve sitting at a desk, wearing a blue oxford and tie, barking orders at someone unseen.

Sam talking to an old woman.

Mike kneeling in a church.

Bernard playing catch with two young kids.

Jake dancing with a long-haired blonde.

I stiffen.

Who's that girl? Why's he dancing with her?

"Emma!" Walker waves his hand in front of my face. "Hello in there. Can you focus, please?"

"Yes." I swallow my fear and uncertainty.

"Okay, then." Walker backs up to the edge of the road.

Hands quivering, I begin, trying to perform everything exactly as before. I don't want any surprises.

"I call upon the elements of Air..."

I light the incense bowls. The flames take hold and dance with the shadows.

"Earth..."

Soft thuds echo in my ears as I drop river pebbles along the dirt road.

"Water..."

Leaves rustle overhead as I place Grandma's wooden bowl at the base of the tree.

"And Fire... Watch over me."

Grandma's bowl glows yellow-orange. Delicate carvings of flowers, flames, wind, and water dance and swirl together. It's beautiful, mesmerizing.

Funny, that didn't happen last time.

"Guard me. Guide me. Protect me during these my Rites."

Candlelight illuminates Walker's profile. He doesn't look the least bit scared, but I'm terrified. I step back and hold the *Book of Shadows* high in my hands. By now I know the words by heart:

"Reveal to me
The treachery.
Expose the crime
From back in time.
Bring forth, bring down,
Let truth be found.
Draw back the veil
That hides the tale.

Make known the fear
That once lived here."

Lightning crashes. The earth shakes. I stumble when the ground rocks beneath my feet. Just as I catch my balance, a beat-up van's headlights blind me.

"Get out of the way!" Walker yells.

But I can't move. I remain rooted in place until Walker drags me into the shadows of the nearest shrubbery.

"Not Grandma's bowl!" I protest. "I have to save it!"

"Be quiet and lay low," he whispers in my ear.

I shudder and watch my worst nightmare unfold anew. I hate that I have to see this again.

The familiar van backs up to the river. Young men pile out, all wearing black bandanas and green plaid flannel shirts. They haul Steve out of the back of the van. His body slumps as they force him to the edge of the river. They pummel him with their fists and kick his crumpled form to the ground.

Tears race down my cheeks. I dread what will happen next.

"I've got to get closer. Stay here. I don't think they can see you, but hide anyway." Walker whispers. He crawls through the underbrush toward the river.

I flinch every time Steve cries out.

The tallest man doesn't touch him. He stands off to the side, staring out across the river. He's turned away and I can't see his face.

When I can't take any more, the shortest of the men smashes the bent metal rod down on Steve's head. He shudders a few times, then remains still. Just like the first time I worked this spell, the group dumps Steve's limp body into the river, spray-paints the Smiley Face on the tree, and piles back into the van.

Only two men remain on the path.

The tall man gazing over the river is slow to leave. His face comes into view as he approaches the van, mumbling to himself with a mouthful of crooked teeth.

My pulse races. I *knew* Eva Garcia's murderer had something to do with Steve's death.

Once he disappears into the van, only the shortest man is left, still clenching the bent metal rod in his hands. The others call for him, but he remains motionless.

He looks young and scared. His dark eyes focus on the rod for a long time before he lifts his gaze—to mine. He stares right at me, unsmiling. I can't breathe. Should I run? Can he really see me? Is this real or another hallucination?

Steve's murderer approaches as the van peels away in the opposite direction.

He edges closer.

And closer.

I hunch down in the bushes. But he reaches in and yanks me to my feet. My legs quiver and my heart explodes in pain. My chest feels like a vacuum sucking in everything around me. My head snaps back and I gasp for air, arms flailing like an injured bird. Grabbing the nearest tree, I struggle to stand. When the world finally comes back into focus, the last gang member has disappeared.

I wheel around, searching for him. Where did he go?

"Emma!" Walker snaps his fingers in my face. "You're a million miles away. Come on, let's go. I'll drop you off quick before I head down to the station. I need to run through the file again, pronto. Okay? I was right about my hunch. I just have to prove it."

"Oh... yeah. Fine." The noise of a million insects buzzes in my ears.

I rush around to collect all my supplies, relieved to find Grandma's bowl intact and undamaged. Then I scamper behind Walker's quick strides to the car.

As he drives, Walker taps impatient fingers on the steering wheel. "Thanks, Emma. You're the best."

"Then you got what you needed?" I hold my breath, silently praying he won't ask me to do this again.

"Yeah. I think so," Walker says. "At least I can identify all their faces now."

"The guy who killed Eva was there." My throat tightens shut.

His eyes widen. "The guy with the crooked teeth? The one called Shadow?"

I nod, unable to speak again. There's so much to say, but some unseen force stops me from telling Walker any more. I barely got out what I did.

"Why didn't you point him out? I never saw him."

I clear my throat a long time before I'm able to mutter, "Good question."

Minutes later, he parks in front of my apartment building.

"I'll keep you posted." Walker turns to me as I step out of the car. "Thanks again. You know how important this is to Steve—and to me."

"I'm glad I could help." But never ask me to do this again. It's too dangerous.

I watch him drive away, dreading what comes next, because I know the spirits won't leave me alone after I called on them. And there were so many of them this time.

"Were you guys out on a date?" a grating voice asks from behind. Phoebe stands on the sidewalk, a bag of groceries in her hand.

"I told you," I growl. "We're not dating."

"Then why are you always together?" she asks, one hand on hip.

I sigh. "It's late, Phoebe. Good night."

I trudge up the stairs to my apartment, my legs weakening with every step. I unlock the door and stagger inside, as if drunk or drugged, or both at the same time. The apartment floor begins to teeter and the hallway fills with a black smoke.

The room temperature plummets.

An unseen force drags me into the bathroom, then lifts me, shoving me toward the mirror.

Silver hands reach out from the glass and pull me into another time and place.

CHAPTER SIXTEEN

THE SACRIFICE

wake in an unfamiliar bed, in the middle of a nightmare that's not my own. A green and black flannel shirt hangs over the bedpost by my extra-large man-sized feet, which stick out past a flimsy blanket.

I killed him. I crushed that guy's skull. With that metal rod.

Don't worry. They dumped him into the river. No one will find him.

No one has to know. Except the Cobras. I only did what they asked. I had to do it. And that guy doesn't matter.

Nothing matters except now I'm a King Cobra at last.

"Hey, wake up, loser." My sister waltzes in the room and punches me in the arm. "Rise and shine, Butt Head."

Pulling the covers over my head doesn't stop Carmen. It never does.

"Where've you been the last few days, Dominic?" She pops her gum. "You weren't at home. Or school. And you don't have a job."

"Leave me alone," I grumble from under the sheets.

She sighs with exaggeration. "No can do. It's time for school."

I see the dead man's face. I hear him crying out in pain. I ended that pain by ending his life. Bile rises up the back of my throat. I'm going to be sick.

I cover my head with the pillow. "Leave me alone."

I can still feel the metal rod in my hands.

Carmen punches me again. "No can do." She smells like cinnamon.

"Stop it! Why are you always on my case?"

"Can't handle a punch from a girl? Aren't you supposed to be all tough now, with all your *new* friends?"

I sit up. "Why do you hate them so much?"

She frowns. "They're no good for you. Why do you want to be one of them?"

I need them for protection. How come Carmen doesn't get this? "Be careful," I warn. "The King Cobras are dangerous." And now… so am I.

"Then I guess I better watch my back." Carmen narrows her dark eyes. "I won't lose you to them. I won't allow it."

"What are you gonna do about it?" I snap, yanking on a wrinkled green t-shirt.

"Did anyone ever tell you that green and black aren't your best colors?" She smacks her gum. "You look terrible. Like death warmed over."

Big sisters suck.

Waiting with two other King Cobras in the tattoo parlor, I stare at the ground fighting to remain calm. Am I doing the right thing? What if Carmen's right? Maybe I should get out while I still can.

Shadow peels off bills from a large roll of cash and stuffs them in the tattoo artist's hands.

"Brand him." He sneers with crooked teeth. He laughs and slaps me on the back, but when Shadow's gaze falls upon me, my stomach lurches and flails like a mouse in a trap.

The tattoo still burning on my arm, I follow the others into a run-down building, then down to the basement. Water trickles in the background. The air around us hangs dank and damp. We descend deeper into the underground sewers on metal ladders attached to walls. I glance around, my heart racing. I've no idea where I am. I can't run away now even if I want to.

Shadow glances in my direction. "Your first time to the Inner Sanctum, isn't it?"

"Y—yes" my voice cracks.

He coughs, his crooked teeth leering close to my face, and slaps me on my sore arm.

I wince, both at the pain and the smell of his breath. It's like he swallowed Death.

"Like your tattoo?" he asks.

I nod, not daring to say any more.

"Good. Now you belong to us." His cackling makes my skin grow cold.

Finally we reach a large open sewer. I flinch at the smell, but hide my disgust. Tall black candles line both walls, leading up to a large stone altar. The ceiling arches far above us, dripping with moisture.

I step on something soft. I pause and pick up a limp black cat.

What's a dead cat doing here? With a shudder, I discover the body of a crow next to the cat. Bile threatens to come forth once again. My head spins and my stomach convulses.

I shouldn't be here.

Shadow grabs my tattooed arm, sending pain up to my shoulder. I drop the cat. It makes a soft thud on the floor.

"Master wants to see you now," he growls. He drags me toward a raised stage in the front of the room. A tall man faces away from us on the stage, standing in front of what looks like an altar.

My feet stick to the floor. I glance down to find I've stepped in blood. I bite down hard on my lip to keep from crying out.

"Master, you wanted to see Dominic?" asks Shadow, with a bow.

"Oh, yes." The Master turns and my stomach lurches again. Blood trickles from one side of his mouth. His lips peel open in a grimace filled with long, sharpened teeth.

I step back involuntarily.

"Welcome, my boy. You did well during your Initiation, or so I am told." Master's eyes are wide and black as an insect's. "And, Shadow, my faithful servant, I understand you have important news for me."

Shadow steps forward. "Yes, Master. As you requested, I've been searching the Chippewa River Valley for the strange power source you detected."

"Yes. Please continue."

Shadow's eyes glow with excitement. "I found her at last. Her name is Emma Roberts."

"How wonderful." Master folds his hands together. His nails are long and black. "Show me."

"As you command." Shadow enters a circle of tall red candles. Each wick bursts into flame. The rest of the crowd hovers close, murmuring and watching.

Master descends from the stage, waves his hands, and Shadow disappears into a thick mist. As the haze disperses, an image appears of three college-aged women walking across a parking lot.

"Let's sit over there," a blonde, teenaged girl points toward a cluster of trees, a bag bouncing on her hip.

"It feels strange to be outside this late at night," whispers a young woman with a ponytail, nervously tugging on her shirt.

"Do you think the campus cops will drive by and stop us?" a pretty girl in a short skirt asks.

"Why would they stop us?" the blonde responds. "It's just a little love spell."

The mist shifts to reveal the same three women sitting near a large rock illuminated by lit candles under a full moon.

A few crickets chirp, a lone frog bellows, then silence.

The blonde hands the pretty one a spell to read:

"Oh moon, upon me shine.
Steal his heart and make it mine.
Guide his eyes so he will see
The only one to love is me.
Seize his voice and make him say
That he will never go away... "

When the spell ends, the anxious girl turns around. She searches behind her, a puzzled expression on her face, then shakes her head and turns back to the others.

Master waves his arms, dispelling the vision. Shadow reappears and exits the Circle.

"Ahhh, my faithful servant." Master places a long-fingered hand over his heart. "You have done well."

"Then you agree it's the quiet one you want?" Shadow hesitates. "I'm ashamed to admit that at first I assumed the witch working the spell must be the cause of the sudden power shift in the air. But when the nervous one turned around—I swear she sensed me watching her—then I knew that *she* was the one you wanted."

"Yes. She is the one." Master pauses. "She's unaware and untrained, but ripe with power. I must have her."

"I'll go at once," Shadow replies.

"No. The girl is not yet ready to serve me. She must be transformed. Follow her. Make the most of any opportunity. She should be easy enough to break once the time comes."

"As you wish, Master." Shadow nods.

"Be patient, my faithful son. All good things take time—or bad things, in this case." Master chuckles, splaying his fingers together. "So much needs to be done. We must prepare the Inner Sanctum. Purify the workers."

Shadow bows his head. "I am your servant."

"Obsidian. I'll need more of it. As much as you can find." The Master gestures toward the wall over the altar. A vision of a beautiful Brazilian woman wearing a necklace of black stones appears for a moment in the empty air, then fades. "While you're in Eau Claire observing young Emma, take a moment to relieve the beautiful Eva Garcia of her obsidian collection. She possesses a mirror which I would find quite useful."

"Anything you ask, I will do."

The two of them bow their heads together, as if in prayer. Master places a hand on each of Shadow's shoulders.

I step back, away from the altar. I hate both of them. I hate myself. I hate this room, and everyone and everything in it. What am I doing here? What's Master going to do with those girls? And that beautiful woman? Is he going to kill all of them, too? Or ask Shadow to do it instead? Or demand it of me? No way. I'm not killing anyone else. Not even a cat.

I want out.

The two men move apart. Shadow's eyes have fogged over.

Master raises his thin, dark brows. "We must be patient."

"She needs time... and training," Shadow speaks slowly, as if in a trance. "Yes..."

"The *Book of Shadows* must become hers," Shadow murmurs. "She must be compelled to use it... she must become attached, let it control her... then *I* will take over her mind... and bring her here."

"Exactly, my son. I have no need of her until she masters the *Book*. And to arrange all this we need a sacrifice. A young sacrifice."

My skin prickles. What sacrifice?

Master's gaze falls upon me. Then he extends his long arm, pointing my way.

My legs turn to melting ice. Does he mean me?

In a flash, Shadow stands in front of me. "This one has too many questions running through his head. I hear his uncertainty. He's not one of us. He never will be. He hasn't accepted his fate. He's fighting it, but it's a battle he will lose."

"Then be done with it." Master turns back to the steps, and ascends to his altar as if disinterested.

Shadow reaches for my neck.

I turn to run but I'm not fast enough. Ugly faces leer at every turn, blocking my escape.

Shadow's foul breath burns my neck. "It hurts more when you resist."

The edge of a knife flashes. Sharp pain shoots into my stomach. The fire inside melts into a cool pool of liquid.

My legs give way. I drop onto the floor, grabbing at my belly. Blood sticks to my fingers.

Disfigured faces rush at me, but I'm too weak to turn away.

There's blood.

There's pain.

Then I feel... nothing.

CHAPTER SEVENTEEN

HELP

I wake on the floor of my own apartment. The good news is that I'm me again. The bad news is that there's another disgusting dead black crow on my chest. Wincing at the foul smell, I grab the nasty thing by a stiff wing and force open a window. Another dark moth flies in the apartment as I toss the crow outside.

In slow motion, it tumbles to the ground, as if sinking through liquid instead of air. Down below stands Phoebe, the oblivious target. I consider warning her, but don't. A silly grin on my face, I watch the bird splatter on Phoebe's shiny black hair a second before it explodes into a dark cloud of smoke. I back away from the window before she spots me.

Phoebe's startled scream echoes through the parking lot. As her screech thins to nothing, the familiar noise of a spinning cup screeches in the bathroom.

"Oh, shut up!" I storm into the bathroom, grab the cup, and smash it on the floor. It breaks into a million pieces, each shard skittering across the black and white tiles.

There's a snake in the mirror. I lean closer. No. Freaking. Way. The snake is me—or, at least, part of me. My left shoulder has been inked with a ginormous tattoo of a hissing green snake. I still have bruises all over my body. And the bite wound on my wrist hasn't healed yet.

What next? I shudder, revisiting in my mind the dank sewers inhabited by Master and his minions, including Shadow.

The images Shadow revealed weren't of strangers. Those three girls were my roommate Chrissy, her sister Angie, and me performing a love spell to make Mike's older brother Kevin fall in love with Chrissy forever.

My heart races. It's hard to catch my breath. That vision was about *me*. Angie threw away the *Book of Shadows* because she kept having nightmares about Steve's death. The King Cobras gave me Angie's book—it *had* to be them. The Shadow said I'd need a reason to use the *Book of Shadows*. Mike's death gave me enough reason. Master said I'd be easy to break. What if he was right?

My mind spins as fast as the broken shards on the floor.

Words written in blood appear across the mirror. *You belong to the Master now. He will never let you go.*

The words fade away, and a garish Smiley Face sneers at me from the mirror instead.

I grip the bathroom counter, my gut heaving. I poke the tattoo, still fresh and sore to the touch, inviting the pain.

It doesn't matter how much it hurts. I have to get rid of the spirits possessing me.

I won't let the King Cobras have me.

I'd kill myself before I became the Master's slave.

I rush out of the bathroom. It's time to take that exorcist priest up on his offer. I grab my purse and stuff it with the leftovers of my failed exorcism. After I ensure that Phoebe has retreated to her apartment, I sneak out the back and speed to church. Thankfully, my brakes work this time. When I arrive, a handful of white-haired ladies gossip on the front steps.

It looks like morning mass just ended. I rush up the front stone steps. This time, the doors stand open so I don't have to fight them. Entering the gathering space, I cough on the incense-laden air. I press forward, searching for the exorcist. He's stacking missals in the far corner.

"Father Joe?" I ask, my voice cracking on his name.

He turns around and his eyes widen. "You're back."

"Yes." I glance around, waiting for a voice or an image to stop me, but all is quiet—for now.

"Does this mean you're asking for my help?" He sets the missals aside.

I nod, silent, still unable to look him in the eyes.

Without warning, he places a small crucifix on the back of my neck. I spasm in pain, falling to the ground. My head snaps back, forcing me to look the priest straight in the eye. My vision glows red and I growl like a caged animal.

Father Joe raises his eyebrows a notch, but otherwise seems unperturbed. "I'm sorry about that, but I had to know what I'm—I mean, what *you're*—dealing with. Did you know you were possessed?"

He reaches out a hand that I don't take.

"Yes. I knew," I spit out. "That's why I'm here. You didn't have to do that."

"Oh, I think I did, not that I wanted to." He offers his hand again, and this time I accept, but with hesitation. "Let's sit for a moment."

He leads me to a middle pew, where I collapse. He lets me catch my breath before he continues. "I *can* help you, but I'm afraid you're going to feel a lot worse before you feel any better."

I laugh, but the noise sounds miserable. "I'm not sure I can feel any worse than this."

"I'm afraid you can, but you've made an important first step in seeking me out. I'll help you through the rest. What's your name?"

"Emma Roberts."

"Now, Emma, in order to properly perform an exorcism on a... young woman, I need the assistance of another woman. If you're better now, let's go find the secretary. She's been quite helpful in these types of situations."

I struggle to a stand, but can't trust my weak, wobbly legs. "Can I stay here while you get her? I'm so dizzy." I grasp the pew.

Father Joe pauses. "Are you sure you'll be okay alone?"

"Yes." I take a jagged breath. "As long as you keep that crucifix off my neck, I'm good."

"Okay." He scans the church as if reluctant to leave my side. "Don't move. I'll be right back."

He pats my tattooed shoulder in a fatherly fashion and hurries off. The pain which shoots through my arm is bad enough, but my rising panic is even worse. This time, the exorcism has to work—otherwise I'm out of ideas. As I wait for Father Joe to return, the gaggle of elderly women shuffle into the church. Instead of choosing other pews, one by one they file into mine.

I ignore them as they silently edge toward me. Why can't they find another pew?

A moth lands on my hand. I brush it off.

The church fills with the stench of rotting meat.

I glance up and suppress a scream. Only one of the demonic old ladies still has a nose, and only half of one. Their white hair transforms into writhing green snakes. Melting eyeballs drip yellow pus onto colorful flowered blouses. Closer and closer they stalk toward me, evil words emitting from their gaping mouths.

"Slave of the Master, give in to your fears."

I scramble over the backs of pews, my hands knocking missals and choir books to the floor. The pages hiss and crumple as the demons trample them with their feet.

They chase after me, clutching dead hairless kittens in their raised hands.

"Be the channel. Use the Book."

Racing past the pews into the gathering space, I pick up speed and leave their cackling voices behind me. I burst out the front doors, into the glaring sunlight. I glance back at the church steps as the evil spirits transform. Flowered blouses flutter and reform as green flannel shirts. Black bandanas wrap around their snake-covered heads. All three forms melt into one.

I halt in the middle of the road as Shadow levels his steady gaze at me. His eyes shine solid black, like stone. He has no irises. Just black.

He holds out a bloodstained hand. "I sense your loneliness, Emma," he says, his voice warm, slippery, and inviting. "The Master can raise from the dead whomever you want. You do not have to be alone."

Jake. He's trying to use my feelings about Jake to manipulate me.

"Never." I choke out the word, my throat tightening down.

His black, soul-less eyes narrow. "Don't be so sure. Master's seen the future in the obsidian mirror, and you are by his side."

"Why did he want obsidian?" I back away. "It's supposed to ward off bad spirits."

An evil chuckle rumbles in his veiny throat. "Don't be a fool. Anything pure can be made foul, if one is brave enough to pay the price. Such is the case with you."

My chest heaves, as the spirits inside me lurch against my ribs like insects trapped in a glass jar.

Shadow steps closer, a hand still outstretched. His black nails lengthen into claws. "Show me the *Book*."

I sneak a hand in my bag and grasp a leftover bottle of holy water instead. My movements hidden by the bag, I unscrew the lid. With one swift move, I yank the bottle of the bag and fling the blessed water in Shadow's face.

He howls in agony as I race for my car.

I gun the engine and peel out of the parking lot. I scream through the window at his malformed face, "Never! The *Book* is mine!"

Shadow recovers quickly, his words haunting me as I speed away, "You are mistaken. I gave you the *Book,* and I can take it away again."

CHAPTER EIGHTEEN

MOMMY DEAREST

Something shakes my arm. **"Wake up! Wake up!"** a female voice urges.

Leave me alone. I'm so tired. Go away.

"Come on! Wake up!"

A sharp smack cracks across my cheek.

"Ouch! That hurts!" I sit up, brushing sand off my face, startled to find myself in the cool shade under the bridge on campus.

Phoebe kneels next to me, scowling. "Well, it's no wonder."

"No wonder what?" Ugh, my mouth is so dry and my eyes feel crusty. Wait a minute… How did I get here? Wasn't I driving home? Where's my car?

She narrows her dark eyes, perfectly lined in kohl. "No wonder your mom thinks you're on drugs."

I take a deep breath and beg the world to stop spinning.

"Well, are you?" she asks.

"No, of course not." I hallucinate enough on my own. I don't need any outside help.

Phoebe shrugs. "You certainly *act* strange enough."

I stand shakily and brush sand off my pants. "You're one to talk."

She crosses her arms. "What are all those crazy noises coming from your apartment?"

"I like alternative music." I wonder if she knows I had something to do with that dead crow.

"It's not music, and you know it." Phoebe gestures for me to follow. "Come on, your parents are waiting."

"What?" Oh no. Not today.

"They're worried because you haven't returned any of their calls." Phoebe urges me forward. "They asked me *tons* of questions."

Oh, great. "Like what?"

"Your mom wanted to know if I had seen anyone *suspicious* hanging around here." Phoebe's voice falls to a whisper. "Like drug-dealers."

"What did you tell them?"

"That the *only* person I ever see you with is that cop."

I groan. "His *name* is Walker."

"Yeah, him." Phoebe pushes onward. "And another thing. Why are you always wearing turtlenecks? It's June, for crying out loud."

Another wave of pain surges through my body. I fight against it, but it rages everywhere—in my swollen throat, under my ugly tattoo, and radiating from what feels very much like a sharp blade twisting in my gut.

Phoebe watches with suspicious eyes. I glare back. That girl needs to quit trying to figure me out.

"What's wrong with you, Emma? You can barely walk."

"I'll be fine," I lie, covering the abdominal pain with a hand. I'm so very far away from being fine.

Her gaze lands on my protective hand over my belly. "Maybe you have appendicitis. A friend of mine had that. She was in agony."

"I don't have appendicitis." I continue my stilted walk to my parents, hoping that my pain tolerance will improve by the time we reach them.

When my mother spots me, she sprints the last ten yards in our direction. Her worry rolls over me in waves. Dad stands silently nearby, as if dazed.

Mom grasps both my upper arms in an excruciating stronghold and hugs me. I want to scream against the pain.

"Thank you, Phoebe," Mom dismisses her with a bright false smile, never releasing the vice-like grip on my shoulders.

Mom waits until the three of us are alone in my apartment before she lets me have it. "Emma, you look terrible! Are you on drugs? You said you weren't at Christmas, but what the Hell's wrong with you?" She follows me into the kitchen. "We're so worried. Your father even searched the Internet for clues to your weird behavior."

"I did not," insists Dad.

"Oh, you did, too," Mom spits back. "I only helped a little."

"Don't worry. I'm fine." I limp over to the cupboard, swearing under my breath as I tip over an empty five-hundred-count bottle of ibuprofen. Now what am I going to do?

"What have you been doing this summer? You never come home anymore." Mom taps the kitchen counter with her perfectly manicured fingernails.

"Actually, I've been volunteering with the police department," I say.

"Well, whatever you're up to *down there*—it isn't good for you." She says "down there" as if I was doing something dirty. I chuckle at the irony. Too bad she's not right. Whatever she's imagining would probably be a lot more fun. And considerably less painful.

"What are you trying to do... kill yourself?" Mom inches toward me as if trying to sniff out the answer.

"Cheryl, aren't you overreacting a little?" Dad wrings his hands.

"Why are you running in a turtleneck in June?" Mom plucks at my collar. "You're asking for heat stroke."

I recoil from her touch. "Running?"

"That's what Phoebe said you were doing."

"Oh." Thanks, Phoebe. I owe you one.

"Are you trying to lose weight by sweating more?" Finally, an excuse my mom can understand.

"Yes, that's it. Are we going out to eat? If so, I need to shower first." I rush into the bathroom. Nothing seems to be spinning or dripping.

No Smiley Face appears on the mirror.

"I don't think she needs to lose any more weight," Dad says as I shut the door.

I undress, wincing with each movement. Thank goodness no one can see all my bruises and injuries. Dad thinks I'm anorexic. Mom thinks I'm trying to kill myself. If they knew about my dreams and the voices in my head, they'd probably commit me for schizophrenia.

We sit at an elegant dining table. Mom glares over her frosty drink. I cower behind a wine menu. Not that I'm planning to order anything—me, the only college student on the planet without a fake I.D. Plus, my parents only let me drink at home.

"Is somebody out there?" Eva Garcia's familiar voice interrupts the sultry jazz music and sizzling steak aroma of the restaurant.

I slam back in my chair, scanning the burgundy interior of the restaurant for old lady zombies. So far, the place looks normal.

It just doesn't sound normal.

"I can't breathe!" Jennifer Pearson gasps, and I spin around to look for her.

"Enjoy your meal." The waitress presents our plates and leaves in a hurry.

"Too bad you ordered shrimp." Mom frowns. "You look pale. Maybe you need more red meat in your diet."

"She will be easy enough to break," the Master mutters in my ear.

My eyes widen as I attempt to focus on the food and ignore the inner voices. "So, Mom and Dad, how was your trip?"

Mom clears her throat. "We're not here to talk about our trip."

Thin trails of smoke from the tapered candles on our table encircle my head. I fake a cough. "I'm sorry. These candles are bothering me. Maybe I'm allergic." I blow them out as the wine steward pauses at our table.

Dad waves him away. "So, Emma, how's summer school going?"

I swallow another shrimp. "It doesn't start until next week."

Mom stops dissecting her fish and glances at my father. "Classes started *this* week, Emma."

The shrimp turns into a heavy rock in my stomach. I missed school? I don't even know what day it is? That's insane!

The restaurant begins to spin and tip.

Dad's eyes narrow. "Emma, you'd better tell us what's going on, right now."

Mom points her knife in my direction. "Starting with: *why* haven't you returned our phone calls?"

"I think there's something wrong with my machine," I begin weakly.

She raises a doubtful eyebrow. "What about your cell phone? I called that as well."

"That phone's been acting up, too," I mumble.

The room still twists around me.

Only I stand still.

My parents whirl past like a carousel, with me as the center.

Dad rubs his arm and breathes hard, sweat on his brow. "If you decided against taking summer classes, you should just say so."

"I *am* sort of tired," I admit, trying to keep my voice calm and my hands steady.

"Then come home and rest for a while!" Mom pleads.

"I'll consider it." I envision Mom tying me to the sofa and forcing me watch shirtless Patrick Swayze movies until I make a full recovery. Hey, maybe that's not such a bad idea. But I can't leave town until *after* I get back to Father Joe.

After an hour of chewing in chilly silence and forced conversation, the room finally sits still, so I can walk in a straight line out to the car. My parents drive me to the apartment. Thank goodness they always stay at the Marriott when they visit, or things might get tricky.

When Mom hugs me good night, I almost cry out in pain, but manage to hold back. Dad hugs me, which isn't typical for him.

"I'm worried about you," he whispers into my ear before standing back and tucking his large cross necklace under his shirt.

"I'll be fine," I lie to my parents, and perhaps even myself.

CHAPTER NINETEEN

HOT DATE

After they drive away, I limp to my own car. Things can't go on like this anymore. I need help. It's time to tell Walker the truth. He's the only one who knows enough to understand, and he doesn't even know the half of it. I drive to his house at a senior's pace in case the brakes die on me again. I park on the street because a fancy red sports car occupies the extra spot in front of his double garage.

A low-rider rolls by as I exit my car. Its booming stereo vibrates in my gut. I glance over, and recognize the familiar green snake tattoo on a muscular arm hanging out the window on the passenger side.

My own tattoo begins to throb under my turtleneck. My gaze drifts up from the tattooed arm to Shadow's crooked tooth grin.

He sneers, leaning out the window to point a finger at me, gun-style.

"I'll be back for you. Don't bother trying to escape." Shadow's threat floats back to me on the wind as the King Cobras' car disappears into a thick mist.

My legs collapse. I lean against the Lexus to steady myself. Did I just imagine that? Real or hallucination—it's getting hard to tell. I stumble up the driveway to the front steps. Every light in Walker's house appears to be on. I ring the doorbell repeatedly until the door swings wide open.

"Stop it already!" Walker opens the door and removes my hand from the ringer button. "What the heck do you want?"

"I have to talk to you!" I blurt out. "And I don't care if your mom is still here. This is important."

"Now isn't a good time." Walker tugs at his shirt collar. I've never seen him this dressed up before. A shirt he had to iron. Pants with creases. Shiny, black shoes instead of cowboy boots. What's all this?

I shake my head. "I don't care. I need your help. Right now. Your mom will just have to deal."

"Mom went home. I told you this already." His eyes bulge. "Can't it wait until tomorrow? Please?"

I glance at the extra car in the driveway. "Who's here, then?"

A Victoria's Secret model saunters to the door, a drink poised in her elegant hand.

Damn it! Walker's on his hot date. He's not going to help me now. I back away from the door and flee to my car.

"Who's that?" Model Chick asks Walker.

"Someone from work," he tells her. "Give me a minute. Okay?"

"Of course." She sounds annoyed.

Walker's dress shoes clatter after me. "Emma, wait!"

I struggle through tears to unlock the car.

He places his palm on the door to stop me from opening it. "What's going on? Why are you crying? I know you're hiding something from me again, but I can't figure out what. You're going to have to tell me the truth. Right here. Right now."

I start coughing but force my voice through it. "I need your help. Why do you have to be on a date right now?"

He sighs, but never looks away from my tear-streaked face. "I didn't realize I had to check your schedule first."

"Is somebody out there?" Eva asks, a tremor in her voice.

I slump against the car as a wave of nausea hits me. "I can hear them, Walker." I try not to vomit as a force clamps down on my throat.

His hand shoots out to steady me. "What do you mean? Who can you hear?"

The world fades. Sparkling lights swarm in my peripheral vision. I turn to face Walker. He has to know the truth so he can help me. Sweat trickles down my cheeks and my stomach flips over. "I can see them, too. And I feel everything that happened."

His face is blank. "I don't understand."

"They're inside me, and they won't leave." Toppling forward, I grab the front of his dress shirt. "You've got to help me get rid of them. They're after me."

"Who?" His eyes darken into something dangerous.

"The King Cobras... they're coming for me and my *Book*. They already got Eva Garcia's obsidian mirror and whatever else they need to prepare their lair."

His mouth falls open. "What lair? Where?"

"Excuse me." Little (and I do mean little) Black Dress preens in the driveway. She crosses her perfectly toned arms and swings out her hip seductively. "Should I go now?"

"Emma, Give me a minute. I'll be right back. *Don't* leave." Walker disengages my hands from his now crinkled shirt and hurries over like an obedient dog to his date.

I open the driver-side door and dig in the car for tissues. Instead, I find my *Book of Shadows*. Exhausted, I sit down and caress the soft, fabric-covered book with my hands.

The *Book* rises into the air.

Pages flip back and forth.

My tattoo burns as the King Cobras chant in my head: *"Use the book. Be the channel."*

"That's it!" I growl. They can't have me and they can't have my *Book*. I'll destroy it before I let them have it, and I don't need Walker for that.

Let the Victoria's Secret model have him.

I rev the engine and peel away.

Never thought I'd end up a book burner.

I'm not even that religious.

CHAPTER TWENTY

PLAYING WITH FIRE

My tires squeal to a stop at the nearest gas station. I rush inside and grab three cans of lighter fluid, a large box of matches, and a thick pile of newspapers. The cashier's eyes widen, but she doesn't comment on my purchases. Through the darkness of night, I drive to Carson Park where Jennifer Pearson was attacked.

I glance over at the *Book of Shadows* in the passenger seat, regret in my heart.

"I'm going to miss you." Great. Now I'm talking to a book. Just lock me away.

A sob catches in my throat as I pull into the empty parking lot. I jump out of the car and haul everything over to a stone fire pit. Metal swings creak, rocking back and forth in the warm summer night breeze. I stare at them for a moment, wishing to be a child again.

Then I crumple up the newspapers, throw them in a fire pit, and douse them with lighter fluid. I toss lit matches into the pile, watching the fire climb higher and higher, until it rages blue, white, and orange.

Candles spill from my purse as I step back from the flames. I brace myself for what I must do here tonight. The King Cobras will leave me alone if I can't do magic. I toss the candles into the flames. The wax melts and transforms.

My hands pause on Grandmother's bowl. No. I can't destroy it. This bowl is the only thing I have left of her. I slip it back in my purse and gaze into the white heat of the fire. The flames leap and dance around the pile of colorful candles, melting together.

For the last time, I hold the *Book of Shadows*.

It trembles in my hands.

Why do I feel guilty destroying this? In a moment of doubt, I flip the book open. The pages glow with light; symbols flicker and spin in circles.

The *Book* is possessed, too.

Contaminated.

Just like me.

I grit my teeth and pitch it into the hungry mouth of the fire.

A tower of flame shoots into the sky, three stories high.

Like a volcano, it builds and grows. The heat radiates onto my skin.

With a powerful whistling noise, the fire collapses on itself, taking with it the glow of every streetlight in the parking lot.

Total darkness envelopes the park.

A twig snaps nearby.

"Who's there?" My throat scrapes out the words. I freeze in place.

Someone else is in the park.

I can hear their breath. Which means they're close.

Really close.

Almost right next to me.

"Hello?" a male voice calls out. "I can't see. Is somebody there?"

I know that voice! But it can't be. "Mike? Is that you?"

"Emma? Where are you? What's going on?"

Finally! Someone's here to help me deal with the demons. Tears of relief fall, and I gulp in breath, my chest shuddering.

I just have to find Mike in the darkness. Then everything will be all right.

I light my last match with shaking hands. Its small flare illuminates only the fire pit in front of me.

More twigs snap. I swing around and the match blows out.

Behind me, the fire pit whines and crackles as the fire takes hold and grows.

A thin, high pitch escalates into an inhuman scream. A cat is howling, or maybe a bird of prey.

I spin back to watch the *Book of Shadows* writhe amongst the flames.

Oh, no. Not that.

What have I done? My heart slams in my throat.

I need it. I *need* it. I must have it.

My fingers itch to feel the soft, fabric cover of my *Book*.

Drawn against my will, I reach into the smoldering fire pit.

PART TWO

WHERE THERE IS DARKNESS,

LET ME BRING LIGHT

CHAPTER TWENTY-ONE

HAPPILY EVER AFTER?

Church bells ring. Is it Sunday already?

Sand. Tiny pebbles on my jeans.

The campus bridge towers overhead. I kneel in the cool shadows underneath.

Ahead flows the river. Always the river.

The gentle current. Soothing. Inviting me to come in.

Glaring sun. Too bright.

An orange sun streaks across the sky. Then nightfall.

Moonlight dances upon the water. Someone swims the Chippewa River.

He's wearing a red shirt. I need to follow him. Protect him.

Cool water climbs my ankles, my thighs, my chest.

My hand catches on a lost sock. I struggle to remember.

What is it? Have I been here before?

The trees hide in shadows and whisper the answer.

The river swallows me whole. I can't breathe, but it doesn't matter. Not anymore.

I sink, uncaring. Giving up the fight. Giving in to the river.

Light glitters in the distance.

I hear voices. I flow toward the sound.

The water lightens to turquoise.

Fuzzy figures dance in the distance, underwater.

I resurface, blinded by overhead lights and a bright yellow sign hanging on the far wall. Blurry blue letters proclaim, *NOT Sweating to the Oldies.*

I rub my eyes. Something brushes across my left side. I spin around to find a vibrant senior citizen, pumping water weights to the beat of *Big Boss Man* by Elvis. Beautiful old biddies wearing colorful flowered swimming caps swarm around me, like bees at the hive.

Everywhere I turn I'm in somebody's way. The ladies' faces radiate joy, but they aren't smiling at me. They're focused on the workout. These exercise enthusiasts are at the very least pushing seventy, and yet they're all in much better shape than I am.

I escape into a corner of the pool, but the ladies dogpaddle after me, migrating to the sides for flutter kicks. Seeking refuge from their synchronized swimming, I flail back into the middle of the turquoise pool.

Through my noisy thrashing, I hear laughter.

"Good grief, Emma. Why are you always so awkward?"

Wait—I recognize that voice! Turning to the instructor, I blink in amazement. For a second, I'm too stunned to speak. A giant smile breaks across my face.

It's Jake! My heart leaps. I missed him so much. What's he doing here? Where am I? Is this real or a dream? A million questions race through my head as I splash toward him. One stunning senior citizen after another crashes into me.

"Jake! What happened—" I sink below the surface, my mouth filling with water. I come up sputtering, "Get me out of here!" Emma Roberts, graceful to the core.

He yanks me out of the pool, suppressing a laugh. Water pours from my clothes, forming a small lake across the tiles.

"Nice shirt." He smirks.

I glance down at the Doors shirt he left behind, layered over a turtleneck. "Oh, I..." I flush, raising my eyes to meet his.

"It doesn't matter. You're here." He pulls me close and kisses me hard, much to the delight of the old ladies, who clap and cheer their approval.

After we break apart, I collapse exhausted into his arms. Jake hugs me tight. It feels so right. This is where I'm supposed to be. But where am I?

After a pleasant moment, Jake tenses. "Wait a minute... Emma, why *are* you here? What happened to you?"

My memories blur. "I don't know. I mean... I'm not sure. The last thing I remember is Mike going back into the river and now I'm here," I mumble into his chest, breathing in his familiar smell. I never want to let go. I'm safe here. Safe from what, I can't remember.

"Oh..." His tone sounds off, disappointed.

"What's wrong?" I back out of his embrace, a tight feeling in my throat. "Aren't you happy to see me?"

"Well, of *course* I'm happy to see you again." Jake doesn't sound like he means it. He steps to the side and grabs me a towel. "I just thought it would take you a little longer to get here. Um, are you here because of Mike, then?"

"I didn't come here on purpose, if that's what you're thinking." I wrap the towel around my shivering frame. "Actually, I have no idea how I got here. Right now I'm too cold to care."

Jake pauses, his expression puzzled. "Then go to the women's locker room and warm up. Colleen will help you find some dry clothes."

"Who's Colleen?" Don't tell me Jake has a girlfriend. I'll smack him upside the head if he does. Especially after kissing me in front of all these people.

"Skinny. Long dark hair... "

This doesn't sound good. Who is this chick? And what about the blonde he danced with in my vision?

Jake continues, "Always wears shirts with unicorns on them."

Unicorns? What the heck kind of girl is this?

He smiles. "You can't miss her. She's about four feet tall, eleven years old, and never stops talking."

Oh. Got it. She's just a kid. Phew.

He gives me a gentle shove. "Go get warmed up. I'll see you later at lunch."

"You still eat here?" I glance around. Where am I, anyway?

"Yeah. Isn't it great? I would have missed eating. It's one of my favorite hobbies. But I've got to get back to the ladies." He stage whispers the last part, egging on the old biddies who giggle in return.

How ridiculous. I can't believe Jake teaches water aerobics to senior citizens. That's not a very Frat Boy thing to do.

Jake's eyes dip down to the towel wrapped around my body. I tighten my grip, straining the towel against my dripping clothes. Why do I feel so naked? I gotta get out of here.

"A warm shower and dry clothes sound fantastic," I say, a false bright tone to my voice. "Where's that locker room again?"

Jake points toward a set of silver doors. I scurry across the tiles, slipping occasionally (and hoping Jake doesn't notice), then push through the heavy swinging doors without a single backward glance. Warmth envelops me, and Enya plays in the background.

The locker room is so warm and cozy this *must* be Heaven. The lockers glisten in pearly rainbow hues. I spot a unicorn shirt across the room and approach the young girl combing her long, dark hair in front of a large mirror.

"Are you Colleen?" I ask.

"Yes." She eyes me up and down, pushing a pair of glasses up on her nose. "Where's your swimsuit?"

"I don't have one. I just got here. Jake said you'd help me find some dry clothes."

She nods. "What's your name? Let's find your locker."

"Emma Roberts." I feel like I'm announcing myself on some game show. This is weird.

Colleen consults a clipboard hanging on the wall. "Let's see. Emma Roberts, number 4514."

I find the locker number and swing open the metal door. Inside the locker sits a pair of purple Converse low tops, jeans, and another turtleneck. Everything I like—except for the turtleneck. Something flickers in the back of my mind, but I can't quite reach the memory.

"Locks aren't necessary here. Stealing's not an option." Colleen perches on a nearby locker bench. "How do you know Jake?"

"That's a long, confusing story." I avoid her question by asking one of my own. "How do you know him? Do you take his water aerobics class?"

"Me?" She giggles and blushes. "No, I swim laps whenever he has class."

"That sounds great." Not really. It sounds exhausting.

"Can I tell you something?" Colleen whispers, "I have a secret crush on him."

The flush rises in my cheeks, and I overreact. "You're eleven. He's *way* too old for you."

"Yes, I know it's stupid." She crosses her arms and juts out her chin. "But I think he's cute. Don't you?"

"Um..." I pause as flashbacks of my drunken last evening with Jake flood my mind.

"Well?" She clears her throat. "Do you think he's cute or not?"

How funny. She's trying to feel out the "competition." I try not to laugh because I remember how I wanted to be taken seriously at that age. "Oh, yeah, well, Jake's hair *does* look better now that he stopped using that nasty hair gel. He used to spike his hair up all the time. I *hated* that."

"There's no hair gel in Heaven," Colleen informs me.

I glance around the locker room. "So this is Heaven?" *And why am I here?*

"Well, sort of. Jake says it's not quite Heaven, but a heck of a lot better than Hell." She blushes again. "He calls it 'Almost Heaven,' after a song he used to like."

"So this is purgatory?" With water aerobics and warm locker rooms? Weird. *I should be more upset about this. Why don't I care that I'm dead?*

"Sort of, I guess. You wait here until you're ready to move on."

I remove the contents from my locker one by one. "When do you move on? And where do you go?" *Am I really dead? How can I be dead?*

"It depends," Colleen says, with an air of superiority, as if I'm a small child and she's old and all knowing.

"What happened to the long white hallway?" I ask.

She cocks her head to the side. "What white hallway? Oh, yeah. It's been remodeled."

"There's remodeling in Heaven?" That doesn't make any sense, either.

"Of course. There's remodeling everywhere." Colleen pauses. "Are you sad about dying?"

"Am I really dead? I don't *feel* dead." *How did it happen? Is this even real?*

Colleen shrugs. "I *still* don't feel dead, and I've been here a lot longer than you. But sometimes I miss my parents."

"Oh, no... my parents." I sink down on the bench next to my new shoes. "What are they gonna think happened to me?" I look to her for answers, but she doesn't have any. A dull ache grips my chest, and it hurts to breathe. I need to get away from her watching eyes. "Maybe I'll take a hot shower and get ready for dinner. I'll think about everything else later."

"Yeah." She crinkles her nose. "You should get cleaned up. You look horrible."

Great. Thanks for the compliment, kid.

The water aerobics brigade parades into the locker room, pumping their arms and humming Elvis tunes. I watch them in wonder. I can't find a single varicose vein, cellulite patch, or swollen knee among them. They look stunning.

After they pass, I raise my arms and peel off the soaking wet turtleneck and T-shirt.

Colleen gasps. "What happened to you?"

"What do you mean?" I glance at the ugly collection of bruises on my arms. "Holy crap. No wonder I'm sore."

She points at my shoulder. "That's the ugliest tattoo I've ever seen. Why'd you pick that?"

My upper arm has been branded with a green cobra. An image flutters to the surface for a moment of a snake under my couch, but the vision disappears before I can figure it out.

I shudder. "I've no idea how that happened. I don't even like snakes."

Colleen cocks her head to the side. "Jake doesn't like tattoos."

"Then don't tell him." I smile, trying to win her over. "It will be our little secret."

CHAPTER TWENTY-TWO

DINNER WITH THE DEAD

Colleen chatters as we leave the locker room, but I barely hear a word. My head is too crowded with questions. Am I really dead? What happened to me? Where did the ugly tattoo and bruises come from? My mind races, but gets nowhere. I have no answers to my many questions.

"The Eatery's just up ahead." Colleen points as we round a corner between two long stone buildings.

The bright lights of an arched doorway glisten on a cobbled street. The smell of garlic bread and roast beef beckon us inside the dining room, which resembles a German pub. I trail after Colleen, who races ahead to a sturdy wooden table where Jake and Claire's dead husband, Bernard, sit eating.

As we approach, Bernard jumps up, still as handsome as Christopher Plummer and always the gentleman. He pulls out a chair. "Here you are. The seat of honor for our special guest."

"Thanks, Bernard," I begin, "It's so nice to see—"

Colleen interrupts, arms folded across her slight chest. "All you Emma-fanatics should know that it looks like someone beat her up seven or eight times before they killed her."

I turn on her. "You promised not to tell!"

"No, I didn't." Colleen narrows her eyes. "And she's got the ugliest snake tattoo *ever*."

"Thanks a lot," I mutter, as Jake clenches his jaw.

Bernard frowns. "Emma, what's this all about?"

"Who beat you up?" Jake's hand forms a fist.

"I don't know—" I begin.

"She acts like she doesn't know anything," Colleen stage whispers. "Do you think it's true?"

I throw her a dirty look. Are all eleven-year-olds this annoying? "If you don't mind, I'd like to eat something before you all attack me with your questions. I'm hungry, okay?"

"Sure thing." Jake pushes back his chair and escorts me to the buffet line. He elbows me. "So, where's your tattoo?"

"Very funny, Jake." I flush. "It's not anything sexy, I swear."

"Why am I not surprised? You avoid anything sexy like the plague—except for me, that is." Jake smirks. "Here, grab a tray. You're up next."

My mouth waters as I observe the selection, my heart rate elevated by how close Jake stands beside me. "This place *must* be Heaven. Look at all this. There's lasagna, cherry pie, fresh peaches, French toast, cinnamon rolls, and ice cream. I want to eat it all."

"The cooks here are first rate because they love it," he says, leaning close enough to raise the heat in my cheeks. "That's what it's like here—everybody has a job, but it's enjoyable because it's whatever you really like to do."

I chuckle, trying to keep things light. "So Jake Cunningham really enjoys coaching old lady water aerobics?"

He nods, picking up a bun and setting it on my tray. "Yeah. It's fun. Besides, those are Healing Waters."

"Healing Waters?" Something tells me I might need Healing Waters. Would Jake take me there again if I asked? Would we finally be alone, then? The thought makes me flush deeper.

"Yes, I help those fine old ladies fix whatever's wrong with their bodies before they move on. I'm curing arthritic knees, diabetes, and heart disease. Yes sir, Jake Cunningham's the best doctor ever, and I didn't even have to go to med school."

He's as egotistical as always, but maybe he's right. After all, my bruises look worse than they hurt. "That's a silly job for a Frat-boy." I select a generous helping of lasagna. "But why do you have to heal up bodies that are already dead?"

"Not everything changes when you die. Besides, water aerobics isn't my only job here. But I suppose you'll need a fancier job than me, Miss Smarty Pants."

"Maybe I could tutor. I liked doing that." I grab a bowl of chocolate pudding. "Does anyone even go to school here?'

"Yeah. Some people are just *dying* to learn." Jake pokes me in the ribs. "They never had time for it before, I guess. The math professor's name is Parker. You'll like him."

As we cross back to our table, I spot another familiar face. "Sam. It's you."

Sam. The first soul I pulled out of the river and the first one to jump back in. He glances up. Not one thing about his demeanor suggests he's glad to see me. I bite my lip, concerned that he appears even worse than before.

Sam clears his throat. "Emma, why are you here already? Are you okay?"

I start to reply with an automatic "yes," then pause. "I'm not sure," I say instead.

He grabs his tray. "I'll come sit with you, if you don't mind."

"Of course. Why would I mind?"

Bernard smiles as we settle down at the group table, his eyes crinkling. "How does it feel eating lunch with those you raised from the dead?"

I return his friendly grin. "It's pretty surreal, seeing all of you together in your own 'skins.' It's like the full moon is out again."

Bernard pats my hand. "You must have a lot of questions."

"I do." That's for sure.

"And we have plenty of questions for you, not that it sounds like you have any answers." Jake pushes the lasagna in front of me. "But you're hungry. So eat."

I attack my layered pasta, shoveling it in like I haven't eaten in days. After a few bites, I look up, feeling Sam's quizzical eyes on me. He glances away.

Jake leans toward Colleen. "How many laps did you swim today?"

Colleen flushes. "I lost track."

"How do you know when you're done?"

She pushes her mashed potatoes around her plate, eyes down. "I don't know."

"You must swim about 45 minutes, because that's how long my class is, and you're always there, swimming the whole time."

"Um..." Matching roses bloom in Colleen's cheeks.

Poor girl. Even though she kind of bugs me, I better help her out. "Swimming is supposed to be the perfect exercise," I interject.

"How would you know?" Jake turns to me. "You hate exercise."

"No, I don't." Okay, yeah, I do, but it's so hard not to argue with him.

"Whatever you say, Emma." He folds his arms, glancing at my empty plate. "Since you're done eating, tell us what happened to you."

"I already told you I don't know," I say. "The last thing I remember is Mike going back into the river." I glance around the room. "Where is he, by the way?"

"That didn't take long," Jake mutters, leaning back in his chair.

I glare at him, annoyed. What does he have to be jealous of?

The elderly man's fingers drum the table. "It's strange. I couldn't find Mike anywhere today."

"Oh..." Suddenly the lasagna feels like a bowling ball trapped in my gut. I'm forgetting something. Something important. What is it?

"So what happened after Mike left?" Jake asks. "Come on. Tell us."

"Not much. Walker asked me to help him with some murder cases." That's right, isn't it? My mind feels like a sieve.

"Steve's case?" Bernard asks.

I nod. "Yes. We're going to solve it. We promised."

"That's good," Bernard says.

I turn to Sam. "Do you know who all these people are? Or do you need me to introduce you?"

"Don't worry. Sam's up to speed," Bernard winks. "He knows all the dirt. It's like gossip central around here. We've told each other everything."

"Everything?" I sneak a quick glance at Jake.

He smirks.

Colleen swoons. "Yeah, Jake told me how he donated both his kidneys to his sister Laura."

I roll my eyes. Thank goodness Jake didn't tell her we've kissed, or she'd probably strangle me with a unicorn shirt.

"And Mike told the others about Claire taking in Abby and Steve's baby." Bernard runs a hand through his white hair. "Of course, all Steve talks about is whether or not Officer Walker has figured out his murder case yet."

"Speaking of Steve, where is he?" I ask.

They all trade meaningful glances, then Bernard clears his throat. "After Jake informed me you were here, I invited Steve to dinner, but he said he couldn't make it tonight. He's very busy these days, but makes an effort to eat with us when he can. He'll send for you when he's available, though. I guarantee he'll want to see you."

"Why's he so busy?" I ask. "And what do you mean by 'when he's available'—what's up with that?"

"You'll see," Jake mumbles.

Sam stands. "I'm sorry, but I gotta go right now. Can I talk to you later, Emma? Alone, if you don't mind." He throws a significant look at Jake.

"Sure, Sam. That's fine." *But is he fine?* I wonder.

"See you later." Sam hurries away.

After Sam's out of earshot, Colleen whispers, "That guy is kind of strange."

I glance at Sam's retreating back. My mind fills with a flashback of him jumping off the bridge, trying to kill himself for a second time. "He doesn't seem any better."

"Don't worry." Bernard pats my shoulder. "He'll be fine. It takes time."

I stare at my empty plate.

"Are you done eating?" Jake asks.

"Yep." I pat my content belly. "I'm stuffed."

"Okay, then." Jake pushes back his chair. "You look exhausted. You should rest."

"Yes, go take a nap." Bernard smiles, his eyes just as kind as I remembered. "We'll figure out the details later. And I'll find Mike. Don't worry."

Jake stands and holds out a hand. "Emma, you're coming with me."

"What?" A half-thrill, half-fear races through me. He's going to ask to see the tattoo, I just know it.

I follow Jake out of the dining room, waving good-bye to the others, and pretending I don't see the half-shocked, half-hurt expression on Colleen's face. Good grief, Jake still walks too darn fast. Two turns after leaving the cafeteria, I'm lost amid a sea of stone houses. The cobbled roads twist and turn every which way. I trail Jake's steps, not wanting to fall behind. After about ten minutes, he halts and I run smack into him.

"Here it is." He sweeps his arm before yet another boxy white building and opens a small wooden door.

I step into a small cozy room. Georgia O'Keefe posters hang on the wall, and a worn red Asian rug covers the floor.

"Georgia O'Keefe? I'm impressed." And a tad surprised.

"Don't get too excited. This place was already decorated when I got here, but now it's 'Home Sweet Home.' Your old clothes are piled on the bed, all clean and dry. Your personal items are on the dresser." He ventures over to snoop.

"You said everyone up here has a job that they truly enjoy, right? Who likes doing laundry?" And who went through my stuff?

"It takes all kinds, I guess." He picks out the small picture of him from my wallet. "Where'd you get this?"

"Your sister. We've been writing each other."

"Really?" His eyes widen. "How is Laura?"

"She's great, but I guess your dog Nani's not doing so well. She's sick or something. They were taking her to the vet last I heard."

Jake sighs. "Poor Nani. She was the best dog." He sets the picture back down, then walks over to a lit panel in the wall. He pushes a few buttons and a Beethoven sonata floats in from invisible speakers.

"I thought you only liked rock and roll." I fidget with the pile of clothes, then notice I'm standing right next to the bed and move away.

He chuckles. "Rock music's still the best, in my opinion, but I saw those piles of classical piano books you had at your house, and figured you'd like this better."

I remember practicing piano at home, my parents' proud faces at my recitals, decorating the Christmas trees, going ice skating. When would I see my family again?

Tears fall before I can stop them. "Jake, I'm worried about my parents, and I can't remember *anything*. This is horrible."

He hurries to my side and I lean on his shoulder.

I sniffle. "I don't even know how I died."

He hugs me close. "I wouldn't have known either, without you."

"This is what it's like when you die? You don't get to know?"

"Everyone has a different story how they got here. Only ours are the same—the ones you brought back."

My shoulders droop. "Sometimes I wonder if I didn't make things worse, especially after seeing Sam tonight."

He squeezes me tighter. "You don't make things worse. You only make them better."

"How can you be so sure?" I breathe in the familiar smell of him. I still miss him, even when he's right here in front of me. My chest still aches, like I'll never be happy.

"Because I know you. You're practically perfect."

I flush. "Practically? As in, not one-hundred percent?"

"Yes, Miss Perfectionist, you do have some lingering issues. For example, you're still dressing like a boy." He points at the Doors shirt on his dresser.

"But you like that band," I point out.

"Okay. That shirt can be the one exception." He smiles, more gently this time. The room stills, except for Beethoven and my heart.

Jake gazes at me until I get dizzy with waiting.

Kiss me already! A voice inside of me begs.

"So... " His voice is gruff. "... about that tattoo."

CHAPTER TWENTY-THREE

SWITCHED

show him the stupid tattoo.

He grimaces. "What the Hell happened to you?"

I shrug. "I told you, I don't know—"

"It doesn't make sense that you're here already." Jake backs away. "Not that I'm not happy to see you. I just thought it would take longer."

I cross my arms. "Gee. I'm so glad to hear you don't actually want me around."

He paces the room. "Be serious, Emma. Aren't you the least bit concerned what happened to you?"

"Of course I want to know what happened, but I can't remember." I give up. My mind won't work right.

"Then try harder," he urges, stepping close and grabbing my arms.

"Okay." I close my eyes, attempting to focus, but it's as if something it blocking the light. I can't see anything but a tiny flicker in the back of my mind. "I'm sorry, Jake. I don't know."

"Never mind. We'll figure it out. I'm just glad you're here." Jake takes my face in his hands. "Because, no matter what happened, now you'll be safe."

I clear my throat. "Safe would be nice."

"I worry about you." Jake sighs.

I attempt a laugh, which catches in my throat. "I don't blame you."

"Then don't blame me for this, either." Jake pauses a moment, his eyes troubled, before he kisses me.

This time I'm not drunk. This time I know what love is. I feel every flutter of my heart, every breath on my cheeks, every movement of his hands. And it's perfect.

Until I open my eyes and discover I'm not kissing Jake anymore.

It's somebody else.

What the heck? I step back.

Mike stands in front of me instead.

He morphs into Dominic. Blood soaks the front of his shirt.

The vision shifts once again. Shadow appears, his sneer crowded with crooked teeth. *"No use resisting. You're one of us now."*

I choke as black, acrid smoke fills the room. The floor beneath me shifts, and the walls disappear.

I fall on my hands and knees in the park where I burned the *Book of Shadows*.

My own voice asks the dark night, "Mike? Is that you?"

But I'm not the one speaking.

"Emma?" Mike's voice comes from my mouth instead. "Where are you? What's going on?"

The small flare of a match ignites, then swiftly burns out. The world hushes, as if waiting. As if it knows what comes next. From across the park, I watch myself bend over the fire pit, reaching out my hands toward a glowing presence.

How can I see myself? Am I Mike, now?

Does he possess me, too?

An explosion rips the ground, scattering dirt and rock and branches.

I crawl over to my body, and brush off debris. Try to find a pulse. Nothing. Put my hands to my chest, and push once, twice, three times. Blow warm breath into the cold mouth, then listen.

No response.

I push on the chest again, but can't remember CPR. Is this right? Can't remember.

Crows scream, circling overhead.

Even this late at night they can smell Death.

Sirens tear the night in two, ringing in my ears.

Headlights race into the park. Cursing, I jump up and run away.

I can't stay. Not supposed to be here.

I race through the woods, someone close behind me.

Are they dead or alive?

And what am I? Am I Mike? Am I Emma? Who am I?

And what have I done?

CHAPTER TWENTY-FOUR

BIG BOSS MAN

MIKE!" I break away from Jake's embrace. **"Oh my** God, what have I done to him now?"

Jake freezes. "Emma, what's going on?"

"Oh, no." I sink to my knees. I've ruined everything.

"I've gotta tell you. There's nothing more flattering than when your girlfriend screams out some other guy's name while you're kissing her."

Wait a minute. "I'm your girlfriend?" I ask weakly, my heart taking a limp leap, as if it doesn't have the energy to soar.

Jake sighs. "I don't know. Maybe I should ask you."

"Sorry, Jake, but I can't talk about us right now." I take a shuddering breath, the images in my head swirling. "I've got to focus, to remember it all. It's important." Unfortunately, more important than kissing Jake. At least right now it is. "I had a vision."

"Sounds like it was a good one," he mutters.

I glare at him. "Shut up and let me finish. I remember what happened now."

He sits on the bed, first glancing away, then turning back and patting the spot next to him.

I pace the room instead. "Did the others tell you about the séance I performed at the site of Steve's murder?"

"Yes." He folds his hands together.

"Walker had me do the same thing again—and not just for Steve, but for two other women who were murdered as well."

His shoulders slump. "I have a feeling I won't like this story."

I pause, trying to clear my muddled mind. "This time, when I worked the revealing spells for Walker, instead of just *watching* the events like before, the attacks started *happening* to me instead."

Jake's jaw clenches. "What do you mean by that?"

"Brace yourself." I stretch down the collar of my turtleneck to offer a glimpse of yellow, brown, and purple bruises. I make a weak joke. "Too bad I didn't hang out longer in that healing pool, right?"

His eyes widen. "What did Charlie say about this?"

"Well, I didn't exactly tell him what was happening... at first." I fidget with shirtsleeve.

Jake jumps off the bed. "You let him continue with his experiment, even though it hurt you?"

"Trust me—I wanted to tell him, but every time I tried to explain, something inside me wouldn't let me speak. I thought I was going nuts. The voices of the victims and the attackers argued in my head. I kept blacking out, losing time, and ending up somewhere I never remembered going in the first place. My totally annoying neighbor Phoebe even found me passed out under the Chippewa River Bridge once when my parents came to visit."

Jake doesn't say a word. He doesn't have to.

I take a deep breath. "Things were getting way out of hand, and I went to Walker's house determined to tell him everything and get him to help me."

Jake clenches and unclenches his fists. "And then what?"

"Things didn't go well, I'm afraid, and it was probably all my fault. So I decided to destroy the *Book of Shadows.*"

He raises his eyebrows, clearly surprised. "Really? Why would you destroy it?"

Tears moisten my eyes. "I had to stop the voices before I went back to Father Joe."

Jake waves his hands in the air. "Wait. I'm lost. Who's Father Joe?"

"He's an..." I pause, dreading Jake's reaction. "He's an exorcist."

He grabs my shoulders. "Are you kidding me? You need an exorcist?"

I glance down at my hands. "Yes. I do."

"What's wrong with you?" his voice cracks. "You take far too many risks."

"I never claimed to be normal." I fake a smile.

He shakes his head. "That's not even funny, Emma. When you first got here, it worried me. But I didn't say anything to Steve, because I was selfish and wanted you for myself. I should've known you were in trouble."

My shoulders droop.

Jake tugs on my arm, leading me toward the door. "Let's go see Steve. Maybe he can help."

"Is he really in charge up here?"

"I'm afraid so." Jake takes my hand and we hurry down the narrow streets, passing row after row of white stucco buildings.

"Are we in Greece?" I ask.

"You're dead. It sounds like you're possessed. But you're still in denial about what's happened, aren't you? This isn't Greece, Emma."

"But there's an ocean nearby," I argue. "I can smell it. And these charming little homes look like the ones in Mom's Mediterranean travel guides."

Jake urges me forward. "Come on. We're almost there. Hurry."

"Stop rushing me. I think Heaven's made you even bossier than before."

"This isn't Heaven, either. You're not there yet." Moments later, Jake halts before a tall stone building and gestures at a huge wooden door. "Here it is. Make sure you knock hard, or they won't hear you." He turns to leave.

"Where are you going?" I grab his arm and Jake flexes. "Why aren't you coming in with me?"

His gaze flickers from me down the street and back. He's evading something. "Steve and I don't see eye to eye on most things. You should probably visit him on your own. I'd get in the way."

"But I—" *I want you to stay with me.*

"This is what's best." His gaze darts toward the massive door swinging open. "You need help that I can't give you. But Steve can."

A security guard dressed in black glowers down at me. "You're late."

"How can I be late? I don't even have an appointment. I just came to see Steve."

Without a word, the tall guard grabs my arm and drags me inside. The door slams shut behind us, Jake's face disappearing with a loud *thud*. The guard yanks me down a long gray hallway, my feet slipping on the glossy floor. I stumble trying to keep up. Sheesh. No wonder Jake didn't want to come along. After a few twists and turns, the guard pushes me into an office filled with high-end furniture.

"Mr. Lawrence will be with you soon."

"Okay. Thanks—" The door slams shut in my face. "Thanks for nothing, I guess!" I thought people were supposed to like their jobs up here. That guy must enjoy being a giant a-hole. I rub my sore arm and circle the office. This place is enormous. It doesn't feel like the Steve I knew at all. He seemed like a regular guy, and this looks all official. Brass lamps, a mahogany desk, and leather chairs. The best that money can buy. That is, if money even exists here.

Twenty minutes later, Steve strolls in, wearing a crisp blue oxford and power tie.

"Emma! You're here!" He embraces me in a professional hug, with the proper amount of back slapping involved. Two pats, not three. How odd. Like I'm meeting a senator to petition for women's rights or something.

"Wow, Steve, this is one impressive office. What exactly do you do here?"

"I'm in charge." Steve points at the chair across from his massive desk. "Have a seat."

"So I've heard. That happened quickly." I settle into the buttery leather. "You're dressed so sharp, I hardly recognize you. What happened to the real Steve? You look like a big boss man, or something."

"Thank you." His smile stretches like a plastic politician. "I've been told that I'm a natural for the job."

I pause. That wasn't meant to be a compliment. What's going on with him? This is uncomfortable. And somehow I don't like asking him for help. I clear my throat. "Listen, Steve. I have a problem."

"Yes. I can see that." Steve's curled lip makes me feel dirty. "You've brought undesirable company with you."

"You can see them?" I jump out of my seat, searching the room for signs of possession—spinning cups, dripping faucets, and the like, but find nothing. "You're *sure* they're still with me?"

His steely eyes stare right into me. Can he see Dominic? No wonder he's upset.

"You're *not* alone, Emma. Let me assure you of that."

I sit back down. "Shoot. I thought maybe they were gone. I haven't heard them at all since I got here. In fact, I didn't even remember about them at first."

He frowns. "They're subdued, but certainly not absent. God won't grant you an audience in this condition."

My head swirls. "What are you talking about?"

Steve leans over his desk as if I am his wayward pupil. "People always want to know when they get to see God. Part of my job is to keep them away until it's the right time."

"Well, it's the right time for me. I've got a million questions."

He shakes his well-groomed head. "Sorry. You're not ready yet."

I clench the arms of the chair. "No. I'm more than ready!"

"You'll need to spend more time in the Healing Waters first."

I roll my eyes. "What are you saying? That I have to do water aerobics with the old ladies? What is *wrong* with this place?"

A smile plays across Steve's lips. "Funny Emma. You always did get upset over nothing."

"Nothing? This is *not* nothing." This is exasperating. Some help talking to Steve turned out to be.

"No, it's not." Steve crosses his arms. "They told me you killed yourself with witchcraft. What did you expect—God would welcome you with a parade? It doesn't work that way."

I flinch as if Steve slapped me, then come roaring back. "What I *expected* was that God would be more understanding." I slump in my chair, exhausted by Steve's lack of sympathy. I thought he was my friend. I guess I was wrong about a lot of things. And I didn't mean to kill myself, but shouldn't God be merciful anyway? "What about Sam? Has God seen him yet?"

Steve nods, tapping his desk with a pen. "I'm told Sam was seen right away."

"That's not fair! I didn't kill myself on purpose. I was trying to get rid of the *Book of Shadows* before *it* killed *me*."

Steve frowns. "You never should have harmed such a valuable item."

I feel small now. "I didn't trust it anymore. It was starting to take over."

"And you don't like it when you're not in control." A flicker of a smile plays on his lips. "But your job was to protect the *Book of Shadows*."

"Not at my own expense." Why is this turning into a fight? He's so different than before. Or is he?

Steve folds his fingers together. "I have to say I'm disappointed."

"Don't start with me, Steve. I tried to help Walker, partly to solve your murder, I might add, but all these spirits started attacking me. I tried to get help from Father Joe—"

"I know about the exorcist."

This takes my breath away. "How?"

"I know a lot of things, and yet, it's not enough. There's always more." He leans forward in this desk chair. "Now what *exactly* happened with the book?"

I take a deep breath. "When I threw the *Book* in the fire, I think I brought Mike back. Again. That's what I came here to tell you. I need your help."

"You're sure about this?" Steve checks his watch. What kind of schedule is he on?

"At first I couldn't remember what happened, but it came back to me in a flash. I saw it in a vision just now."

Steve pauses before asking, "You're positive this vision was real and not just a dream?"

I level my eyes at him and scrunch up my shirtsleeve to reveal the snake tattoo on my arm. "None of this has been 'just a dream.'"

He flinches and adjusts his silver cuff links. "Have you told the others?"

"I've only told Jake so far, but at lunch Bernard said he couldn't find Mike anywhere, so I know I'm right."

Steve drums his fingers on the desk, then pulls out a pad of gold-embossed paper and a thick black pen. "I'll have someone look into it. But don't forget you're possessed. We have to be *absolutely sure* this isn't something the spirits want you to believe." He presses a buzzer. One of his guards rushes in and stands at attention as Steve's pen scratches across the paper. He rips the sheet from the pad and hands it to the man, mumbling directions I can't hear.

"Yes, sir." The messenger dashes off with the note.

Steve turns back to me. "How's Charlie coming along with my case?"

"What about Mike?" I ask.

"I told you—I'll have someone look into it." He leans back in his chair, a commanding presence. "Now, I asked you about Charlie."

"You're not my boss, Steve. Try to remember that. You're *supposed* to be my friend." But is he? I take a deep breath, trying to calm the fire in my belly. I want to slap him, not be treated like his employee. "All the leads went cold. Charlie had me rework the revealing spell. Then I died. I don't know what happened after that."

Steve taps his pen. "Have you seen Abby and my son?"

"Yes. I'm sorry." Heat flushes my face. "I should've told you that right away. They're doing great."

"So he's healthy?"

"Yes," I assure him. Poor guy.

His face relaxes. He looks like the old Steve at last. "And Abby's okay? She has enough help?"

"Of course. She has Claire and your parents. Maybe someday her parents will come around, too."

"That's good." He puts the pad of paper and pen back in the drawer. "You know. I'd give anything just to see them one more time."

Poor Steve. All this power and he still can't have what he really wants. "Listen. I had a picture of Stevie in my pocket when I got here. If it isn't ruined, I'll bring it to you."

"I'd like that. Thanks, Emma." Now he sounds more like the Steve I used to know.

Someone raps on the door.

"Come in," Steve commands.

Another imposing guard enters. The strange ogre of a man leans to whisper in Steve's ear. I pick at the sleeve of my turtleneck. Suddenly, I feel very unimportant. Steve's dressed like the President of the United States, and I look like I'm going to the mall.

"He's here *now*? That's wonderful." Steve's voice sounds angry rather than happy, despite his choice of words.

Steve rises and turns to me, avoiding my gaze. "I'm sorry, Emma. Something's come up. We'll continue this another time."

I stand. "Let me know what you find out about Mike, and don't worry about Abby and little Stevie. Claire will take good care of them."

"I know she will. Bernard is content to wait for her until she's no longer needed. Good-bye." He dismisses me with a wave of his well-manicured hand.

His words strike me as peculiar. Does Steve have some power over Claire and Abby's situation?

The big guy in a dark suit immediately escorts me out of the fancy office, down the hall, and outside.

"Wait." I try to put on the breaks, but he keeps dragging me along. "I have another question."

"Your appointment is over," he snaps, as we reach the door and he tosses me out.

I spin around. "But how long does it take Steve to find out something? When can I come back?"

"The Boss will call for you when he wants you. Don't bother him until then. He's busy." He closes the door in my face again. The bolt slides into place with a loud *clunk*.

CHAPTER TWENTY-FIVE

PROFESSOR PARKER

Wandering alone on unfamiliar streets, I lose all sense of direction. Every curved stone alleyway appears the same. What should I do now? Where should I go? Since I appear to be stuck here—and I'm still not quite sure what "here" means—and Steve only seems to care about himself now, I'm not sure where to and who to go to for help. I pause at the intersection of two streets, biting my lip. Maybe that math professor Jake mentioned could help, but I've no idea where his office is. Too bad Jake didn't tell me.

After walking a bit farther, I spot a corner kiosk with the word *INFORMATION* blazed in red letters across the top. I hurry over, searching for directions.

A college-aged woman sets aside her bottle of bright pink nail polish. "How can I help you?"

"Hi. I'm Emma Roberts. And I'm sort of lost." My eyes are drawn to her fingernails. So, even though there's no hair gel here, there's still nail polish. I guess someone has their priorities in order.

Cari (or so her name tag reads, with a star over the "i") peers at me as if I'm a curiosity at a sideshow. Or else she can see the extra spirits I still carry around. "Emma Roberts? I heard about you."

"Great." I clear my throat. "I have a reputation here already?"

"No." Cari fidgets with her perfect hands. "Someone stopped by looking for you."

"Who? Jake?" Maybe he can take me to the math professor.

"Nope." She lowers her voice. "The Faded Witch. I don't know her real name... nobody does. Except maybe Sam Metzger—he hangs around her like a little lost puppy."

"The Faded Witch? Who's she?" So I'm not the only witch here. Interesting.

Cari leans forward to whisper, "I heard she's cursed."

"Why?" Oh dear. Then I probably am, too.

"She threw something out of balance back on Earth. She's cursed to grow ever more worn and haggard until the balance is restored."

"How's she supposed to do that?" Not that I'm here to help her. I've got enough on my hands already, right?

Cari's eyes widen. "I've no idea. She's never even talked to me before—that is, until she asked about you."

Great. Another dead person with a problem I'm supposed to solve. Trouble is, I'm kind of a mess right now.

"Where is she?" I glance down the nearest alleyway to check for any crouching witches with green skin and a black hat. I don't see any, but we're not in Oz. At least I don't think we are.

Cari shrugs. "Who knows?"

"I guess I'll deal with her when the time comes. But for right now, I need directions."

"I can help you with that." Cari pulls out a shiny yellow notecard. "Where do you want to go?"

"The math professor's office. Is there only one?"

She tucks her hair behind her ear. "Yep. That would be Professor Parker." She turns the note card sideways and writes *information kiosk #2* on the top, and *Prof. Parker's office* along the bottom edge. Then she sets down her pen and waits. After a few seconds, the blank space in the middle fills with written directions in block letters.

Cari hands it to me with a smile. "Here you go."

"Thanks." I read through the instructions, then head down the road in the right direction. Professor Parker tutors in a building on the edge of "town." His office is at the far end of a deserted hallway. Scratchy classical music floats down the hall, tinkling louder as I approach a wooden nameplate with *Professor Parker* printed on it in black letters. I stand in the open doorway and gawk at the mess inside.

The professor doesn't notice me at first. He hovers over his disorderly desk, writing out equations on scraps of paper. Books are stacked haphazardly on homemade wooden shelving. A latch-hook image of a panda bear hangs on one wall. The elderly man wears a gray oxford shirt, sweater vest, and corduroy pants thinned at the knees. He takes off his glasses and leans back in an olive green metal chair, which groans in protest.

I step into the room. "Professor Parker?"

"W-what?" Startled out of his reverie, he tilts back too far. The chair slips out from under him, sending him to the floor with a *bang*.

I jump forward to help. "I'm so sorry. I didn't mean to scare you."

He chuckles. "Oh, don't worry. Happens all the time."

"Why don't you get a new chair?"

He pats the chipped paint. "I like this one." Professor Parker picks up his thick glasses and wipes them with a dirty cloth. "My daughter threw away all this stuff after I died. She thought it was junk, and I got to keep it."

My gaze travels over the Professor's prized possessions. "They always said that you can't take it with you. I wonder if everyone's idea of Heaven is wrong."

He nods, a thoughtful expression on his face as he places the glasses back on his nose. "That's a good question."

"I have about a million others if you've got time. I've lost a friend, I'm worried about my parents, and some Faded Witch person is looking for me. I'm not sure what this all means, or what to do about it."

He smiles. "I think you'll find that around here, every question has more than one answer, and every answer leads to more questions."

Great. Not even professors up here can answer my questions.

How disappointing. Then I remember my manners and extend my hand. "Hi. I'm Emma Roberts. I'm interested in a math tutoring job."

His skin feels papery thin and his cheeks are pale.

"Are you sick?" I ask.

"I had leukemia, but I'm getting better." Professor Parker glances at a big wristwatch. "In fact it's about time for my supplement." He slides open a narrow drawer filled with what look like individually wrapped Snowball cakes. The crinkly wrapper disappears into thin air after he opens it. He takes a large bite of the dessert and his face flushes with color.

He shows me the middle, which looks like red Jello. "I'd offer you a bite, but I don't think you'd be interested."

I grimace. "No, thanks."

He gestures to a small wooden chair. "Have a seat. Let's discuss a schedule. It's nice to have some assistance, but there's not a huge demand for our services."

"But Jake said that lots of people here are eager to learn."

The professor chuckles. "I'm afraid the fine arts folks are more popular than the math and science tutors, but that's nothing new."

"That's just like regular life."

"It certainly is." He finishes up his supplement, then wipes his hands together.

"Except it doesn't feel like regular life to me up here. People don't act the same." I think of Steve, so angry under the surface. "Do you like it here, Professor Parker? I don't mean this in a bad way, but I expected something different when I died. I'm not sure what exactly, maybe a few clouds, or harps, or winged creatures."

He smiles. "I haven't spotted any flying horses or unicorns, either, if that's what you mean. But to answer your question—I'm quite content here while I wait for my wife." He glances around his office. "She's going to throw out all this stuff once she gets here."

"How long have you waited?"

He reaches for a framed family photo of him at a younger age, surrounded by a wife and daughter. Black electrical tape holds the frame together.

"Time isn't important here." He points at the wall in front of him. "Have you seen my clocks?"

I turn to look. There hang five dials, the hands all whirling and twirling back and forth. Below each clock is a rectangular silver box stating month, day, and year.

"What's wrong with them?" I ask.

"They're not broken, if that's what you're thinking. Look closer."

I read aloud the small nameplates under each clock. "New York, San Francisco, Paris. The last two have question marks. What does that mean?"

"They're yours to choose. Tell the clocks what you want to see."

"Eau Claire, Wisconsin," I say in a clear, loud voice.

The hands of the two clocks shiver, then spin wildly. The last clock on the right halts at 10:45 pm and a date that sends shivers down my spine.

I point, my hand shaking. "But that's when I died."

His eyebrows rise. "Is it? How interesting."

The hands of second to last clock continue to whirl, moving forward through the next couple days, pausing, then rushing back to the exact time of my death, then forward again. The two clocks work in unison—one spinning ahead while the other twirls behind, over and over again, always pausing on the same dates and times.

I plop down in my chair, a sick feeling in my gut. "That's creepy."

"I've never seen them do that before." Professor Parker taps a coffee cup.

I shudder to think what he must be drinking. I hope it's not blood. I'm not sure I can work with a vampire. Wait, maybe that would be sort of cool.

"What do you think it means?" I ask.

He pauses. "Are you *sure* you're dead?"

"I don't *feel* dead." I pinch myself and do feel the sting, so this can't be a dream. "Did you?"

"Yes." He gives me a sad, wise smile. "But before I died, I couldn't even tie my shoes without losing my breath. I pretty much felt halfway dead long before it actually happened."

"How dreadful." I shudder.

He smiles brighter. "Don't worry. I had a good life before that. And up here, with the help of these tasty morsels, I can even go hiking in the woods again. I missed that."

He points at another picture of himself, with mountains in the background. The glass is cracked in one corner. "I just wish my wife were here to go with me."

What a nice guy. "I'm sure she'll be glad that you waited for her."

"God said I could move on if I wanted, but I couldn't do it. My wife will need a lot of help when she gets here. She forgets things. She's got Alzheimer's—or 'old timers,' whichever you what to call it. But she'll get better once she gets here."

"I'm sorry about your wife." I'd hate to lose my mind—it's all I have.

"Thanks. But let's talk about you. Do you have any more questions? It can be pretty confusing here at first."

I lean forward in my chair. "Is Steve Lawrence really in charge up here? I've got a serious problem and I want to be sure he's the one to talk to. And do you know someone called the Faded Witch? And have you spoken to God already?"

He chuckles. "You *do* have a lot of questions. I'd have to say 'yes' to all three. Any concerns *should* go directly to Mr. Lawrence. He'll take care of it, that's for sure. I'm not sure I'd go so far as to claim the Faded Witch and I are friends. The best I could say is that she occasionally tolerates my presence. She's an interesting woman, but she likes to keep to herself—except for that new protégé of hers."

"You mean Sam?" I ask.

He nods, taking another sip from his cup.

"I wonder why she wants to talk to me," I ponder.

"That *is* interesting. I know she's been waiting for someone for a long time, but I got the impression that person was a middle-aged man, not a young girl."

"Why is she cursed?" I ask, even if it's none of my business. "Is it just because she's a witch?"

"No. It's some private matter between her and God. She claims she stole the apple from Eden, but I'm not sure I believe her." He leans back in his chair, and I tense, waiting for him to fall again.

A knock on the office door interrupts our conversation.

Professor Parker waves. "Come on in, kids."

Two young students linger in the doorway of the office, a boy and a girl, carrying notebooks and pencils. They giggle and lean into each other.

I smile at them. "It'll be different tutoring non-college students."

"I've found that college-aged kids often seem the least interested in learning," the professor muses. "I look forward to your help, once you've settled in, of course."

"I'll be back. I promise." I excuse myself from his office. The sun warms my back, but doesn't do much to console me. I'm not sure Steve will do anything about Mike. I don't want to do water aerobics. And I still haven't figured out how to dispel my demons.

Questions bounce around in my head like wayward super-balls. Why won't God see me? Is it the witchcraft thing? It can't be the killing myself thing because God saw Sam right away, and he did it on purpose. If it's because I'm carrying all these spirit-demon things inside me, then why doesn't God want to help get rid of them? And who's this Faded Witch person, anyway?

As I approach the kiosk, Cari smiles. "Did you find the professor okay?" Her glossy pink nails glisten.

"Yeah, but now I'm looking for Jake Cunningham."

Cari giggles. "He's hot."

You've got to be kidding me. People shouldn't still be able to use the word "hot" to describe someone up here. "Yeah. Can you help me out?"

She whips out another shiny card. "I'm sure he's at practice this time of day. He always is."

Oh great. Jake's got another fan. We'll line them up in a row: Colleen, Cari, all the water aerobics ladies...

"Have you seen God already?" I try to sound casual, but I really want to know.

"Yes. Right away. She was beautiful. Her blue gown glittered like the stars." Cari's face glows with the memory.

"God is a She? Interesting." And cool. "Anyway, thanks for the directions." I grab the card and take off. Even Cari, the nail polishing queen, got to go right away.

Along the way, I find myself stopping everyone I met on the street. "Hi. I'm Emma Roberts. Have you talked to God yet?"

I question over a dozen people, and the answer is always "yes," but Who or What they saw varies from person to person. Most of the older people met a tall slender man sporting a willowy long beard that glowed like a shiny pearl. Two kids talked to a wild lion. A man with long hair spoke with a giant elm tree.

How come people see different things? Maybe the better question is: why do some people all see the same vision? And how come I'm the *only one* not permitted to see God?

CHAPTER TWENTY-SIX

FADED WITCH

After walking farther, I come to the end of the white stone buildings. The cobbled streets spill out onto a series of large grassy fields dotted with kids in baseball caps. Far to my right, a gradual slope leads to a distant beach. Sparkling sapphire waters stretch to the horizon. Warm, salty breezes caress my face.

My mom would love to be here. Or would she? My stomach lurches. How are they doing? What do they think happened to me? Did I just ruin the rest of *their* lives? My old friend, guilt, is going to have a party in my head for an eternity over this.

I pull at the turtleneck and fan myself while searching for Jake past grade school football games, junior league baseball, and tiny tot kickball. Past the green fields, tall trees sway along baseball fence lines. The weather is warm and perfect, like July in Wisconsin. Pausing out in the open, I glance back at the compound where everyone sleeps and eats. Pristine white boxes stack upon each other, climbing the side of a mountain far up into the sky.

I jump when someone taps me on the shoulder. I whirl around to find Sam.

"Hey, you scared me." Where'd he come from?

"Emma, someone wants to see you." His gaze darts toward the woods.

"I know. I heard. The Faded Witch. That's fine, but let's talk first. Are you okay, Sam? I'm worried."

He shakes his head. "Boy, do you have things backward. *You're* the one in trouble. I'm fine now."

I frown. "You don't look fine."

"You should talk, with fifty thousand bruises and an ugly snake tattoo." Sam crosses his arms. "I made Colleen give me all the details."

I sigh and shrug. "Take me to the Witch then, if you don't want to talk."

"I will." He points toward some nearby trees. "She's worried. She's been watching you."

"Why?" I head for the shade of the trees. "Do you know if I'm the one she's waiting for?"

"You're not. In fact, you shouldn't be here at all, but I'd better let *her* tell you the rest. I don't understand how things got so screwed up for you."

I tense. Why is everyone against me? "You're beginning to sound like Mike. He begged me to give up the *Book of Shadows* months ago." My heart sinks as I envision my precious *Book* shimmering and shivering within the fire.

A croaking voice startles me from my reverie. "Maybe he was right. Or, maybe not."

Out of nowhere, the Faded Witch appears in front of us. I didn't see her coming, but perhaps that's the point. Her unkempt gray hair looks like a tornado styled it. A shapeless, faded flowery dress hangs from her bony shoulders. Despite her lowly appearance, her blue eyes study me with the fierceness of a wild animal.

Sam squirms beside me. What has him so on edge? "Do you want me to leave?"

"Not yet." She raises an unruly eyebrow. "You're *really* Emma Roberts?"

I nod, mesmerized by her gaze. My arms and legs freeze, as if without uttering a word, she cast a spell to make me immobile. But I can still speak. "Are you the Faded Witch?"

She cackles. "I'm much more than that to you, my dear."

"What do you mean?" My eyes catch on a gemstone-encrusted cross necklace hanging beneath the lace edging her faded dress. "Why do you have the same necklace as my father?"

"Oh, good. You're starting to catch on. I'd rather hoped you'd be smart."

My heart pounds. "How do you know my dad?" Don't drag him into this.

"Let's put it this way…" She smiles, as if pleased with herself. "I understand you've been using *my* wooden bowl and getting yourself in all sorts of trouble—probably because you're using that inferior *Book of Shadows*, and nobody's coached you properly."

I unfreeze to cross my arms. "That's not *your* bowl—it was my grandmother's."

She pauses with a frown. "Oh, dear. Maybe you're not as smart as I'd hoped."

I hate it when people insult my intelligence. But what is she talking about? Oh, no. Not that. Really? Could this be?

"Oh, my gosh!" I whisper, glancing at the silent Sam. "The Faded Witch is my *grandmother?*"

He shrugs. "It makes perfect sense to me. I mean, where'd you get all this power from, anyway?"

I turn to stare at my disheveled grandmother. "Wait a minute, did you just insult my *Book of Shadows?*"

"Mine was better. *Much* better." She holds out a hand, floating a leaf three inches in the air above it. "And you must not care very much for yours if you tried to destroy it."

"Yours is better?" I glance around. "Where is it? Do you have it here?"

She removes her hand, letting the leaf fall. "That's between you and your father."

My breath catches. "You mean Dad *knows* you're a witch?"

"Of course he does. Don't be silly. Where do you think he got his necklace?" She clasps the jewelry. Then her bright eyes dim as if I've just run over her dog and she can't bring herself to yell at me for it.

The ground sways beneath me. "Why didn't anyone tell me about you?"

She shakes a finger at me. "I can't believe my son raised such a reckless daughter. You shouldn't be here already. John must be heartbroken."

Tears spring to my eyes. "I know. I'm sorry about that."

A dark moth settles on my shoulder. I brush at it absentmindedly.

"What's this?" Grandma grabs up the insect to hold it quivering in the air. "Why would you bring this evil here?"

"I didn't mean to. It was an accident." And I'm so tired of feeling guilty.

She taps on my chest, hard. "How many spirits are trapped in there?" They squirm beneath the pressure of her fingers.

I tremble. "I'm not sure, but not all of them are bad. Eva was murdered for her obsidian mirror. Jennifer was killed while cheating on her husband. Dominic took out Steve before his own gang cut out his liver in a sacrifice."

She leans in closer. "But which one of them would be strong enough to poison you?"

A chill runs through my core. "*Shadow*. It has to be him. He works for the Master. He killed both Eva and Dominic. Probably lots of other people, too."

Her eyes narrow. "I don't like the sound of this. Let me see what I can do." She turns and disappears into the trees, the moth still trapped between her fingers.

"Where are you going?" I call after her.

"I've got to talk to a Man about a Dog," her words come back to me on the wind.

"That doesn't make any sense." I turn to Sam. "Is she always like this?"

He nods. "Pretty much."

I glance around. "Does she expect me to wait around here until she comes back?"

"Yes. She does."

I put my hand to my hip. "How long is this gonna take?"

He shrugs. "Could take hours. Who knows?"

I'm not waiting that long. "Well, I need to find Jake. Want to come along?"

He settles down on a nearby fallen log. "Nope, I'll wait. She expects it."

"Really, Sam? You're like her little puppy."

His jaw clenches. "I know and I don't care. I *want* to help her, especially if it will help you."

I smile, remembering the days we spent together last fall. "I always knew you were a good guy, Sam."

"Go on, then." He waves me off. "I'll see you later."

I hurry off and spot Jake coaching some kids on a playing field. I hurry toward him, trying to shake off my discomfort. As I near the fence, a boy standing out in left field removes his bright orange baseball cap to scratch the brown stubble growing on his head.

None of the kids have long hair, not even the girls. Every single one of them has sallow skin, bony legs, and so little hair that none sticks out below their baseball caps. Except for the girl at bat. Her fiery hair falls in a curly ponytail down to her waist, but this isn't what attracts my attention. Her right arm shines like a light bulb. It doesn't look like a real arm at all, except for its shape, but it isn't a prosthetic arm, either. I can't stop staring. Is it a new arm? What happened to the old one?

Then just beyond the ball-field, something darts between the tall, swaying trees.

Not something. Someone.

More specifically, my grandmother.

I rush past Jake's team, pausing long enough to catch his eye and give him a quick wave before taking off after the Faded Witch—I mean, my grandmother. I need to know what she's up to, and so I enter the dense woods. The worn trails crisscross at random intervals. Within ten minutes, I'm so lost I'm not even sure how to get back to the game fields. I pause at an intersection of five paths, not sure which one to take. I follow one on impulse, then trip on a tree root and fall to the ground, scuffing my hands. As I brush dirt off my jeans, heavy footsteps thud nearby. Twigs crunch and snap in the brush.

My heart rate triples.

I race down a narrow path leading to yet another fork in the woods.

A low growling noise follows me. Blood pulsates in my ears.

I pause in confusion, searching for the source of the strange noises. Where is it? *What* is it?

I spot the Faded Witch standing between the trees in the distance. Her voice projects as loud as a radio held next to my ear: "If you don't fix this, I'll *never* forgive you."

Then she disappears.

"I've always loved your ultimatums." The words sound more like an animal growl than a human voice. "And I'm pleased to hear you *do* care about someone other than yourself."

All I can see are the trees. Where are these voices coming from?

"Ha!" She cackles. "That's how I got here in the first place. Don't you remember?"

"You didn't follow the rules." The words shake the ground.

"I didn't agree with the rules." Her voice flies in and around the trees, stirring the leaves. "So I made some of my own."

Their words crash down on me from every direction. Branches creak and rustle as rabbits, squirrels, and chipmunks scatter across the woodland floor.

"You haven't come to see me for some time now." The growl turns almost to a purr. "Why do you stay away?"

A haze drops, then lifts. All the trees disappear. I stand in a sandy clearing, with trees far in the distance. The Faded Witch is right in front of me. She glares up at a pit bull the size of an elephant.

I gasp. I've seen this Creature before, when I attempted to contact Jake a few months ago. Grandma releases her hold on the moth. It drops to the ground and the Creature crushes it under its mighty paw.

Black smoke rises from the spot, then disappears with a whimpering noise.

"Greetings, Emma. How nice of you to join us." The words rumble like thunder, crash like the ocean, and echo like the fall of a tall tree. The giant dog advances on me, on muscular legs at least six feet tall.

I can't breathe. Black sparkles fill my view. My legs turn to water. I'm going to faint and this enormous thing is going to eat me. I hope I taste nasty.

The blocky head lowers and exhales, warming me with sweet breath that smells of freshly mowed grass. My vision clears just in time to notice the endless array of large white teeth in the creature's gaping jaws.

The better to eat you with, my dear. The words from a fairy tale dance in my head. I'm not sure if anyone actually said them aloud, but the meaning is clear. The dark brown eyes come closer, considering me without malice or friendship. I stare deep into the eyes. Deeper and deeper I fall, lost in a pool of darkness.

CHAPTER TWENTY-SEVEN

WHERE DID THEY GO

Emma! Where are you?" Jake calls out, crashing through the brush.

At the sound of Jake's voice, the trees return with a windy rush. The clearing and its occupants disappear in a white mist. Released from the spell, I fall to my knees like a rag doll as Jake approaches.

"They were right here." I flail about. "Where did they go?"

"What are you talking about?" Jake helps me to my feet. "Are you okay? You look spooked."

"Maybe I am." My legs shake. "Did you know that the Faded Witch is my grandma? And that she keeps a pet monster here in the woods? Wait. That's not right. It seemed to control *her*."

Jake stifles a chuckle. "There's no such thing as monsters in Heaven."

"But this isn't Heaven. Don't look at me like that! I didn't imagine it and I'm *not* crazy." I hope not, anyway. "A huge dog with eyes like a human's was talking to my grandma. I *saw* it, I swear."

"Maybe the sun's getting to you." Jake peers into my face. "Or did a fly ball hit you in the head?"

"Why don't you believe me?" I step away. "I'm telling the truth. I'm a witch because of my grandma, and she has a pet monster. Or else it's the other way around."

Jake raises his arms in mock defense. "All right. Fine. There's a giant dog roaming about Almost Heaven who enjoys the company of old lady witches."

I glower at him.

"Come on, Emma. The kids are done playing. Let's go to dinner, okay? You should eat. Maybe you'll feel better." He leads me along the paths. Soon the trees thin and the bright green playing fields come back into view.

He keeps trying to take my hand, but I pull away.

"Why don't you believe me?" I cross my arms to keep him at bay.

Jake puts out his hands in his typical *quit freaking out on me, Emma* gesture. "Why would there be monsters? And what if you're latching on the Faded Witch because you think you have something in common?"

"Trust me. We're related. She *told* me, plus she's wearing the same cross necklace as my father, and she knows about the wooden bowl I used for my spells."

His brows rise. "That's strange. She's doesn't look a thing like you. I heard she's been here longer than anyone else. I always see her wandering around, like she's searching for something that doesn't exist. It's sad."

I stop walking. "Sam brought her to see me."

Jake's steps also come to a halt. "Do you think she's been waiting for you?"

"No, I don't think so. She barely talked to me before she took off to see that dog-thing, whatever it was."

"So you're her granddaughter? I guess it kinda makes sense—the whole witch thing, I mean."

My stomach swirls with mixed energies, both fear and excitement. "That's what Sam said—that my power had to come from somewhere."

"Maybe I should introduce myself." Jake flashes his one-of-a-kind grin. "I bet she'd like me."

"Don't be so sure of yourself, buddy," I say. He's so full of himself, even now. How ridiculous. And now I wish he'd hold my hand again. Ugh. I'm so mixed up I don't even know *what* I want half the time.

He winks. "Why not? You two are related, and *you're* crazy about me."

"I wouldn't be so sure of yourself." Of course, my Mom loved him right away, so he's probably right. How frustrating. Must be nice to have everyone like you right away, the first time they see your face. Except it wasn't that way with me...

"You love me. You know it." He pauses, waiting for an answer.

My stomach clenches. I've no idea what to say. "You're a very annoying person." I put my hands on my hips. "I should kick you." But part of me wants to kiss Jake, instead. Kiss him, and forget about everything else that has happened. But I can't. I'm responsible for everything, and I need to fix everything.

"Stop flirting with me, girl, and get over here." He grabs my hand. I give in and let him hold it.

As we cross the playing fields, a young boy in an orange cap walks far ahead of us back to the stone compound.

Jake points. "That's Tommy. He died from a brain tumor. Bernard adopted him along with Colleen."

"That's cool. I mean the adoption, not the brain tumor." I think of home, of those I left behind. Abby and Claire must be wondering what happened to me. "I'm glad both Bernard and Claire got a chance to have kids. But I don't get why the kids are here, anyway. Why don't they go straight to Heaven? They're not old enough to have done anything wrong."

Jake takes a few deep breaths before answering. "Moving on is a funny thing. Sometimes it's physical illness that keeps you here. But it could be mental. Whether you want to call it 'sin' or not, lots of people aren't healthy when they get here."

Without meaning to, I flinch.

Jake releases his hold on my hand. "I'm sorry. I forgot you're injured. Did I hurt you?"

"No. That's not it." I step back. "Did you mean me? That I'm not right in my head?"

"I, uh..." Jake pauses to frown. "Maybe *you're* the best one to answer that question."

My eyes tingle with tears.

"Come on." He puts an arm around me. "We'll figure everything out, okay? But not on an empty stomach. How about some ice cream? Ice cream can fix anything, right?"

"I'm not so sure I believe in the mighty power of ice cream like you do." I muster a smile. "But it sounds good. I'm officially starving to death." I choke out a weak laugh. "You're probably not supposed to say that up here, right?"

Jake grins and my stomach flip-flops.

"Let's go, then." He gestures down the next walkway. "We'll hit the snack bar. But first I need to go back to my room to shower and change."

We turn down another street, which resembles all the others. "Okay. I need to pick up something for Steve anyway."

He sighs. "Him again."

I elbow Jake. "You don't like any of my friends."

He shakes his head. "Not true. Bernard's great. Sam's depressing as Hell. Mike's so-so. But Steve—I don't trust him. There's something almost alien in his eyes. It's creepy."

CHAPTER TWENTY-EIGHT

ICE CREAM FIXES EVERYTHING... ALMOST

Sitting together on a wooden bench eating an ice cream cone, I lean my head on Jake's shoulder. "Why do you think God won't see me?"

"I don't know. He saw me right away. He looked like my junior high school football coach."

I lick my cone, stomach growling. "Why is it different for some people and the same for others?"

Jake puts an arm around me. "Maybe God shows up in whatever form is easiest for us to accept."

I pause to stare at my cookies and cream. "I wonder what that will be for me."

He laughs. "Can I guess?"

I glare at him. "No! You're just going to say something that makes me sound stupid."

"Stupid is not a word that suits you." He smirks. "Super-motivated—yes. Over-achieving—definitely. Accident-prone—that's for sure. Hey, maybe God will be a librarian—you know, everything alphabetized, like all your books and CDs."

I scowl. "Why do you enjoy aggravating me so much?"

"I'm pretty sure it's my job." He gives me a quick squeeze.

I stiffen my back against his gesture. "Then get a new one."

"You're the one who needs a job." He drops the arm he had around me, and I immediately miss its warmth.

"I tried. I went to meet the professor."

"Did you like him?" he asks.

"Yes, very much. He's waiting to help his wife when she gets here. She has Alzheimer's." I glance around at the people milling about nearby. "This place is good for fixing what's wrong with you. The cancer kids like Tommy play outside until they're strong again. The old ladies take water aerobics until their arthritis is gone. I wonder what I'll be like when I'm done."

"Some of the ladies like my classes so much they keep coming long after they're healed. I'm just that fun to be around. As far as the professor's wife is concerned, she'll need more than what's offered here. He'll have to take her to the Healing Islands."

"The Healing Islands. Where's that?"

"I don't know." He shrugs. "I didn't have to go there because my mind is *perfect*."

I snort. "That's debatable. Now take me back to Steve's office so I don't have to ask Cari for directions again."

Jake stands, done eating already. "Why don't you like Cari? She's a friend of mine."

"So I've heard." My cheeks flare as he grabs my hand and we walk that way together.

"You're jealous." Jake squeezes my hand. "Good. I was beginning to wonder about you."

I stop walking. "Listen, Jake. I'm sorry if I don't know how to be a good girlfriend—if that's what this is, I mean. It's all new to me, and I've got a lot on my mind right now."

"Emma, I don't expect you to drop everything and turn into some perfect girlfriend. In fact, I don't want you to turn into anything. I like you as is."

I flush under his intense gaze, unable to say a word. *Please kiss me*, I silently beg of him.

His eyes seem more troubled than loving. "But I'm worried you're in serious danger."

Ugh. "Why do you all keep *saying* that?" Darn. I guess that means no kissing.

Jake exhales. "You're here way too early. You're possessed. You've sent Mike back—for the second time. You're seeing monsters and witches in the woods. To be honest, I don't know what to think. Which is why—even though I don't like him—I think you better get Steve to help you. He owes you, right?"

"Yes, he does. And the Steve I remember likes to pay his bills." But I'm not sure I trust him anymore.

"Then let's go." Jake nods in the general direction.

We keep a brisk pace until I spot the huge wooden door.

Jake pauses. "What if he won't see you without an appointment?"

"He will. I've got this." I pull out a picture of his son.

"Why were you carrying around all those pictures anyway? Why didn't you put them in frames like normal people?"

"I wasn't supposed to know any of you, remember? You were all dead before I met you. Except for Mike, of course."

"Of course, Mike." Jake looks at his feet. "Okay, then. I'll see you at supper."

I knock as Jake strides off in the other direction. The heavy door echoes, announcing my visit. A bodybuilder dressed in an Armani knockoff opens the imposing door to glower at me.

I clear my throat. "Tell Steve that I have important information about Officer Walker."

He crosses his beefy arms. "You already had an appointment with him this morning."

My eyes narrow. "Well then, Mr. Helpful, why don't you inform him that I have a picture of his son in my possession?"

He reaches out a massive hand.

I hide the picture behind my back. "He's not getting it until I talk to him in person."

"Fine." He ushers me into the fancy office.

A minute later, Steve enters smiling, hand outstretched to accept the picture. His eyes soften as he gazes at his son. "Thank you, Emma. You're the best."

I shift my weight between my feet, stalling momentarily. "I feel bad ruining the moment, but there's something important I forgot to tell you earlier. When Walker had me repeat the séance, I entered the mind of your killer."

Steve's smile disappears, replaced by an unreadable expression.

"He's dead now, too," I continue. "His name was Dominic. He'd joined a gang, and they sacrificed him a short time after he killed you."

Steve steps behind his desk, gaze averted. "Yes, I know."

"You *know*?" This floors me.

He places the picture into a long slim drawer. "He's here now."

"Dominic's *here*? But he killed you. Does everyone get to come here, regardless of their sins? That doesn't seem fair."

Steve pauses, resting his fingertips on the glossy desk. "I *brought* him here."

"How?" My stomach drops. "Or don't I want to know?"

"Trust me." He turns away. "You *don't*."

"But how did you find out about him before I told—"

"I've got feelers out," his voice is calm, smooth, disconnected. "I discovered the gang that killed me, and sooner or later, its members always end up dead."

I gasp. "Steve, what's going on here? Things are getting crazy—"

"Thanks for your concern, but you have to go now." Steve grabs my arm and forces me to his office door.

"I'm not leaving yet!" I wrench my arm out of his grip.

"Don't judge me, Emma. You should hate them as much as I do. They were after you, too. For your powers. Who knows what they would've done to you if you hadn't..." He pauses mid-sentence. "But enough about that. Thanks for the picture of my son. I do appreciate it."

"Steve, are you in over your head? If you need help, ask."

"Trust me." He straightens his shoulders. "I've got this under control. Now, I'm late for an important meeting. We'll have to continue this discussion another time." His eyes shine cold and unfamiliar.

The door swings open. Another guard stands outside.

Steve clears his throat. "Emma Roberts was just leaving."

The guard grabs my arm, yanks me through the doorway, and drags me down the hall.

"No!" I scream as Steve disappears around a corner. "What about Mike? What did you find out? You've got to tell me—"

The guard tosses me outside. I crumple in the road like a discarded rag. The heavy door slams shut with a *thud*. People step around me as I rise to my feet, gawking at me, and scurrying out of my way.

I glare at the wooden entry door.

Steve's quest for revenge has driven him mad. He's not even going to help Mike.

I'm going to have to do this myself.

But how?

CHAPTER TWENTY-NINE

GHOST DANCING

I rush into the dining hall. Breathless, I plop down next to silver-haired Bernard and his adopted kids.

"Hey, are you busy tonight?" I ask him. "We need to talk."

"Sorry, Emma." Bernard puts an arm around his daughter's shoulders. "I promised Colleen we'd attend the 'father-daughter' dance down on the beach. And this here's Tommy. Jake said he could hang out with the two of you while we're gone."

My eyes stray toward Jake up at the food counter, heaping sandwiches and drinks onto trays. I bite my lip and turn back to Bernard. "It's about Mike. Are you're *sure* you haven't seen him since I got here?"

Bernard winks and chuckles. "Still got a thing for him, do ya?"

"No. That's not it—" I protest.

Jake's tray clatters on our table.

Bernard glances around the room. "Well, I haven't seen him. I don't know where he is. Sorry to eat and run, but we're late for our 'date.'" He and Colleen hurry off, leaving Tommy behind.

I push the food Jake brought me around my plate. I can't believe Steve isn't going to help, that he only cares about himself now. Actually, I can believe it, but it doesn't make me any less disappointed.

"Are you going to eat that?" Tommy asks. His plate looks like it has been licked clean.

I slide my untouched tray across the table toward him.

"Gee. Thanks!" He wins me over with a crooked smile.

"No problem. I'm just not hungry." My stomach feels heavy, like a giant piece of concrete.

It doesn't help that Jake has fallen into a sullen silence. After supper, the three of us meander onto a wide terrace overlooking the ocean. The breeze carries beach party music up to the patio. The catchy rhythm of the steel drums beckons my feet to move.

"I'll be right back." Jake excuses himself to go speak to a tall blonde I haven't met yet on the other side of the terrace.

The woman giggles and a jealous pang stabs me. She's probably the one I saw him dancing with in my vision. That's just great.

Tommy taps his foot to the music and glances shyly at me.

I smile. "Tommy, are you going to ask me to dance?"

He grins. "Okay, if you insist."

This kid has spent way too much time with Jake. Where else would he learn lines like that? We sway awkwardly to the beat due to our height difference. From the patio, I gaze down toward the beach and the sparkling waters stretching far into the distance.

"Do you like living with Bernard and Colleen?" I ask.

"Yes, they're nice to me." He pauses for a moment. "We're waiting for Bernard's wife. Do you know her?"

"Yes, I know Claire. She's super nice, too."

Tommy takes a deep breath. "Do you think she'll like me?"

I smile at his sweet uncertainty. "Of course she will."

"Good." He exhales. "I'm waiting for my mom. But God said I have to wait a long time."

This is so weird. People here *want* their loved ones to die. It's not like that on Earth.

"You're lucky you don't have to wait." He grins at me. "Coach is already here."

Jake waited for me? My heart hiccups as he saunters back our way.

"Tommy, I saw your friends down on the beach." Jake thumbs toward the sandy dunes.

The boy scurries off and Jake smoothly cuts in. "Shall we dance?"

"Uh... I guess so." The blood pulsating in my ears drowns out the music.

His muscular arms wrap around me. "This is much better. I've got you alone at last."

I tense. Why can't I relax around him? "Don't expect much—I'm not a very good dancer."

"Don't worry." He whispers in my ear. "I know you're not a graceful ballerina. We've danced together before, remember?"

"Yes, I remember." My steps falter.

Jake tries to continue dancing, but I've stopped moving. "Emma, what's *wrong*? Every time I touch you, you freak out. Do you want me to leave you alone, or what?"

My head is pounding along with the beat. "I'm... distracted. I'm so angry at Steve and worried about Mike that I can't think about anything else right now."

He steps back. "Emma, you're the one who got beat up, tattooed, and almost killed, but still the only thing you care about is that you sent Mike back to Earth once again."

I bite my lip. "But who's going to take care of Mike this time? I'm not there to help him."

Jake clenches his hands. "Mike's a grown man. He should be able to take care of himself. Honestly, sometimes I wonder if you're just disappointed that you're *here* and he's *there*."

What? My mouth falls open. "That's not it at *all*."

"You know." Jake lowers his voice. "I feel like there's a conversation we started and never got to finish. And maybe it's too late. Maybe you've changed your mind already. I mean, you were drunk that night..." His voice trails off.

"That's not it—"

"It's not? Don't forget I read your diary. All this witchcraft business happened because you insta-loved on Mike before he drowned. I just came along in the aftermath. And everyone says stupid things when they're drunk. You could've thought you were talking to Mike, for all I know."

"No. I said what I said because I meant it." I cross my arms. "Not because I was drunk."

Jake stares at me. "Then say it now."

I avert my gaze, watching all the other people dancing around us on the patio. Are they listening in? "Can't we talk about this later?"

"Do you love me?" Jake's eyes narrow. "Or not? It's a rather simple question."

My heart races. I'd like nothing better than to go home with him, but I'm not that kind of girl. I'm a Trixie Belden kind of girl, fixing problems, solving mysteries. Duty first. "I do, but I can't focus on this right now. Steve's turned into President Psycho up here, I'm still loaded with disturbed spirits, and Mike is stranded back on Earth with no one to help him."

He throws up his arms. "How come you can't see that *you're* the one here who needs the most help?"

I flinch. "Well, God could help, but He, She, or It won't see me."

He grabs my arms, but with a gentle touch. "What if you're wrong? What if Mike didn't go back? Maybe he moved on." Jake pauses. "What if it those spirits possessing you *want* you to believe this? Maybe it's a trick."

"Haven't you noticed—Mike's *not* here! That's proof enough for me. He's stuck back on Earth, where he didn't want to be even the last time around, and once again I'm responsible."

"Mike wasn't waiting for you, just so you know." He takes a deep breath. "I was. Not that it matters to you, apparently."

"You're jealous over nothing. I just want Mike to be okay. I can't *stand* the thought of hurting him. And Steve's not helping at all. He's being a total jerk."

"Of course he is. That's no surprise. But, despite what you say, I think you still care about Mike a little too much for my comfort."

My heart spasms. Am I having a heart attack now? Does that

happen here? "Can't you accept that you're not the only person in my life who needs me?"

"Oh. Is that it?" He glances away. "Then I guess I understand everything."

"Then explain it to me, because I don't understand a *thing*. Why won't God see me? Why is my grandma cursed? What was that Creature she was talking to? It was the scariest thing I've seen yet. Is that who I'm going to turn into someday? My grandma, I mean. Not the dog."

Jake stares at the ground. "Answer me one thing: when you threw that *Book* in the fire pit, were you trying to get rid of it or were you hoping to get Mike back again? Be honest."

I cross my arms. "No, you idiot! I was just trying to get rid of the demons."

He keeps talking as if he hasn't heard me. "I thought I knew you."

"You do know me. You read my whole stupid diary, *remember*?"

He glances back up, right in my eyes. "Yeah, I did. I guess that means I should've known better." Before I can respond, he walks away.

I watch him head down to the beach. I want to say something, but it has to be the right thing. My mouth is dry and wordless, but this time I can't blame the demons inside me.

I can only blame myself.

CHAPTER THIRTY

BACK TO CHURCH

Fighting tears, I skirt around the dining hall and rush in the opposite direction, cruising down the winding streets without a destination in mind. With each turn, I get more lost. The cobblestone paths lined with stone buildings all look the same. Why does Jake drive me crazy? He makes me so angry I can't even say what I should. If only he'd just shut up once in a while.

Tears blind me as I turn another corner.

Angry voices cry out, "Witch! Evil! Filthy abomination!"

Startled, I wipe away tears. People cluster outside a beautiful white church with a curved blue roof. They're all staring at me. Each person clenches a cross, a rosary, or some other religious token, as if to protect themselves.

"Willing harborer of the demon!"

"Daughter of Darkness!"

"Satan's Slut!"

My mouth falls open. No one calls me a slut! That's not even close to the truth.

"Don't say that!" No one's bullying me ever again, no matter who they are. "Who said you were all so holy? Let the one who is without sin be the first to cast a stone, or whatever." I glance at the rocks lining the road.

Bad choice of Bible verse on my part.

The church doors swing open and a woman drifts out, a blissful look on her face. The next person in line darts inside before the doors crashes shut. Wait a minute. Could this be...?

"Is this the waiting line to see God?" I ask.

The people back away.

"Is it? You better answer me." I stride toward the waiting line and the hecklers stiffen. A curly haired woman dressed like a flight attendant purses her lips.

I point at her. "And if you *dare* call me a slut again, I'll turn your hair green *permanently*."

Laughter bursts forth behind me. I spin around.

"You tell them, my Little Witch." Grandma laughs, her bright blue eyes flashing.

"What are you doing here?" I ask.

"Looking for you, as usual," she responds.

The crowd murmurs its disapproval. A mother covers her child's eyes with the edge of her robe, which makes me feel guilty. Why does she believe I'm that bad? I was only trying to help. That's all I ever do.

"Come with me, girl." Grandma gestures toward the side of the church, away from the main line. "Our kind uses the *side* door."

"Oh, thanks." I follow her into a small garden filled with burgundy peonies.

Grandma touches my arm. "You need guidance. The way you're headed, you'll get lost."

"Who's going to help me?" I ask.

She points to an ornately carved wooden door. "Seek and ye shall find."

I grab the handle. The second the door opens, my feet slide like skates through the open doorway and halfway down the hall before I come to an abrupt stop. The temperature plummets. My breath hangs in the air like I'm in a walk-in freezer. I run my hands along the wooden wall for support until I reach the red curtains at the far end. I extend both arms in front of me as I approach the red drapes. I struggle through layers of thick velvet fabric, but instead of entering a sanctuary, I descend the aisle of an empty college lecture hall.

I whirl around, searching for signs of life.

"Where are You?" I call out. "Why won't You talk to me when You'll talk to everyone else?"

Elegant script appears on the white boards at the bottom of the lecture hall. *YOU DON'T BELONG HERE.*

"But I need to talk to You. I've so many questions. Something's wrong with Steve and I need to help Mike."

The floor shifts and shakes below me. I stumble, growing dizzier by the second. The room morphs into the wooded park near my parents' house. My feet crunch leaves on a shady dirt path. A brindled pit bull with cropped ears approaches.

My heart thuds as I take an involuntary step back. "Please help me."

The gray-muzzled dog wags his tail as his voice growls in my head. *FIRST YOU MUST HELP ME.*

"I don't understand. Why are You a dog?"

STEVE WILL REVEAL ALL YOU NEED TO KNOW.

"Steve? He's *totally* out of control. Why aren't You doing something to stop him?"

ALL THAT CATHOLIC SCHOOLING, AND YOU STILL DON'T UNDERSTAND THE MEANING OF FREE WILL?

The dog and trees disappear as the room tilts again. I fall to my knees as a glossy black grand piano materializes in front of me. A man who looks like Billy Joel plays a beautiful, yet haunting, melody. After I regain my footing, I place my hand on the cool, smooth surface of the piano.

"What about the demons?" I ask Billy Joel. "Aren't You going to help me with them?"

I THOUGHT YOU WANTED TO DEAL WITH IT ON YOUR OWN.

So it's true. God does know everything. I flush, embarrassed. I don't really want anyone to know all of my thoughts.

"Please tell me what to do," I beg.

The pianist closes his eye, nodding in time to the melody. *BE GOOD TO YOUR MOTHER.*

"What's that supposed to mean?"

YOU'LL SEE HER SOON.

My breath catches in my throat. "What happened to her? Is she okay?"

ASK HER YOURSELF.

I whirl around. "Is she here?"

NO. YOU'RE GOING BACK.

"What? But I don't want to go back!" I'll lose Jake for good. But maybe I have to, to fix the mess I made.

The music ends. The Pianist turns His terrible eyes on me. Within the shimmering irises, I see babies crying, a sea of arms flailing, and wolves howling at the moon.

A low growling fills the room.

The piano stool falls with a crash as He sprouts fur and morphs into the aged pit bull, which grows taller and broader, transforming into the Giant from the forest. The Creature flings Itself at me, knocking me to the ground.

I writhe and fight to escape the enormous bared fangs. Its hot breath surrounds me. My body burns, both inside and out. I scream for the pain to stop, but instead of speaking, my mouth spews red and orange flames.

I choke as smoke pours out, followed by moths, and then a crow, all from my open mouth.

The room around me fades away. Sprawled on the smooth wooden floor of an old church, I retch, feeling like I've been turned inside out. My head spins when I attempt to sit up and look around at the empty room.

"Where *are* You? I have more questions!" My plea echoes off the walls.

The front doors of the church burst open. Two men in black suits hurry toward me. Each grabs an arm and hauls me out of the building.

I fight their grip as they drag me past the grumbling crowd. "Did someone call the cops on me because I cut in line?"

Neither of them answer.

I realize the truth.

"You goons work for Steve, don't you?" I hope they don't beat me up for saying that.

Streets flash by as they herd me to the familiar stone building. They throw open the massive door, drag me down several hallways, and toss me into Steve's ostentatious office. I stumble and fall, rubbing my sore arms. Now, I've got *new* bruises on top of the old ones. Dizzy and weak, I collapse into a chair.

Steve enters without a word. He crosses the room to a minibar where he washes his hands. He wipes flecks of blood off his face with an elegant handkerchief and rolls down his crisp white sleeves. Cold anger oozes from every exfoliated pore.

"What's going on, Steve? Why are you covered in blood?"

Instead of answering, he settles down at his desk and writes a letter. I clear my throat, shuffle my feet, and otherwise try to annoy him into speaking, but he ignores my efforts to capture his attention.

After he fills several pages, he folds them lengthwise, stuffs them in an envelope, and hands it to me. "Give this to Officer Walker. It's important."

"And *how* am I supposed to do that?"

He rises to his full height. "You're leaving. Right now."

"But I don't want to go back." At least I don't think so. Jake won't wait forever.

"You will after I tell you what you've done to Officer Walker."

I scowl. "I haven't done anything to him. All I did was help with a few murder cases—including yours, I might add."

Steve frowns. "You're mistaken. Walker's in jail on charges of attempted murder."

I grip the arms of the chair. "That's impossible!"

Steve glares at me like I'm an idiot. "*Your* murder, Emma."

"*What?*" I jump out of the chair.

"Kevin, Mike, and your new wanna-be friend, Phoebe, are trying to help him, but it's hopeless unless you go back and clear his name."

"No. It can't be true." It feels like I'm breathing into a vacuum and all the air is being sucked out of my chest.

"Congratulations. You were right. You *did* bring Mike back to life again. He exchanged places with you when you came here. This time, he even has the use of his own body. He doesn't have to share one like last time."

I stare at a thin streak of blood staining Steve's cheek. "Whose blood is that?" Looking down at the envelope in my hands, I know the answer. "It's from Dominic, isn't it? You kept him prisoner here, and tortured him until he spilled whatever information you wanted. Is that even allowed up here?"

"You could say that I'm making up the rules as I go." Steve flips open a wooden chest on his desk and plucks out a shiny chain. At the end dangles an ornate silver and gold key. He grabs my elbow and leads me to a metallic door at the far end of the room. Steve unlocks and swings open a heavy golden door to reveal a silver one behind it.

"I can't believe how you've changed." I stare at Steve's clenched jaw. "I mean, who's worse now—you, or the gang that killed you?"

"I'm going to pretend you never said that." He slides the key in the second lock. "Actually, Emma, you should thank me. I'm giving you what you always wanted. Or should I say 'who?'"

Blood is pounding in my ears. "What are you talking about?"

"You're going to the Healing Islands before you go back to Charlie."

I shake my head. "No. Send me straight back. I can't waste time on a tropical vacation."

"We're not wasting anything. The time you spend at the Healing Islands will last only the blink of an eye on Earth. You won't be of any use to me if you're all messed up. And I sent Mike there to tell you everything he knows. Imagine it. You'll be together in paradise. This could be a wonderful opportunity for you."

I want to smack him across his blood-stained cheek. "What's wrong with you, Steve? You're not the person I remember. I'm disappointed in you."

His eyes narrow. "Don't be ridiculous. I'm exactly the same person. Maybe it's *you* who has changed."

"Maybe I have, but I'm not the only one. You're so angry now. You're out of control."

"No." He gives me a tight-lipped smile, more of a grimace. "I'm *in* control. There's a difference. I've always been willing to do whatever it takes to accomplish my goals. And if you don't like that, the take a good look in the mirror, because you're exactly the same way. That's what I always admired about you. You did what had to be done, when necessary, regardless of the consequences. That's what heroes are made of."

"You're no hero, Steve." I clench my jaw. "Not in my book."

"I'm sorry you feel that way." But he doesn't look sorry at all.

"Just open the door, Steve. I'm going, but I want you to know that I'm doing this for Walker. *Not* you."

"Fine. If that's how you want to see it."

He opens the last door and I plunge through the opening.

WHOOSH!

The wind stings my eyes as I drop into pale blue nothingness. Falling into the void, I hear Jake's muffled voice from a great distance.

"Where's Emma?" he demands.

"Oh, great, it's the God Squad," Steve scoffs.

"What did you do with her?" Jake yells. "And where do you think you're going?"

A series of two doors slam shut, one right after the other.

Once again, Jake and I never got to say good-bye.

PART THREE

THOU SHALT NOT STEAL

CHAPTER THIRTY-ONE

LOST IN PARADISE

After the initial plummet, my descent feels more like floating than falling. I drift through a cloudless blue sky, but its perfection can't calm the turmoil inside. Will I ever see Jake again? Will I reach Walker in time? How can I explain myself without telling the police and (gulp) my parents that I'm a witch? At least Dad shouldn't be surprised, since it does run in the family.

The sky lightens as I soar past the sun and land feet first on a pristine beach, stumbling about as if I've got sea legs. Bright sunlight bathes my skin, warming my hair and soothing my bruises. Steve was right. This is paradise.

Now to find Mike.

I hurry along the beach, leaving a long path of footprints behind. I scan the glittering sea, and sandy beaches lined with palm trees. The heat is stifling. I push up the long sleeves of the turtleneck and approach the water's edge to cool my feet.

Where is Mike? All I can find are swaying palms, skittering reptiles, and screeching birds. Can't trust anything Steve says anymore. Can't trust him. Can barely trust myself. I'm not sure how I'm going to save Walker when I haven't even done a very good job of saving myself.

Still sweating, I climb onto a large flat rock jutting into the ocean and gaze out at the far horizon. Nothing but endless sky and sea. And heat! I can't take it anymore. I strip down to my bra and underwear and jump in. Warm water swaddles me like an infant. Bright blue and orange fish dart through turquoise waters. I pass coral reefs and fields of waving seaweed as I twist and turn in the comfort of the water's embrace.

I could stay here forever. Completely relaxed, I crawl back onto the gray rock warmed from the sun and stretch out to dry. My bruises have faded away. As I melt onto the rock, something cold and wet nudges my hand. My eyes fly open. A Golden Retriever with a gray muzzle, scrawny legs, and rough coat pants over my head.

"Woof!" The old dog noses a worn tennis ball in my direction. The dog's clouded eyes shine with hope.

"You wanna play fetch?" I toss the ball far out onto the beach, causing the old dog to give me the stink eye. "Sorry, buddy. I shouldn't have thrown it so far."

The dog ambles down the rock, every movement hesitant and stiff. Far beyond where the ball landed on the beach, I spot a dark silhouette in the sunlight. As the figure draws closer, my heart stutters. After all this time, why does seeing Mike still make me nervous? Wait, maybe it's because I'm only wearing a bra and underwear. I tug on my turtleneck and jeans as fast as I can over damp skin and scramble down to the beach.

"Hello, Mike," I call out as he approaches.

He throws up his hands. "I *knew* you'd be here somehow."

Oh, boy. He's *not* happy to see me.

"What have you done now, Emma?" He shakes his head. "I keep getting tossed here and there. Why can't you leave that awful *Book of Shadows* alone? I told you it was dangerous. I should've forced you to get rid of it when I had the chance. But I didn't, and you didn't, and now you're dead because of it, aren't you?"

I keep my distance. "I need my *Book,* Mike. And I'm not dead. Not yet, anyway."

"Well, you did a very good impression of a dead person in front of that fire pit. You weren't breathing, and I couldn't find a pulse. I tried to resuscitate you, but there was smoke everywhere, and sirens blaring. Then the cops showed up. And I panicked—so I picked up your stupid *Book* and ran away."

I gasp and warmth floods my being. "You mean the *Book of Shadows* is okay? I didn't destroy it?"

"That *would* be the only thing you care about," he mutters.

My heart races. "No, it's not. And I'm really sorry. I didn't mean to leave you alone."

He waves his hand. "I wasn't alone. I had my family."

"You did?" My jaw drops. "But last time, you said you didn't want to—"

"I know, but this time around I didn't have a choice. And I'm glad I got to spend some more time with my mom, even though twice now I've left without saying good-bye." He grabs a pebble and flings it across the beach. "All because of you and your obsession with witchcraft."

I hang my head. Why can't I do anything right when it comes to Mike? Or Jake, for that matter?

"You've no idea what you've put me through." His shoulders slump. "When is this going to stop?"

A wet nose nudges my hand. Grateful for the distraction, I pick up the old dog's ball and toss it a short way down the beach.

"I'm sorry, but I wasn't trying to call you back this time." I sneak a glance at him, but he's staring at the ocean. "Walker asked me to help with some murder cases, and things got out of hand."

"Out of hand?" He spins toward me. "Is that what you call being possessed by demons? I'm beginning to think you don't care *what* happens to you as long as you can keep using that stupid *Book*."

I take a step back. "How do you know I'm possessed?"

"Father Joe told me. He's trying to figure out how to dispel your demons. He and my mother spend a lot of time at the hospital watching over you."

"*Your* mother?" My gut clenches. "But she *hates* me."

Mike shakes his head. "No, she doesn't. You're just paranoid."

"Yes, she does. Remember what she said to me at your funeral? Oh, wait... I guess you weren't exactly there." My ill-chosen words peter out.

"Well, I don't know what she told you, but I'd forget about anything anyone says at a funeral—especially the funeral of their own son."

I glance at the open water, which looks so much more tranquil than I feel. "Okay. That's fair."

He bends down to pet the dog. "Plus it's not *her* you have to worry about—it's those demons inside you."

I cross my arms in front of my chest, as if protecting them. "Hold on. They're *not* demons— not all of them, anyway. Most of them are victims. Except for one very creepy guy named Shadow."

He tosses the ball a short distance down the beach. "You still need to get rid of all of them or they'll destroy you."

I avoid his gaze. "I'm not sure they're even still with me. I feel so much better now. Maybe they're gone."

"Don't fool yourself, and don't lie to me." He grabs my arm. "What are you going to do now? What's your big plan? You'd better have a good one, or you're gonna ruin Charlie's life."

My stomach sinks. "I don't know yet, but I'll take care of it. I promise. I just don't know exactly how yet."

"Oh, boy. Charlie's doomed." Mike sinks to his knees, burying his face in his hands. "You're in this too deep and can't see your way out."

"First, you've got to tell me everything that happened, so I can help Walker when I get back. That's the reason Steve sent us both here."

Mike talks through his hands. "So this is Steve's fault? Doesn't matter. I can blame you and him all I want, but it's still all my own dumb fault. If I hadn't gone swimming that night and drowned. If I'd convinced you to get rid of your *Book of Shadows*."

I put out a hand, begging him to stop. "I'm sorry I always make you feel guilty."

"Of course I feel guilty. It's my fault this whole thing started." He rubs his eyes. "You treat witchcraft like a game and it almost killed you, but let's stop fighting about it and get started figuring out what to do.

Who knows how much time the Great and Wise Steve gave us? I hardly even know where to begin."

"Did you talk to Walker? How is he?" I hold my breath, waiting for the answer.

"Sorry. I don't know. Never saw him. He's stuck in jail with news reporters swarming the police station. I couldn't risk getting anywhere near him. Someone might recognize me, and I'm supposed to be dead, remember?"

"So he *is* in jail." My stomach sinks. "I wasn't sure whether to believe Steve or not. Walker must be so pissed at me."

"Maybe." Mike shrugs, plopping down on the sand and running it through his fingers. "Kevin's still training with the police. He told me jail has been tough on Charlie. You know, since he's a cop and all."

"So you finally talked to Kevin? That's great!" My sudden happiness disappears, because Kevin hated me even more than Mike's mother. And now maybe Walker's mother, too. Wait a minute... "What did you tell Kevin about me?"

Mike smiles. "You mean: does Kevin know you're a witch? Yes. He does. I told him the truth about everything."

I put a hand to my belly. "Oh no, I think I'm going to be sick."

Mike grabs the ball and tosses it in the air, the dog watching closely. "That's funny. I must have that effect on a lot of people, 'cause Kevin puked the first time he saw me."

I grimace. I hate even the thought of puking. "It must have been quite a shock for him."

"Oh, he bounced back fast. Within a day, he was poring over your awful witchcraft *Book* trying to figure out how to bring you back so you could free Charlie. We were all trying to help, but none of us knew what to do."

A wave of possessiveness rushes over me. "Are you telling me that *Kevin* has my *Book?*"

Mike flinches at my tone. "No. Your neighbor Phoebe does."

"What? Why is *she* involved?" I run my hands through my hair, wanting to rip it out.

"Don't complain—she's been a lot of help." He tosses the ball, and the dog gets up to lumber after it.

No way am I getting jealous over this. No. Way. Okay, I am. I want my *Book* back. "She's not that great. She mostly just gets in the way."

"You're crazy. She was so nice to my family. She was full of ideas about how to get you back, although none of them worked."

I throw up my hands. "Why is it okay for her to be a witch and not me?"

Mike shakes a finger at me. "Phoebe's careful. You're not."

"What do you mean? I always do my research."

Mike scowls. "You don't realize how terrible you looked in that hospital bed. Head-to-toe bruises, broken fingers, and cracked ribs, not to mention the internal injuries. You should've seen your mom's face, wondering if you'd ever come out of the coma."

Tears sprang to my eyes. "How are my parents?"

He frowns, avoiding my gaze. "Your mom's a mess. She's got way too much to deal with."

It hurts to breathe. "Did you tell her that I'm a witch?"

"No." He pauses. "We didn't."

"Good." Because that would be the worst thing he could do to me.

He rubs his temple. "No. Not good. Because now she thinks you and Charlie were dating and that he was abusing you."

"Oh, crap." My stomach lurches. I'm seriously going to get sick.

"What happened?" Mike asks. "I mean, Father Joe could tell you were possessed, but he'd never seen a case like yours."

I sigh, and the skinny old dog takes snuggles close at my side, dropping the ball to the ground. I tangle my fingers in the dog's soft fur. "When I helped with the murder cases, instead of *watching* what happened to the victims, I lived it. I got beat up, choked to death, and then stabbed." My forced smile feels like a grimace. "I'm like a cat with nine lives."

Mike's face pales. "You're insane. No one else would allow this to happen to them."

"Yeah, I know." Can't argue with the truth.

"Why didn't you quit when you started getting hurt?"

"That's what I was *attempting* to do that night at the park. First I went to Walker's house and interrupted his hot date to tell him that I couldn't help him with cases anymore. I tried to explain what was happening, but never really got the chance. The voices kept stopping me. Then I decided to destroy the *Book of Shadows* before I returned to Father Joe for an exorcism, but obviously *that* plan didn't work very well, either."

Mike's eyes widen. "Charlie had no idea what was happening to you?"

I squirm. "Um. Not really."

"That 'hot date' must be the infamous 'female eyewitness' to your so-called 'violent argument' right before your attack. No wonder Charlie's in trouble. The press is making a huge deal out of this, using some stupid 'corrupt police officer' angle. It's crazy. They claim he set the fire to cover up your attempted murder."

I feel faint. "This is worse than I thought. How am I going to fix this?"

"Beats me." Mike stretches his legs out in the sand.

The old dog struggles to rise and gimps to the edge of the ocean to take a long drink.

"Poor thing," I say. "I wonder where it came from."

Mike snorts. "You're more worried about that sick, old dog than you are about yourself."

"Well, who's going to take care of it way out here? It could starve to death, and it's so skinny already."

Mike puts a hand on my shoulder. "Why don't we focus on the *real* problem here? The night of your accident that tower of fire you conjured attracted a ton of attention. Emergency vehicles filled the park. Sirens wailed for hours. There was smoke everywhere. I felt bad leaving you, but I was scared what would happen if I was seen, so I ran off."

My gaze flickers back to him. "I know. I saw the whole thing."

"But you were either dead or unconscious. How could you see anything?"

"I saw it in a vision afterward." While kissing Jake. Not that I'm going to tell Mike that part.

Mike grimaces. "Another vision?"

"Remember how I once told you that my dreams border on reality?"

His eyes widen. "Like that body on the highway to Madison?"

"Yeah. Just like that."

He shudders. "You should quit this stuff, you know?"

"Not yet. I've gotta help Walker first, remember?"

"Things do look bad for him. Charlie was the first to get there. I hid in the woods and watched him race across the parking lot to you. He shook you, trying to get you to breathe, I think. Then he hoisted you up in his arms and carried you across the parking lot toward the other police cars. The other cops spilled out, drew their guns and yelled at him to put you down. But he wouldn't let go. They had to force him. I couldn't hear him through all the sirens, but Kevin said he kept saying you were dead because of him."

I cover my gaping mouth with a hand. "Oh, no! Why would he say that?"

"Kevin spotted me watching among the trees. Of course, he didn't realize who I was at first. He raced after me and I ran as fast as I could through the woods until he caught up and blinded me with his flashlight. That's when he puked."

"You must have scared the crap out of him."

Mike gives me a weak smile. "Yeah, I did. Poor guy. He begged me not to leave, but I couldn't let the other cops see me. I told him to meet me under the campus bridge and took off again."

"Why would you pick there?" I grimace. "That's where you died!"

"It was the only place I could think of on such short notice. And lucky for me, that's where your friend Phoebe found me."

I crush a shell in my hand. "Phoebe's not my friend. She just lives downstairs in Abby's old apartment."

"I know. I stayed with her for a couple days."

Now, she's really not my friend. She's one dead witch. "How could you stand it there? It's everything you hate, all witchcraft books and tapestries."

"You forgot about the awful incense." Mike laughs. "But she was nice and helpful."

"Helpful? Really? All she can do is predict the weather..." My uncertain voice trails off.

"She tried everything she could think of. Yesterday before daybreak, we snuck back into the park. Phoebe lit a fire and set candles and other witchy crap all around the same fire pit you had used. She chanted and cried out and all sorts of nonsense, but nothing happened. The last thing I remember was her getting frustrated and throwing the *Book of Shadows* down on the ground."

Mike traces patterns in the sand. "All at once, everything started to fade. Phoebe screamed and ran toward me, but disappeared as she got close. Everything went gray, like I'd gone blind. When the ocean came into view, I thought Phoebe's spell had screwed up, sending me away instead of bringing you home. But, like you said, it must've been Steve and not Phoebe who arranged all this."

"Yep. Steve's in charge, all right." I reach in my pocket for the letter. "I haven't read this yet, but he told me to give it to Walker."

"Steve's obsession with his murder has gotten out of hand. It's all he talks about, and he's bossing everyone around."

"Yeah. That's what Jake said." I flush as I say his name. "They were fighting as I left. I could hear them."

"I can believe it." Mike pauses. "Jake cares a lot about you, Emma."

My face burns. I blame the turtleneck.

"He must've found out that Steve had you sent back. Don't worry. I'm sure Jake could take him in a fight. Steve's all show, you know. He's actually kind of weak." Mike chuckles. "On the other hand, Jake's pretty built..."

My cheeks are really burning now. "What are you saying, Mike? Don't play some warped game of matchmaker with me. Besides, I've screwed up everything where Jake is concerned, but it doesn't matter now. All that matters is fixing this mess with Walker."

"I suppose you're right." Mike stands to stretch. "But I can't sit still anymore. Wanna walk along the shore with me?"

As we meander along the beach, Mike picks up a few stones and skips them across the water. The dog gimps after us. We remain silent for a while, listening to the waves caress the beach. Not talking is probably the safest thing we can do, since we always seem to hurt each other.

But there's more I need to know, so I ask, "How long have I been in a coma?"

"A whole week. That's a long time, Emma."

Oh dear. "How bad is it to be in a coma that long?"

He shrugs, then his eyes widen. "Something's happening to me. What's going on?"

His image starts to flicker, like a TV station with poor reception.

I grab for his arm, but my hand swooshes through empty air, like he's not even there. "Mike? Can you still hear me?"

He fights to speak as he fades away, his image blinking on and off before me. "Be careful, Emma. There's going to be a battle."

"A battle?" My mind floods with painted warriors from *Braveheart*, but I'm pretty sure that isn't what he means. "What are you talking about? What kind of battle?"

His voice grows faint. "It's... just... beginning."

"The beginning?" The beginning of what? "Then why does this feel like the end?"

Mike is a shadow now. He's almost gone. How many times is this guy going to leave me?

"Tell Mom... good-bye." He disappears as the sky rips in the distance, flapping like a curtain.

My heart aches after he's gone. I miss him already.

A spine-tingling howl carries on the wind and raises the hairs on my arms.

What now? I spin around to find the source. Squinting, I spot two figures on a far off cliff. The Creature and the Faded Witch standing together.

Watching me. Why are they here? Am I supposed to go to them?

Before I manage a step, the Golden Retriever perks up its ears and lopes off in their direction. As the dog runs, its arthritic gait transforms into an athletic sprint, and the thinned coat sheds its gray to regrow in golden waves. Halfway down the beach, a youthful dog swings back to me with flashing black eyes.

Are you coming? it seems to ask.

I finally recognize the dog as Nani—does that mean Jake's here? If he is, then at least I'll have a chance to apologize.

I race after the dog, but the sand slows my steps. It hardly feels like I'm moving.

A loud splash from the dancing waves draws my eyes to the shoreline. The waters swirl in a hypnotic pattern, emitting a low-pitched gurgle.

At my feet, the purple-blue waters churn.

"Emma!" I hear my name, but don't recognize the voice.

Who's calling me? Where are they?

An invisible force drags me to the water's edge. The waves transform into cold hands and yank me into their wet embrace.

I drown once again.

CHAPTER THIRTY-TWO

WELCOME BACK

Yanked into a vacuum of black churning water, I'm entangled by curtains of seaweed. I struggle to breathe, fighting to reach a faint light in the distance. I swim past more coral reefs and brightly colored fish. Drawn deeper into the sea, I scramble through a forest of ragged rock before falling through an opening covered with seaweed.

What if I don't get there in time?

The fish disappear. I am alone. The world holds still. Silent.

My ears pop with a sudden pressure change.

I gulp stale, metallic-tasting air.

Three blurry figures hover overhead.

A man's loud voice bounces off the walls. *"Deliver us from all sin, from the snares of the devil, from lightning and tempest, from everlasting death!"*

Water splashes my face.

"I command you, unclean spirit, along with all your minions now attacking this servant of God, to depart, you seducer, full of lies and cunning, foe of virtue, persecutor of the innocent. I adjure you, profligate dragon, to depart from this woman…"

More water strikes my face, clouding my vision and choking me.

"Stop it!" I croak, wiping my eyes and face.

The dark figures lean closer.

"We did it! She's awake!" Claire's worried face comes into focus. "Look. Her bruises are fading."

"I can't believe it worked." Mrs. Carlson clutches a Bible in her hands.

"What's going on?" I flinch at the sight of Mike's mom just inches from my face—she hates me. She *hates* me. My head spins. Claire and Mrs. Carlson waver in and out of focus.

Father Joe steps forward. "Welcome back, Emma."

"How did you know where to find me?" I whisper.

Father Joe holds a Bible, cross, and a bottle of holy water. "I read about your *accident* in the paper and came to finish what we started."

"You came to the hospital to perform an exorcism?" I scan the room. "Does Mom know about this?"

He clears his throat. "Uh, no. We thought it was best."

"Good." I breathe a sigh of relief. "Let's keep it that way."

"I even told her Mike was my nephew instead of my son, because... well, you know." Mrs. Carlson glances at the floor, as if ashamed.

I turn to Father Joe. "You know about Mike now, too?"

"Yes." He clears his throat. "I recognized him from the pictures at his funeral. There was no denying it was him."

"And you're okay with this?" What a relief. I'd hate to lie to a priest.

"Not at first, I wasn't. And I still have trouble believing you raised all those people from the dead. Exorcism training didn't prepare me for this. But I've taken a vow to assist those in need."

"So you'll help me?" Now I'm really asking for help. What a change.

He flinches, a worried crinkle across his brow. "Oh, dear. You're not asking me to help you with some *witchcraft* spell, are you?"

"No! Of course not! I just need to get out of here." I tug at the tape holding what seems like a hundred tubes to my body.

"What are you doing?" Claire slaps my hands away from the IV lines.

"You don't understand." I rip off the rib brace. "I need to free Walker."

"Oh, no you don't." Claire shakes her head. "You've been seriously injured. You need to rest."

Mrs. Carlson steps away from the hospital bed, her face paling. Is she going to faint? I better keep an eye on her.

"I rested enough on the Healing Islands." I dismantle the finger splints.

Claire fights my efforts. "What are you doing? You need these things!"

"No, I don't." I flex and extend my fingers. "See. Good as new. I'm not even sore."

Her eyes widen.

"Don't worry. I'm fine. But I can't just lounge around in here while Walker's stuck in jail."

"How do you know about that?" Mrs. Carlson asks.

I peel off the chest monitors. "Mike told me what happened."

Father Joe collapses into a chair. "This is too much."

BEEEEEP! BEEEEEP! BEEEEP!

I jump at the wailing alarms.

Claire rushes to silence the sirens. "Good thing I was a nurse. Sometimes it comes in handy."

"You saw Mike?" Mrs. Carlson asks in a hush. "Where is he? He didn't show up today, and I've been worried."

I tense. Every time I'm near this woman I feel guilty. "I'm sorry I'm the one who has to tell you this, but Mike and I switched back again."

"Then he's gone." Her voice shakes. "I wish I could have said good-bye."

"Yes, ma'am." I flush. "And, again, I'm really sorry about that."

"Please call me Julie." She blinks back tears. "I hate that word 'ma'am.' Makes me feel old."

"Makes every woman feel old," mutters Claire, still adjusting the medical monitors. "The word should be outlawed."

"What happened to him?" Mike's mom—I mean Julie—asks.

"Well, Mike told me that Phoebe tried to revive me using witchcraft, but I don't think she succeeded. I think someone else sent me back."

"God?" Father Joe asks hopefully.

I cringe, hesitant to squash his optimism. "No. I'm afraid not. Just someone who *thinks* he's God. I'm sure it was Steve."

His eyes widen. "Is Steve another dead guy?"

"Yeah. He sent Mike and me to the Healing Islands. Which is why I feel so much better."

"The Healing Islands?" Father Joe looks puzzled. "Is that Heaven?"

"Not really. Well, maybe it's *part* of Heaven. It's where things get fixed."

He rests a hand on his Bible, as if for reassurance. "And you needed to go there?"

I succeed in removing the rib belt. "I'm afraid so."

"Interesting. Because of the demons?"

There's so much tape on me that they must've used a whole roll per limb. It's going to take me forever to get out of here. "That and some other things."

Father Joe fidgets with his Bible, averting his gaze. "I haven't involved your mother yet, but I have to ask—what do your parents know about your interest in witchcraft?"

"My mother knows nothing. And let's keep it that way." I release myself from the rest of the tubes and scoot to the edge of the bed, clutching at my hospital gown. "Do I have any clothes here? I can't go out dressed like this."

Julie Carlson reaches into the small hospital closet. "Here they are."

"Thanks." I grab the clothes and head for the bathroom.

Claire blocks my way, arms out. "Please let a doctor check you over first."

"Claire, I'm sorry, but I don't know how much time I have here. I need to hurry."

She flinches. "Oh, dear. Bernard said the same thing when he came back. Say, Julie, maybe you should call Kevin while Emma changes. He'll know what to do about Charlie."

In the tiny bathroom, I yank off the hospital gown. Steve's letter falls to the floor. I pull on my street clothes and shove the letter back into my pocket. I throw my serious bed-head hair into a ponytail. A last glance into the mirror gives me a moment of panic. I may look normal now, but I know I'm not. There's still a wisp of an image hovering next to my reflection, but it's fainter than before.

You can do this. You have to.

I burst out of the bathroom and find the other three standing at attention.

"Let's go." I head for the door.

"Here." Father Joe hands me a white baseball hat with a cross embroidered on it. "Pull it down over your eyes."

"Good idea." I position my ponytail through the hat.

"I'll leave first." Father Joe puts a hand on the door. "You follow me. Claire and Julie will take up the rear. Let's go."

Claire and Julie chat about the weather as we stroll past the nurses' station. My heart races as I use them as a human shield. After Father Joe turns a corner, he holds open the door leading to the stairwell. We hurry down the steps and out to the parking lot.

"Get in." Claire beeps open her car locks. As she drives, Julie talks on the phone with Kevin.

In the backseat, Father Joe turns to place a hand on my shoulder. "Do you feel any different?"

What a strange question. "Yeah, I guess I've always been different."

"No, I mean—did the exorcism work?" He asks. "Are you free of the demons now?"

We pass a row of neon-colored restaurants. My stomach growls so loud it's a bit scary.

"Don't worry. Those weren't the demons talking. I'm just hungry." I lean toward the front seat. "Can we stop and get some food? I'll pay you back later, I promise."

"Sure thing." Claire pulls into a drive-thru. "And it's on me."

After I order, we ride on as I shovel in a burger, fries, and a very large dish of ice cream. Scraping the bottom of the bowl, I still want more. I rub my demanding belly. "I'm so hungry it's making me dizzy."

Father Joe watches me eat. "This isn't the typical response to an exorcism."

"Sorry. It's my first time."

He leans closer. "Are the demons still inside you?"

"Honestly, I'm not sure." I wipe my face with a napkin, because the close way he's watching me makes me feel like I've got ketchup in my eyebrows or something.

He takes out a cross, then hesitates. "I don't want to hurt you."

"That's okay. I'll do it." I grab the cross, anticipating a burning sensation in my skin.

There's nothing. I rub my fingers over the wood and metal. Nothing. Not even a spark.

Father Joe releases a slow breath. "That's a relief."

With a trembling hand, I pass the cross back. I'm not sure if the spirits are gone, or if this is just a trick. I still saw something in the mirror. My stomach churns, and I feel queasy. By the time we get to the jail, I need a bathroom.

Immediately.

I race to the front doors and run smack into Kevin.

"Where's the restroom?" Great. Why do I have to ask him of all people this question?

"Right there." Kevin flinches and points down the hall.

I race to the bathroom, burst into a stall, and hang my head over the toilet.

My stomach gurgles and I want to vomit.

Something heavy falls on top of me, knocking me onto the floor.

Trembling, I scan the stall for my attacker. Am I imagining things or are the demons back?

Mustering my courage, I stand up and stagger from the stall.

"Oh, maybe I ate too much." I groan.

There are three other stalls in the bathroom. I feel a wild desire to kick in every door, searching for my assailant—just like what happens in the movies. Instead, I use my trembling hands. My heart stops short each time I push open a metal door and find nothing. After searching the last stall, my stomach churns. I'm going to be sick again! I rush for the toilet, letting the door swing shut behind me as I heave up empty.

A loud scuffling noise echoes over by the sinks.

My hand trembles as I peek through the door crack.

Across the room a man gets up off the floor and turns to face me. My breath catches in my throat. "Jake! It's you!"

I rush toward him.

"What's going on?" he growls, his face contorted with fury. "Where's Emma? What did you do to her? I swear I'll kill you if you hurt her."

Pain blinds me as his fist makes contact with my face.

CHAPTER THIRTY-THREE

THREE'S A CROWD

What the Hell was that for?" I cradle my bloody nose and shuffle to a sink.

"Cause you're an ass—wait a minute." Jake steps closer. "What's going on? You sound like Emma, but you look like—"

"That's because I *am* Emma! What's wrong with you?" I shove tissues up my flowing nose. "So much for you being in love with me. You just punched me in the face!"

Jake pales. "Are you *sure* you're Emma? Because you look like Steve. Oh, damn it, there's *two* of you in the mirror."

"Huh?" I follow his glare and discover a double reflection in the mirror.

My reflection. And someone else's.

Someone I'm starting to hate—Steve. Plus a sliver of an image of someone else, but Jake doesn't seem to notice that. Only I do.

Jake's hand rises to his mouth. "I think I'm going to be sick."

"No way!" I moan. "You're telling me I have to share my body with *Steve*? Yuck! I can't believe this!"

Steve smirks from within our double reflection. Just like the last time he came back from the dead, he's using a host body. Only this time around *I'm* the host.

"Get out!" I swat at his glimmering image.

"Not an option." Steve smiles his politician grin, flickering to the forefront. "Now, Jake, apologize for punching a girl."

"Wait until the next full moon when you guys separate. Then it will be *your* turn." Jake flushes. "But I *am* sorry, Emma. I didn't realize—"

"That's okay. I know you thought I was Steve. And thanks for reminding me about the full moon, because I'd like to hit him, too."

Steve chuckles. "That's what Jake gets for following me."

"Following you?" Jake asks.

Steve shrugs. "After you rudely barged into my office, I decided to enact Plan B."

I replace the soaked tissues with new ones. "Didn't you think I could deliver your precious note all by myself? I'm perfectly capable, you know."

"Believe me. I had no plans to join you, Emma. It's not safe for me to be here. I'm a magnet for trouble now." Fear flashes across Steve's face in the mirror. "You can blame your dear, sweet Jake here for this little mishap. When he burst into my office and threatened me, I had to make a quick escape. Apparently, he followed."

"So now I'm a host for the undead." I stare at our dual reflections. "That's just great. When I felt sick to my stomach, I hoped it was because I ate too much."

"Trust me." Steve says. "I'd rather be in my own body like Jake. But I'm stuck in here with you."

"How come I'm not in there too?" Jake asks. "Like last time, I mean."

Steve laughs, and the sound makes me shiver. "Yes, everyone knows you'd do just about *anything* to get into Emma's pants."

I flush, pissed and embarrassed at the same time. Wonderful combo.

"I don't know how I jumped into this body," says Steve. "Consider yourself lucky."

Jake clenches his hands. "Steve, I swear to God, I want to punch you again so hard right now."

"Please don't." I fuss with my nose some more, which has almost stopped bleeding. "I can't believe I'm the host body. I never thought *this* would happen."

"Why not?" Steve says. "With you popping back and forth out of life and death, you're the perfect vehicle for the dead. Besides, due to the circumstances, I did enlist you as a potential host in case it was necessary."

"Thanks a lot." I want to flip him the bird, but since we're in the same body—what's the point? "Just tell me one thing: are you in there alone?"

Steve curls his lip. "You mean you're still possessed? I thought God would take care of that."

"I'm not sure they're all gone," I explain. "I haven't heard any voice since I got here, but there's still something in the mirror. Can't you tell?"

He glances around, but I'm not sure what he sees. "I don't know what to tell you. I can't see them or feel them, but maybe it's not the same as before."

I finish wiping my nose and throw away the bloody towels. "I guess we'll find out sooner or later. One more thing: can I assume that normal people will see me instead of you?"

"The only way to find out for sure is to leave this bathroom," says Steve, always trying to be the boss. "Remember to avoid any mirrors. Hopefully, no one can see me. I promise to keep quiet."

I glare at his image in the mirror. "Steve, your promises don't mean much anymore. We need to get out of here without causing a fuss. Jake, let me go first. Wait a couple minutes before you come out. We'll have to play it by ear after that."

Jake nods. "Okay, but holler if you need me."

Steve smiles, showing way too many teeth, like a predator. "Even if no one sees me, I'm delighted to be back. I can't wait to get started."

"You jerk, just shut up and stay hidden!" I snap at him, then storm out of the bathroom, straight into the arms of my mother.

"Emma!" Mom grips my shoulders, probably bruising me all over again.

"How on earth did you get here so fast?" Thank goodness she only sees me.

"I sped." She brushes the hair from my eyes. "What did you expect? When you weren't in your hospital bed, I assumed the worst. But this is a miracle! Your father will be thrilled. Except for the fact that you're *here, out of bed, and not under a doctor's care—WHAT WERE YOU THINKING?*"

Like a deer in the headlights, I panic, unable to answer.

Mom gapes. "What's wrong with your nose?"

"It's nothing. Just a little nosebleed." Actually, Mom, the love of my life just punched me in the face because he thought I was a man. Brilliant. And nothing you need to know.

"But you never get nosebleeds." She examines me so closely I'm certain she can somehow detect Steve under my skin. "Not even as a little girl."

Claire, Julie, and Father Joe hover nearby in a cluster, watching us. Kevin speaks with a police officer on the other side of the room, pointing at some paperwork.

"Mom, where's Dad?" I ask, partly to change the subject, but, really, where is he?

She averts her gaze. "Well dear, you know he's been having some heart trouble..."

"What?" My own heart stalls mid-beat. The rest of the room fades away. "You never told me that."

"The stress has been too much for him." Mom drops my arms and plays with her purse strap. "He felt some fluttering and is having it checked out. Don't worry. I'm sure it's nothing."

I reach for her hand. "Mom, are you okay?"

"That's a silly question." She pulls away to dig in her purse. "My whole family is in the hospital, or *should be* in your case, and you ask if *I'm* okay?"

"I want to see Dad first thing after I free Walker." I'm having trouble breathing normally, and I don't think I can blame that on Steve.

Mom glares. "After what that man did to you, *he's* your first concern?"

"But he didn't do anything to me, Mom. This is all a big misunderstanding. I need to clear him of these bogus charges and then..." My words falter as I watch Jake sneak out of the bathroom and head for the exit. Where's he going? How will I find him again?

The others move toward us en masse, blocking Jake from view.

"Cheryl." Claire pats Mom's shoulder. "Emma *promised* to go back to the doctor for a thorough check up as soon as Charlie was set free."

"Yes, Mom. Just let me do this first. I feel *really guilty* about what he's going through because of me."

"Okay." Mom sighs. "But we're going right back to the hospital afterward." Being raised Catholic herself, guilt is something she respects and understands.

Claire pats my shoulder. "That's the plan."

Kevin approaches, frowning at me as if I'm an alien he has to babysit. "Emma, you need to make a statement. Alone."

"Alone?" I tense.

He nods, business-like. "Don't worry. I'll stay and talk you through it."

I stifle my discomfort with Kevin's plan. Great. I'd love to be left alone with Mike's brother. I feel so much better now. Or not. Kevin probably wants to hit me, too. At least that's what he told me a few months ago.

Kevin waves away the others. "Okay, everyone, this is turning into a circus. I have to ask you to leave."

"But I just got here." Mom gapes. "I'm not going anywhere."

Kevin smiles, and I'm reminded how handsome everyone else thinks he is. "I'll take good care of your daughter, I promise. But this could take hours. You should be with your husband."

Mom blinks back tears. "Kevin, I can't thank you enough. Your whole family—you, your mom, and your cousin have all been *so* wonderful."

"Cousin?" I ask.

Julie catches my eye. "Yes, my nephew *Ryan* was here helping, before he had to leave on his trip..." Her voice wavers.

Oh, she means Mike! Of course, they'd have to call him something else around Mom.

Mom gushes. "You've all been such a help to me this last week."

"We *wanted* to help," Kevin assures her. "Listen, I know my way around this place. I'm the one best suited to help Emma during her statement. You should focus on John right now."

"Cheryl, he's right." Julie takes Mom's arm. "Walk out with us."

It will be easier hiding the truth from Mom if she isn't here. Even if it means I have to hang out with Kevin. Alone. Except for Icky Steve.

"I heard that" Steve mutters within my head.

"Yes, Mom, go ahead," I say. "I'll call you when I'm done, and say 'hi' to Dad for me, okay?"

Mom's nostrils flare, but somehow on her the gesture looks pretty. "Honestly, I don't know which one of you to worry about more. Call if you need me, Emma."

As Mom exits the police station, Steve whispers snide comments in my head. *Doesn't Kevin hate you after what you did to his brother? Why would he help you?*

"Shut up, you parasite!" I hiss out loud, by accident.

Kevin gives me a puzzled look as we settle on a bench. "Have you decided what you're going to tell the police?"

"Uh. No." I swallow, realizing how stupid I am not to have dreamt up a story already.

"You can't just tell them Charlie's innocent," Kevin whispers. "You have a lot of injuries to explain. Or at least you did."

"I know. How about I say that all my wounds were self-inflicted?"

Kevin shakes his head. "Emma, they'll haul you to off to the Psych ward if you say that."

"Right." Of course. Why didn't I think of that? "How about I tell them that I'm clumsy?"

"That won't help Charlie." Kevin frowns. "It makes you sound like a classic abuse victim."

I fiddle with the hem of my shirt. "Um... do you have any ideas?"

"Yeah, I do." Kevin leans closer. I brace myself not to back away. "You're going to tell them you took up mountain biking this summer and had a few tumbles. Phoebe already parked her bike in your apartment, so we're covered in that department."

"We are?" How did Phoebe get in my apartment? And how does she know Kevin? Oh, yeah, through Mike.

"And you were having a 'binder burning' at the park with all your school notes."

"A what?" Why would I burn my school notes? I love school. Oh, wait, that doesn't matter.

"Lots of college kids do that to celebrate the end of the school year. Normally, they don't pour multiple cans of lighter fluid on them at once unless they're totally drunk."

"Could I say that?" I interrupt. "That I was drunk?"

"No. They already checked your blood alcohol level and it was zero. Tell them you were never a Girl Scout, and you didn't know how to start a campfire."

"How did you know I wasn't a Girl Scout?" I ask.

He avoids my gaze by glancing across the room. "I spent a lot of time with your mother at the hospital the last few days. I learned more about you than either of us is comfortable with."

"Oh. I see." I stare down at my hands, flustered. "Can I ask you something?"

"Sure. Go ahead. Shoot."

I clear my throat. "Why are you helping me? I don't understand it. I thought you hated me."

He clears his throat, scratching his head a moment before answering. "There's a couple reasons, actually. One is that Mike *forced* me to help you—so did my mom, actually."

What? "Your mom?"

"Yeah. She said it would be good therapy for me... as if I haven't had enough of *that*, already," he mutters.

"You've been in therapy?"

"Yeah. Nothing serious. I mean it won't end my career as a cop before I even get started, or anything. Church stuff, mostly. You know, grief counseling."

"Oh." Probably a good idea.

"And Mike coming back really helped." He squirms a bit on the seat next to me. "Am I supposed to thank you for that, or something? I don't know."

"No, that's okay." Fire burns my cheeks. I've never felt more awkward. I need to change the subject fast. "So, about Walker. What else should I say?"

"Not much," Kevin answers quickly. "I think we should keep it short and sweet. The more complicated the lie, the more difficult it is to keep it afloat."

No kidding.

Kevin stands as an officer crosses the room toward us.

The uniformed man carries a clipboard of papers and peers at me over his glasses. "Emma Roberts, are you ready to make your statement?"

"Yes." I rise and take a deep breath.

In this case, only lies will set Walker free.

CHAPTER THIRTY-FOUR

INTERROGATION

The stocky policeman extends his hand. "Hello. My name is Officer Snyder."

"Nice to meet you." I shake his offered hand, hoping mine doesn't tremble.

"We'll use an interrogation room to give us some privacy." He spins around and heads down the hall.

"Kevin," I whisper. "Are there any mirrors or cameras in that room?"

"Yes," he whispers back. "Why?"

I grab his arm before I even think about it. "Make him take us somewhere else, *please*. Otherwise weird things are going to happen."

He rushes after the policeman. "Officer Snyder, Emma hasn't been accused of any crime. Can't we do the paper work at your desk?"

He shrugs. "Fine. Suit yourself."

We approach his gray-green metal desk. I rub away the goose bumps on my arms, since the air-conditioning has been set to deep freeze. My heart pounds. Can I really pull this off?

"Have a seat," Officer Snyder orders.

I drop so fast that the chair squeaks several inches across the floor.

Steve explodes in my head. *"Calm down, idiot! Don't blow this."*

Silence fills the room, except for the shuffling of papers.

"Why don't you start at the beginning?" Officer Snyder suggests.

I choke on unspoken words. Should I start when Walker and I worked together? No. That won't do. I can't explain why he needed me without talking about my *Book of Shadows*. I glance at Kevin, but his purposefully blank face doesn't offer much help.

"Oh, right, the beginning." I take a deep breath. "I'm a good student, but even though I planned to take summer classes—"

"Which you never attended—according to your mother," interrupts the policeman.

"My mother?" I gulp, trying to swallow my fear. "You talked to her?"

"Yes, of course." He takes a long sip of coffee.

"Sure. That makes sense." I clench my hands together so hard under the table that I leave painful fingernail dents.

"Please continue." The cop holds his pen poised.

I smile weakly. "I was sort of sick of school. I'd heard of binder burnings, but I'd never attended one before myself. I thought it might be fun."

"Why did you go all by yourself?" Officer Snyder interrupts. "Usually, it's sort of a party."

"Party of one, I guess." I sigh. "You see, I'm a loner, most of the time."

He waits for me to continue.

"I'm so sorry about the big fire. That was an accident. We never went camping when I was a kid. And I was never a Girl Scout."

Steve chuckles. *"Nice touch. Working the pathetic angle."*

Officer Snyder taps his pen on the desk. "Hence the three cans of lighter fluid found by the fire pit?"

"Yes." I pause in fear. "Will there be arson charges, or anything?"

"No, I don't think so. Do you know how you came to be knocked out?" He slides a picture across the desk.

My eyes widen as I pick up the photo. There I lay, bruised and bloody, atop a stretcher with the fire pit nearby.

Steve lets out a low whistle. *"Wow, you look like shit."*

Enough of your running commentary, Steve. I tell him in my head. *You're distracting me.*

He never listens. *"Oh, look, the picture is moving! Did you do that?"*

Steve's right. Within the picture, smoke gathers and swirls around me.

Officer Snyder clears his throat. "I know it must be hard to see yourself this way."

Kevin leans over to block the officer's view of the moving photo.

"Yeah, it is. Sorry." I tear my eyes away. "I remember something flying up and hitting me in the head. That must have been what knocked me out."

"Something or someone? There are several reports of a young man wearing a red shirt in the woods that night."

Kevin shakes his head. "Officer Snyder, I'm sorry I didn't catch him. I still don't know how he got away. If only I hadn't tripped over that log."

"You're in far better shape than the rest of us," the cop chuckles, resting a hand on his belly. "If *you* couldn't catch him, then none of us could."

"Sounds like the other cops eat too many doughnuts," mutters Steve

I force my lying face to appear angelic. "I didn't see anyone else there that night."

"So you didn't see Officer Walker?"

"No, not in the park." I grip the desk edge. "But I did stop at his house before that."

Officer Snyder points his pen at me. "So you admit to knowing Officer Walker?"

"Yes." I hope that's the right answer, but it feels wrong somehow.

Officer Snyder narrows his eyes. "How long have you known him?"

I swallow hard, glancing at Kevin before continuing. "We met last fall, after Mike Carlson died."

Kevin pales.

"I see." Officer Snyder pauses. "And how would you describe your relationship with Charlie Walker?"

"We're... friends."

He raises his eyebrows. "Just friends?"

"Yes. We're friends, like I said." I blush. Damn it! Why do I always have to get embarrassed at inconvenient times? "Actually, he was on a date that night. With someone else, I mean."

The police officer pauses to take another gulp of coffee. "That witness reported a heated argument between the two of you right before you sped off."

I shrug. "I have a bad temper, but that's not Walker's fault."

The cop leans in closer. "What were you arguing about?"

My mind goes blank. "His mother?" Why did I say that?

"Interesting." Officer Snyder covers a slight smile with his hand. "And now we come to the issue of your injuries, which you seem to have recovered from rather quickly." He clears his throat. "Almost *too* quickly."

"Yes, I'm good as new." I flex my hands and arms to prove the point.

"How is that possible?" The policeman shifts through papers. "According to these documents, you had extensive bruising, broken ribs, and fractures to both hands."

I hold up my perfect hands and wriggle them. "I'm a fast healer. And I drink a lot of milk. Perhaps the doctors were over-cautious."

"I am surprised you're walking around already," says Officer Snyder. "But how did you obtain all these injuries?"

I pause. Oh, right. The bike. Talk about the bike. "I took up mountain biking this summer, and I'm not very good at it. I've had a couple of accidents."

He checks his papers. "There are no hospital reports of this."

"I didn't go to the hospital. It was no big deal, really. I've always been clumsy. I fall down a lot."

Kevin frowns. That's right, I wasn't supposed to say that.

"I see." The officer pages through more documents. "Did anyone else go bike riding with you?"

Damn it. Kevin didn't cover this. Was Phoebe supposed to be with me or not? "I usually went by myself." I chance it. "Like I said, I'm a loner."

As the policeman scribbles away, I sneak a peek at Kevin. He winks. Good. I said the right thing.

Officer Snyder clears his throat. "Emma Roberts, are you aware that Officer Walker has been arrested on charges of assault, battery, and attempted murder?"

"Yes," I whisper, a sick feeling in my stomach. When will this be over? "That's why I'm here. I came as soon as I could to clear his name."

"Are you willing to sign a written statement declaring him innocent of all these charges?"

"Yes." I nod, perhaps over-enthusiastically. "Of course."

Officer Snyder collects his papers and stands up. "I'll type this up and be right back."

As he leaves the room, I turn to Kevin. "Did I do okay?"

He leans close to whisper. "Be careful, Emma. Someone might be listening."

I shiver as the walls of the room seem to quiver and close in on me. "I need to see my dad. How much longer will this take?"

"Don't hold your breath. We're not out of the woods yet."

After I sign my name what seems like half a million times, Officer Snyder escorts us back to the lobby. I stiffen the instant I spot Walker waiting near a tall counter to be released. His face droops like he hasn't slept in days. His clothes are wrinkled and his chin unshaven. I cringe when I notice his black eye, no doubt obtained while he was in jail. My heart floods with guilt. I did this to him. It's my fault. Kind of like everything else—or so it seems.

I hold my breath as his entourage crosses near us.

I step toward him. "Walker, are you okay?"

His eyes flick up, but drop back down before reaching mine. His shoulders slump as if the whole ordeal has left him utterly defeated. His mother and sisters surround him like pissed off bodyguards.

Mrs. Walker steps in between us, her arms crossed. "Leave my son alone."

"But I have to talk to him." My hand reaches for Steve's letter. "I have something to give him."

Mrs. Walker narrows her eyes. "Maybe you didn't hear me. I said to *leave my son alone*. He wants nothing to do with you. He's had enough of your kind of trouble." Then she and the rest of her family brush past us, heading for the front door.

Steve screams inside my head. *"Give him the letter! Give him the letter!"*

"Walker, please, I've got to talk to you!" I beg.

Kevin holds me back. "Leave him alone right now, Emma. Give him time to adjust. And give his family some space. They've been through a lot."

"But this is important." I wait for Walker to glance back at me, to let me know that he isn't angry, to let me know that I haven't ruined his life. "It's about Steve."

Walker pauses at the mention of Steve's name, but he doesn't turn back. After a long moment, he walks away from me and into the sunshine.

He isn't going to talk to me.

Maybe not ever.

CHAPTER THIRTY-FIVE

PERSUASION, SPEEDO-STYLE

What am I going to do?" I squeak. "I need to talk to Walker. There's something important I have to give him."

"Whatever it is, I'm sure it can wait," Kevin says. "He doesn't want to talk right now. I don't blame him. Don't make a scene."

I glance around the police station. All law enforcement eyes are on me.

"Then get me out of here," I mutter.

"My car's in the back lot." Kevin ushers me out a side door.

We step into the fresh air. Wait a minute... Where's Jake? I crane my neck but there's no sign of him.

"If you're looking for Charlie, just don't, okay?" Kevin warns.

"No, that's not it. I'm looking for someone else."

"Who?" He beeps open the locks as we approach his car. "Your mom went back to the hospital and everyone else went home."

I pause before sliding into the passenger seat. "You might not like hearing this, but I brought someone back with me." Or else Steve did. Whatever.

Kevin stiffens. "It's not Mike, is it?"

"Not this time. I'm sorry. It's Jake."

He puts his keys in the ignition. "Jake? I don't know a Jake. What's he look like?"

"He's about your height, short hair, sort of muscle-y." I flush and change the subject. "Could you drive me around the main parking lot to see if he's there?"

"You *promise* this isn't about Charlie?"

I cross my heart. "Promise."

"Okay, then." Kevin pulls out of his spot and heads for the front lot. Near the police entrance, several vans are parked at odd angles, with news reporters flocking outside.

"There she is!" a woman shouts.

A dozen reporters charge our car.

I slump down in my seat, heart racing. "Oh, no. Don't let them take any pictures of me. We can look for Jake later. Get me out of here."

"Sure thing." Tires squeal as Kevin speeds away. "What is it with you and cameras and mirrors, anyway?"

I ignore his question, too busy watching to see if anyone followed. After we are several blocks away from the police station, I relax. "I think you ditched them."

"Good. Should I take you to the hospital now?"

"I guess so." I waver. Will I be safe there? "I really want to see my dad, but I'm worried they're going to run tests on me."

"So what?" He makes a turn. "Are you scared of needles?"

"I don't *enjoy* needles, but the real problem is that I'm not *normal*."

Kevin stifles a laugh.

"No, I mean it. There's someone else here with me, maybe more than one spirit."

Kevin glances my way. "I thought you left him back in the parking lot."

"No, that was Jake." I cringe, wondering what happened to him. "Steve's inside my body with me. And maybe some other spirits. Nobody's said anything for a while and Father Joe doesn't think they're in there anymore, but I'm not sure."

Kevin frowns. "You mean like Mike was inside that body suit last spring?"

"Yeah. Sort of. That's why no one can take my picture. They'd see Steve instead, and maybe the others. I'm not sure. I can see Steve perfectly in the mirror, but the others were always faint, like a faint pencil image. But even if I couldn't see them very well, they were still inside, causing me all sorts of trouble."

"That *is* weird." Kevin stares at my chest, which is super awkward, so I focus on rolling up my window. "You're like... possessed."

"I'm afraid so. Weird and possessed, that's me."

Kevin frowns. "I gathered that. So, what happens once we get to the hospital? Should we sneak in the back way, or maybe could you convince the doctors *not* to perform tests on you?"

"What do you mean?"

"Aren't witches supposed to have powers of persuasion?" Kevin asks. "You know, like love spells?"

"Love spells?" I repeat weakly, avoiding his eyes. The first spell I ever witnessed was the love spell my old roommate Chrissy performed to snag Kevin. And it had worked. Big time.

"Or like Star Wars," Kevin suggests. "You know, the old Jedi mind control trick."

I shake my head. "I don't know how to do that."

"Have you ever tried?" he challenges.

I think back. "I don't think so."

"I can't believe I'm saying this, but you could... uh... practice on me."

"Really?" I lean back in the seat. "Okay. Let me think."

"I better pull over for this." Kevin parks on the side of the road and turns to me, his face pale. "You're not going to make me streak naked through the middle of town, are you?"

"No." I laugh. But that gives me an idea. "Don't worry. I'm just going to *try* to make you say something." *Like an apology.* "Now sit still. This shouldn't hurt. At least I don't think so."

I close my eyes and attempt to center myself, but my shoulders remain tense. Flashes of swimming the river, of blood dripping in the shower, and Kevin and Walker fighting in the police station swirl in my brain.

Kevin jerks up in his seat, words bursting from his mouth. "I don't hit girls, but if I did, you'd be the first in line!"

My eyes fly open.

Kevin looks at me, horrified. "What was that?"

I remember. "That's the last thing you said to me before..."

"Before now?" He shudders. "Maybe we shouldn't do this."

"I'm sure it will be fine. I just need more practice. Close your eyes again."

I sit back. This time calm flows through me. Birds singing in the distance transform into violins. A warm breeze caresses my face even though the car windows are shut. My feet dig into a sandy beach. I open my eyes to the ocean breeze and swaying palms of the Healing Islands. Is Mike here? I scan the empty horizon.

"Um, Emma?"

Startled out of my reverie, I spin around. Kevin stands in front of me, red-faced, wearing a bright yellow Speedo.

I try not to stare. Or laugh.

Kevin holds out a dozen red roses. "Emma, I apologize for being such a prick to you. It's not your fault Mike got drunk and wanted to go swimming."

All I can see is the yellow Speedo. It's awful. I take the roses to cover my eyes and mumble. "That's okay, Kevin. I know you were just grieving for your brother."

"But I was a *jerk*," Kevin insists. "There's no excuse. I told everyone it was your fault. I made your life Hell. I made Chrissy move out, and she was supposed to be your friend."

I hold up a hand of protest. "Okay. Got it. You can stop now. Chrissy really wasn't a very good friend, anyway."

The breeze blows back my hair as I'm jerked forward. My head spins and I find myself back in Kevin's car. I sneak a peek in his direction.

"Oh, good." I breathe a sigh of relief. "You're dressed normally again."

Kevin looks dazed. "What *was* that?"

"We were on an island," I try to explain.

He shudders. "Why was I wearing a *Speedo*?"

Steve speaks up. *"Emma, you're even stronger than before. What did God do to you in the church?"*

"I don't want to talk to you," I grumble.

"Why?" Kevin asks. "What did I do now? I said I was sorry."

"No, not you. Steve was bugging me again."

"Steve?" Kevin stares intently at my chest again. I wish he'd stop that. "Why can't I see him? Mike said they took turns in the body."

"Well, I'm not letting Steve take over. You can't see him unless I'm near a mirror. Here, look at this." I bend the rearview mirror so that Kevin can see the double reflection.

Steve waves, a wide, fake grin on his face. Again, I spot the faint outlines of the other spirits—Eva, Jennifer, and Dominic—but their images are so faint, and Kevin's freaked out enough as it is that I don't point them out. For some reason, Shadow is nowhere to be seen. That's a relief, anyway.

Kevin's eyes bug. "This is bizarre. When did you start with all this witching stuff, anyway? Phoebe said you're the real thing. She read your whole *Book of Shadows*."

"What?" Fury flares inside me. "Where is it?" My hands ache for its soft cover.

"She said it disappeared when Mike left again—this time forever, I suppose." Kevin's voice catches.

I hesitate. "Are you glad you got to see him one more time, or does it make things even worse than before?"

Kevin flushes. "You're asking me if I'm still mad at you, right?"

"Yeah. I guess so."

"No, Emma. I'm not mad anymore. And I am sorry about how I treated you." He smiles at my sharp glance. "Don't worry. Your mind control thing worked, but this time it's just me."

"Good." I release a pent-up breath.

Kevin taps the steering wheel. "But where'd you get that *Book of Shadows* in the first place? Seems like a pretty dangerous book."

I hesitate before answering. "I got it from Angie. You know,

Chrissy's younger sister?"

His eyes widen. "Chrissy, my ex-girlfriend?"

"You see—"

Kevin holds up a hand. "I don't want to hear the rest. I'll take you to the hospital, all right? But I've had enough witchcraft for a lifetime, I think."

I only wish I could say the same.

CHAPTER THIRTY-SIX

LISTEN TO MY HEART BEAT

Kevin pulls into the hospital parking lot. **"We're here**. Now what?"

"What I *really* want to do is to see my dad, but I know Mom's going to haul me off to the nearest doctor and watch the whole time I'm being examined. I'd better find a doctor on my own first and get them to sign off on me."

"Okay." He grabs the door handle. "Let's go."

We exit the car and whoosh through the automatic doors of the hospital, greeted by the smell of antiseptic.

"Who do you think we should ask?" I scan the lobby.

"How about that nurse over there?" Kevin gestures toward a pretty woman with long red hair.

"I can't manipulate her out here in front of everyone," I whisper.

"Maybe you can't... but I can." Kevin heads for the front desk.

He smiles wide and leans in. "Hi. I'm Kevin Carlson. I've brought back your escapee." He nods at me. "You know, the one you've seen on TV."

The pretty nurse stares with wide eyes.

"I caught her myself." He winks. "She couldn't resist me."

She giggles. "I'll let her doctor know."

I can't believe what a schmooze Kevin is—not that it doesn't make him useful. "No, I want a different doctor. Someone young." Someone easier to confuse.

"What?" Her finger hovers over the phone. Her eyes cloud over. The mind control is working. I'm getting faster. Kind of scary.

Kevin puts his arm around me. I try not to cringe. "Emma just means she wants to hurry up and get this over with. She's tired. She's been through a lot."

"It's sweet of you to help her." The cute nurse bats her sympathetic eyes.

"Yeah. Thanks, Kevin," I mumble. "You're the best."

"No problem." He tightens his hold on my shoulders.

I freeze in place, forcing myself not to pull away. Even after the apology, I have a hard time believing he really wants to help me.

"Let's see who's available." She turns to speak into a black phone.

Soon she leads us upstairs into an exam room on the second floor. Forty-five minutes (and three out-of-date magazines) later, a frazzled, young doctor bursts in, a stethoscope looped around his neck, and an armload of charts clutched to his chest.

"Good morning," he musters, setting down his load. "My name is Dr. Martin. I was the head resident working on your case."

"Good *afternoon*, Dr. Martin," I reply.

He types into a computer. "I hear you checked yourself out this morning."

I squirm. "Not officially."

"And how do you feel after your..." Dr. Martin peeks into the top chart. "...prostate surgery? No, that's wrong. Wait a minute."

I smile. This is going to be *so* easy.

"Don't worry about the chart," I speak slowly and deliberately, all the better to numb his overactive thoughts. "All I need is a note for my mom saying I have a clean bill of health."

"What?" His eyes scan the first page of my record. "That's unlikely. You sustained serious injuries. You shouldn't even be out of bed yet."

"I'm fine." I catch his gaze and hold it.

"Let's examine you first and then decide, okay?" He grabs his stethoscope.

I take a deep breath. "I said 'I'm fine.'"

"Wh-what?" His eyelids droop.

I will my heart rate to slow and close my eyes. My limbs begin to buzz. Warm breezes brush across my face. I'm floating above the sand, in a cross-legged position. A tan cloak flutters around me, tied at my neck. I open my eyes back on the Healing Islands. The young doctor stands in front of me, his stethoscope still slung around his neck. He wears a red polo, tan cargo shorts, and a shiny black plastic Darth Vader mask.

"Breathe deeply while I listen to your chest," he instructs in Darth Vader's computer voice.

I obey.

"Interesting. You have two separate heart beats."

"That's normal for me," I reply in an even monotone.

"No, wait." He moves the stethoscope around my chest and back, all the way down to my waistline. "Make that *five* different heart beats. They're all over the place."

"Five, not six?" I ask.

He listens again, then shakes his head. "Nope. Just five."

Then Shadow is gone, but the rest of them are still with me. They've been so quiet. I wonder why. God only got rid of the worst one. That's fine, but why'd he leave the rest?

A young boy shuffles up, a sand pail in one hand and a white Storm Trooper mask over his face. "Daddy, are five heartbeats normal?"

"Well, son, an octopus has three hearts and earthworms have five. This isn't that unusual."

"I wish I had five hearts." The little boy waves his blue plastic shovel in the air.

"Go play now," the good doctor says. "I have to write out a clean bill of health."

I take a deep breath and open my eyes.

Back in the doctor's office, the doctor leans against a wall, breathing heavily. "I feel strange."

"Do you need to sit back down a moment?" I ask innocently. "You look pale." Like your legs in those shorts. Time to spend a few more days on the beach with your son.

"No, I'd better go home. I want to see my family right away. Here you go." He scribbles across a piece of paper, shoves it in my hands, then rushes out of the room, ditching his charts behind.

I glance at the sheet. In chicken scratch he wrote: *Emma Roberts is a very healthy girl—Dr. Martin.*

"I hope this works." I show it to Kevin.

He chuckles. "Your mom's gonna love this. And I've got to say, you're the best looking Emperor I've ever seen. You weren't all wrinkled and gross."

Steve chimes in. *"I can't believe Kevin's hitting on you. That Speedo trick you pulled must have turned him on."*

Shut up, Steve, I gripe internally. *Don't be disgusting.*

"What?" I say out loud to Kevin, pretending I didn't hear him.

"Didn't you notice that cloak you were wearing?"

"Oh, yeah. I guess I did." I pause a moment. "But I wasn't wearing a swimsuit last time."

"No, you weren't. That was just me." Kevin grimaces, handing back the doctor's note. "Let's get out of here."

We duck out of the room and hurry through the hallways.

I glance down a hospital wing. "Kevin, do you know where my dad is?"

He tenses. "Yeah, follow me. I visited him with your mom."

"Wow," Steve remarks. *"The Carlson family really goes the whole nine yards, don't they?"*

I follow Kevin up three flights of steps and through a few more hallways until he pauses outside a hospital room.

"You should prepare yourself." He catches my eye, and pauses before he pushes the glossy white door open.

Mom looks up from her metal chair beside Dad's bed. She discreetly wipes her eyes as I enter the room. My hands start to tremble and my arms feel a chill. Dad's shriveled form doesn't take up much space at all in the hospital bed. The hospital gown swallows him. His cross necklace overpowers his collarbones. I touch my own neck, remembering the same cross hanging from Grandma's throat.

His eyes flutters open. "Emma. You're here." Both his welcoming smile and voice are so weak. His hand reaches for me.

"Yes, Dad." I grab his hand and squeeze it. How did his skin get so paper thin?

"But not for long." Mom stands up, still blotting with a tissue at her running mascara. "Emma's going back to her doctor to get checked out right away."

"No, I already did that. See?" I hand her the sheet.

"What's this?" She scans the note then glares at me. "Some kind of joke?"

"No, he was the head resident working on my case. Don't you remember him?"

Dad coughs. It sounds wet, like he has the river in his lungs and can't get it out. Mom tosses the paper aside and pours him a glass of water.

"Cheryl, don't fuss so." He sputters between ragged breaths. "Why don't you get a coffee or something? Now that Emma's here, she can keep me company."

"I'll join you, if you want," Kevin offers.

"I'm not leaving," she replies in her don't-mess-with-me voice. As Mom tucks the sheets around him, Dad stares at me so intently I know he wants to tell me something.

Alone.

And I have a few questions for him myself.

Starting with that necklace.

CHAPTER THIRTY-SEVEN

WHERE'S MY BOOK?

Mom, you should really take a break and go get some coffee. I'm here now." Please don't make me use mind control on my own mom. It's probably a sin.

She scowls. "Why is everybody always trying to get rid of me? First Kevin at the police station, and now you."

The door bumps against the supper tray as a nurse enters. "Sorry, folks, it's time for visitors to leave. Mr. Roberts needs his rest."

"Hello, Mary." Dad winks at her. "Have you got more 'magic pills' for me?" His valiant effort to act normal defies the depressing backdrop of the white hospital sheets and beeping monitors.

The nurse hands Dad a cupful of medication and a glass of water. "Now take these and wave good-bye to your visitors."

"Fine. I'll go." Mom kisses Dad on the head and hooks a purse over her shoulder.

I squeeze Dad's hand good-bye, not wanting to leave.

"Come back soon," he says.

"I will." I try to smile, but it's like I've forgotten how. "I promise."

My heart drops as we leave the room. I keep looking back at Dad's ashen face. We regroup in the hallway, Kevin texting furiously.

"Can't we tell them I just woke up?" I ask. "I want to talk to Dad."

"You heard the nurse. Your father needs his rest." Mom sighs, her shoulders drooping in exhaustion. "Should we go out somewhere for dinner or grab take out and head back to your apartment?"

Kevin glances up from his phone. "Sorry, Cheryl, but Phoebe says you'll have to find some other place to sleep. There are news vans surrounding the apartment building."

"Emma, you're famous!" Steve mocks. *"Must be your good looks."*

"Where should we go?" I ask.

"We could check into a hotel," Mom offers. "I've been sleeping here in a chair, but you might want something more comfortable."

Kevin shakes his head. "The press will find you there. What about Claire's house?"

Steve chants in my head. *"Yes! Go to Claire's! Go to Claire's!"*

"Sounds good to me," I agree, then mutter to Steve, *Don't think I'm doing this just for you. I don't owe you any more favors, remember?*

Mom digs the car keys out of her purse. "Kevin, are you coming with us?"

He slips the cell into his back pocket. "No. I'd better go home to my mother. She's waiting for me."

"Of course." Mom smiles. "You've done too much for us already. I can't thank you enough."

"It's been my pleasure." Kevin glances at me, a sudden sadness in his eyes. Then his tall form disappears down the long hallway.

A wave of remorse hits me. Is he going home to mourn Mike for the second time?

Mom stifles a yawn. "I parked the car out back."

"Do you want me to drive?" I ask. "You look tired."

"Are you kidding?" She throws me a scathing glance, holding the keys far out of my reach. "I'm not letting *you* drive. You shouldn't even be *walking* right now."

Honestly, she's difficult. "But the doctor said I was okay, and I feel fine."

She exhales, blowing a curl of hair away from her face. "Do you now?"

"Yes, I'm back to normal." I dance around in the hallway, to show her all my limbs work. "No worries."

Mom eyeballs me. "Emma, do you even *recognize* the meaning of the word 'normal?'"

I feign innocence. "Why don't you believe the doctor?"

"You may have tricked him, but you can't con me," she huffs. "After all that's happened, I won't be shocked by *anything* anymore."

Hmmm. I seriously doubt that.

She taps my chest with her finger. "At least I *finally* got to know some of your friends. They're very nice. Kevin, Phoebe, and Laura—"

"Laura *Cunningham?*" I glance down the hallway, as if Jake's sister is hiding around the next corner. "How did you meet her?"

"What a sweet girl." She cocks her head to the side. "Why haven't you mentioned her before?"

Tricky question. "We're just pen pals, Mom."

"Well, she's lovely." Mom gestures for me to follow, and we head down the hallway. "She sat by me for hours, watching over you."

"Why was she here?" I ask. This is getting strange. And that's saying something.

"She drove up because you were supposed to give her a campus tour. When she found out about your accident, she stayed on to help."

"What did you two talk about?" Laura knows too much.

"Oh, this and that. Nothing special. She's not one to dwell on herself."

That's good to hear.

The closer we get to Claire's house, the more agitated Steve becomes. He moves so much it gives me indigestion. I squirm in my seat, trying to get comfortable.

Mom eyes me. "Are you in pain? That's it. I'm taking you back to the hospital."

"No! I told you—I'm fine," I speak through gritted teeth.

Steve, I'm going to kill you if you don't knock it off! I warn him.

He chuckles. *"You're too late. I'm dead already, remember?"*

Mom's phone rings and she passes her purse to me. "Can you

answer it?"

I bring the phone to my ear. "Hello?"

"Emma?" Phoebe squeals like she's at a rock concert. "Is it really you?"

After turning the volume down, I answer. "Yes, Phoebe. How are you?"

"I'm great! I'm at Claire's. Kevin asked me to bring some clothes from your apartment."

"Are you staying at Claire's, too?" I inquire. And how much have you nosed through my apartment?

"I've been here on and off the past few days." Phoebe lowers her voice. "I've got *tons* to tell you. See you soon."

My eyes narrow. There's only one thing I want to know. Where is my *Book?* I hang up and watch the houses pass by until Mom pulls into the driveway.

Claire meets us at the door. "Come on in. Abby's still at work and little Stevie's down for a nap."

"I can't wait to see him!" Steve's impatience hangs heavy around my neck.

You're just going to have to wait, I scold.

Claire ushers my mom into the nearest chair. "Sorry I don't have dinner ready. But I'll whip it together, lickety-split."

"Thank you." Mom sinks into the chair and closes her eyes. "This has been the most *exhausting* day."

"How are *you* feeling, Emma?" Claire asks.

"Physically, I'm fine." Mentally, I'm not so sure. "Thanks for taking us in."

"You know I love company," Claire reassures me. "As does Bernie. Even though I'm the one who feeds him, I suspect *you're* his favorite human. He lights up when you come over."

Claire's cat turns and twists around my feet. All of a sudden, he backs up and hisses, then goes back to purring. Has he developed a split personality? Both Bernie and I trail behind Claire as she bustles from closet to closet, pulling down extra pillows and sheets. She hands me an armful of cedar-scented pillows.

"Your mother looks beat," Claire whispers. "After supper, I'll give her the spare room. Then you can talk with Phoebe in private."

"Did I hear my name?" Phoebe pops her head around the corner. "Don't worry. Cheryl's already asleep. We can chat now."

"Poor thing," clucks Claire. "Why don't you two use the living room and shut the pocket doors? I'll watch over Cheryl in the kitchen."

Phoebe and I settle on the sofa. At first, she perches too close, overwhelming me with the smell of incense. I reposition myself at the far end of the couch. Bernie jumps on the loveseat across the room to groom.

"Kevin told me what happened at the police station," Phoebe says, her brown eyes wide. "You were brave."

"Thanks." I'm surprised at the compliment. "And thanks for helping Mike."

"It was no problem. He's great."

Even now, I feel the familiar stab of jealousy. This shouldn't bother me anymore. "Mike told me most of what happened, but maybe you could fill in the details."

"Sure thing." Phoebe settles into a cross-legged position on the couch. "I found Mike under the bridge waiting for Kevin. He stayed at my place, and Kevin brought his mom over. He tried to warn her she'd be shocked, but how on earth do you prepare a person for seeing somebody come back to life?"

I suck in my breath. "How did she take it?"

"She clutched her purse and stared at Mike for the longest time, without saying a word. I thought she was going to faint. Finally, she looked at me and said, 'I'm so glad you aren't pregnant.' Isn't that funny?"

I shrug. "A Catholic mother's worst fear, I guess."

"After that, Julie bear-hugged Mike, laughing and crying at the same time. Then she got all business-like, asking questions and making plans. She's a cool lady."

"She does seem different this time around," I admit.

"Now it's your turn." Phoebe narrows her eyes. "Tell me *everything*. How did you bring Mike and all the others back? How did you talk to him afterward? Which spells did you use? I couldn't figure out your *Book of Shadows*."

I stiffen. "Where is it?"

"It disappeared along with Mike. But don't be sad. Kevin says you probably don't even need it. He told me how you controlled that doctor at the hospital."

Steve chuckles. *"How about the Speedo? I'll bet Kevin didn't tell her about that!"*

I grab Phoebe's shoulder. "But I need my *Book of Shadows*. I've got to have it." It feels like I'm falling.

She moves away. "To be honest, I'm relieved it's gone. It was taking over. When the *Book* was in my apartment, it was all I could think about. It's far too dangerous."

"Then you know how much I need it." I'm lost without it.

"Fine." Phoebe hesitates before continuing. "Ask Laura then. She drove back to the park today before she went over to the police station. Maybe she found the *Book* somewhere."

I stiffen. "Laura went back to the fire pit?"

"Yeah. Didn't you see her at the police station? She seemed eager to find you."

"No. Where is she?" I glance around the living room, but it's only us. And Bernie the cat, who keeps alternating between purring and hissing as he grooms. Maybe he's possessed, too.

"I don't know." Phoebe checks her phone. "I haven't heard from her in ages. I left three messages, but she hasn't texted or called back yet. That's weird."

"Call her again. Ask if she found my *Book*."

"I can't understand it." Phoebe's eyes narrow as she scans her phone. "She was frantic about you in the hospital. I'm shocked she isn't here already."

A cold, numb feeling crawls over me. "Not if she has something to hide."

CHAPTER THIRTY-EIGHT

SECRETS, SECRETS, EVERYWHERE

Evening falls as we wait for Laura to show up. I stare out the window. No full moon tonight—looks like someone took a swipe out of it. Bernie hisses behind me. Maybe he's the culprit, swinging his sharp claws across the sky.

Headlights flash across the driveway.

"That's Abby." Phoebe turns to me. "Have you decided what you're going to tell her?"

Steve clears his throat, but I ignore him.

"No." I'm not sure I want to follow Steve's orders anymore. Why does everything I do have to involve a secret?

The kitchen door opens and shuts, voices banter back and forth in the kitchen, then Abby bursts into the living room.

"Emma! What a relief you're all right!" She rushes over to hug me. The end table light casts a soft glow on her smiling face. She's already lost most of the baby weight. My eyes linger on her soft hair, long legs, and curves.

Bernie jumps up on the sofa and hisses, interrupting my (or rather, Steve's) adoring stare.

Stop it, Steve! I hiss. *No more checking Abby out while you're inside me. You're pissing off the cat!*

"Bernie, get down!" Abby scolds. "What's wrong with you?"

The fat orange cat stalks into the corner of the room to glare at me. Abby gives me another fierce hug, which Steve enjoys much more than necessary. I throw a warning glance at Phoebe over Abby's shoulder, hoping she'll keep her mouth shut until I'm ready. For what, I don't know.

"You gals catch up." Phoebe exits the living room. "I'll help Claire in the kitchen."

"Thanks, Phoebe." I actually mean it. Maybe she's not so bad, after all.

"How are you feeling?" Abby sits beside me. "You look... great."

"*She's lying, you know,*" Steve digs. "*She looks great. You, on the other hand, look like shit.*"

"I feel fine." I force a bright smile. I'm really starting to hate Steve.

"What happened to you?" Abby asks. "I don't understand any of it. The newspapers say—"

"It's not Walker's fault," I interrupt. "It's mine."

Abby frowns. "I don't get it. Why were you setting fires in the park? And why were you hanging out with a thirty-five-year-old cop?"

"Well..."

Her eyes widen. "Do you *like* him? It's okay if you do. I mean, he's old and stuff, but he's still pretty cute."

"That's not it at all." Although life would be a lot easier if that were true.

"Emma, are you blushing?" Abby giggles. "Listen, I'm sure you had feelings for your friend Mike who drowned, but it's okay to care about someone else now that he's gone."

"*I don't like where this conversation is heading,*" Steve grumbles.

"WAAAAAAAAH!" A baby's wail from the back bedroom interrupts us.

Abby smiles. "I swear he can smell when I'm here. He'll sleep for hours for Claire, and the minute I come home he knows it's dinner time."

"I'll come with you," I say, but not on my own. Oh, crap! Steve's figured out how to speak through me. I have to stop this right away.

I follow Abby into the bedroom, hanging back to avoid the mirror over the dresser. I don't want her to see our double reflection. Steve's heart races within me as he watches Abby lift their son out of the bassinette. Little Stevie turns his face to me, cooing.

"Oh look," Abby says. "He wants you. Emma's your *favorite* babysitter, isn't she, Stevie?"

"It's me he wants," Steve insists. *"Let me take over."*

My right leg shakes involuntarily. *Not until she's out of the room, you idiot!*

Abby brings the baby over to the changing table and swiftly switches his smelly diaper to a fresh one.

"Could you hold him a sec while I toss out this stink bomb?" she asks.

"Of course," I reply, Steve tense with anticipation inside me.

Abby carries him over, and I cradle him in my arms. Except my arms are tingling, because Steve keeps trying to take over. Abby whistles as she walks away, garbage bag in hand.

"I can't believe I won't be here to watch him grow up." Steve forces his way to the forefront, burying his face in his son's hair, breathing in his sweet baby smell. *"They stole everything from me that night. Abby wouldn't be alone if I were still alive."*

She's not alone, I remind him. *Claire's here. Just like you wanted.*

"I know, but it's not fair!" Tears spring to both of our eyes due to Steve. *"It could be better than this."*

Memories flood my mind. Pictures and feelings that aren't mine. Steve and Abby on a date, eating at a restaurant. Strolling hand in hand along the bike path near campus. Abby's hair, shining in the moonlight. Steve talking on the phone to her late at night. Abby smiling as Steve kissed her.

I try to dispel the images, but Steve is too determined.

Give me back control, I order. *You shouldn't fight me when we're holding the baby!*

"One more minute. Please. Why can't you understand?"

Footsteps approach in the hall.

We don't have time for this, I warn. *Abby will see you—*

239

She sweeps into the room and locks eyes with us in the mirror. Her face goes white. "Steve?"

She sways a moment before toppling onto the floor, unconscious.

Great job, Steve. You made her faint. Give me back the body NOW.

We switch. Faint glimmering reflects off the dresser mirror. I bend down, cradling the baby in my arms.

"Abby, are you okay?" I shake her shoulder.

She sits up, rubbing her head. "I'm sorry. What a mess I am! I could have sworn Steve was here for a moment—which is ridiculous, and now you'll think I'm a freak."

"No, I don't think that." Poor Abby. All the lies I've told her. Why does she believe anything I say?

She gets up and scurries around the room. "It's all because of that strange picture his mother took a few months ago. It freaks me out every time I look at it. Did I ever show it to you?" She rustles through dresser drawers, searching.

I don't have the heart to tell her Claire showed me ages ago.

"Isn't this strange?" Abby's hand shakes as she holds out the photo. The image shows Steve asleep in a rocking chair, holding his baby. It should have been impossible, since Steve died seven months before little Stevie's birth.

"Tell her," Steve insists. *"Tell her cameras and mirrors show who's inside."*

I thought you didn't want her to know, I remind him.

Abby stares at me. "Emma, what's going on? There's a strange glow about you. Why are you shimmering?"

"You should sit down," I advise. "Maybe you hit your head when you fell."

"No, I'm okay. My eyes must be playing tricks on me." She puts away the picture. "But I have to sit down anyway to nurse Stevie."

I follow her to the rocking chair, trying to avoid the mirror, but Steve forces me forward.

"Please, Emma, just this once..." begs Steve.

This is the last thing I'm doing for you, but it's your choice to tell her, I relent and move into full view of the dresser mirror.

Abby's eyes lock onto the mirror image of Steve holding their baby. She moves close to the reflection, and raises a hand to Steve's face.

"This isn't possible." Abby takes a shuddering breath. She snatches little Stevie out of my arms, making him squirm in protest. Her eyes narrow. "What's going on? Who am I talking to now?"

"Maybe this wasn't such a good idea," Steve says.

"Steve's being a coward, so I guess you're talking to me," I answer Abby.

"You know, Emma, I'm not *entirely* stupid." Abby's eyes fill with tears. "I suspected you were hiding something. I saw all those witchcraft books in your apartment, and wondered why you never talked about it. And Claire's not as quiet on the phone as she thinks she is. But I didn't know what to expect. You've got a lot of explaining to do."

"You're right. It's time to come clean. Steve's been with me since the police station."

"With you?" Abby takes a step back. "The police station? I don't get it."

"That's where Steve found me. He's..." I can't help but grimace, but I try not to look repulsed. He used to be her boyfriend, after all. "...sharing this body with me. And our friend 'Sam' wasn't really Sam, either, at least not most of the time."

Abby and Steve gaze at each other in the mirror. I sense both of them asking me for some great favor I can't fulfill.

I bite my lip. "I'm sorry, you guys, but this isn't *Ghost* and I'm not Whoopi Goldberg. Good movie, though."

Abby stares at the reflection, a strained look upon her face. "Was Sam actually Steve in disguise the whole time?"

I shake my head. "No. First it was Sam. Then Jake. And then—"

"You're right. I better sit down." Abby collapses in the rocking chair. "Okay, start over from the beginning."

My chest tightens and the words rush out. I tell her about how I tried to bring Mike back after he died. That instead of resurrecting Mike, I brought back Sam. Then Jake. Then Mike, Steve and Bernard all at the same time right after that.

Abby interrupts. "Claire's husband, Bernard?"

"Yeah." I watch the expressions cross her face, one after the other: confusion, frustration, anger, and acceptance.

"I thought so." Abby helps her baby nurse. "That makes sense somehow. But why is Steve using *your* body? What happened to the other one?"

"It fell apart when Mike went back. Now I'm the borrowed body." *Will I fall apart, too?* "I'm sorry that I didn't tell you before. But you were pregnant. Everyone thought it was best at the time."

"Everyone but me," she counters. "Why did Steve come back again? Did he want to see us? Why didn't he tell me the truth last time?"

How about you swing these questions on your own, big guy? I push Steve forward and our glimmering sparkles throughout the room. *Here's your big chance, Steve. Don't make me regret being nice to you.*

Steve kneels in front of Abby. He puts a tentative hand on her forearm. "More than anything, I wanted to see both of you, but I also had to give Officer Walker information about the gang that murdered me."

Tears race down Abby's cheeks.

"Can I hold him again?" Steve asks, his own eyes threatening to spill over.

"For just a minute because he hasn't finished nursing yet." Abby hands over the baby, who snuggles in Steve's arms.

"But why didn't you tell me?" Abby asks. "Claire got to know, didn't she?"

"Yes." Steve hangs his head. "I'm sorry, Abby. You had enough to deal with already and I didn't want to hurt you anymore. I did what I thought was best, getting you to move in with Claire, and writing to my parents."

Abby's mouth falls open. "That was all *you*?"

Steve nods, running his fingers over his son's hair.

She laughs. "You're kind of a manipulative bastard, aren't you?"

I halfway glimmer back. "It's even worse than you think." And I'm not sure it's a good idea to get Steve in the habit of taking over my body.

Abby points her finger. "Don't go anywhere, Emma Roberts. I'm not done with you yet."

Steve allows me to assume full control as Abby takes back the baby.

"I can't believe that the whole time I've known you, everything's been a lie. Why didn't you tell me any of this? Didn't you trust me? I thought we were friends."

"Maybe I'm not always such a good friend," I mumble.

Steve glimmers forward. "You've been pretty good to me."

"Better than you deserve!" I retort.

Abby holds up her hands. "Ack! Stop all this shimmering nonsense. It's hard on my eyes. And why are you guys fighting? I'm the one who should be upset, not you."

"Emma's not happy being the host body," Steve says.

"I just don't like sharing it with you," I argue. "You're too bossy."

Steve smirks. "So you'd rather share it with Jake?"

"That's not what I said!"

Abby waves her hand. "Wait a minute! I'm lost. Who's this 'Jake' person again?"

"He's the second one who came back. Right after Sam. He sort of blew you off at first because—"

Abby waves a hand in surrender. "Never mind. I get it. But I have a few more questions for the two of you."

Hours later, after doing our best to answer her, we fall asleep, lounging across Abby's carpeted floor.

I dog paddle, splashing through purple waves.

Jake backstrokes through a school of dolphins.

"Are you a mermaid?" I ask. "Or a merman?"

Steve buzzes by in a speedboat, separating us in his wake.

"Emma, I've got a package for you." Jake waves my *Book of Shadows* in the air as he floats away.

"Jake! Come back!" I jolt awake, sweating as night pales into dawn.

Exhausted, I fall back into a restless sleep. My nightmares jump from one murder to another—the bloody shower, the chase across the parking lot, and the dirty white van filled with hatred. An endless array of flickering candles light up the woods under a starlit sky. Painted Smiley Faces leer from every direction. Steve lights fires at the base of each tree. Flames lick up the trunks to consume the sneering grimaces and transform each tree into a blazing column.

When I wake for good, the smoke from my dreams lingers.

No, wait, something actually smells like it's on fire. I stand too fast and stumble, my feet entwined in a blanket. After shaking it off, I dash to the kitchen. Claire sits at the table, clutching a mug of black coffee. At the stove, Mom jabs at pancakes with a spatula as if she's trying to hurt them. A stack of charred flapjacks rests on a plate nearby.

"Some idiots claim that cooking is therapeutic," Mom growls. "I certainly don't feel any better."

"Cheryl, why don't you have a seat? I can finish that." Claire cracks open a window, and takes over at the stove. The burnt odor fades. "Breakfast will be ready in a jiffy. Phoebe already left for the day. The rest of you can sit where you like."

Abby hurries in and passes Little Stevie into my arms. "Ooh, pancakes. Claire, you're the best!"

I sit down in the nearest kitchen chair and let Steve gaze at his son through me.

But stay quiet in there! I warn. *Mom's watching.*

"Mmmm. These are great!" Abby murmurs as her eyes flicker to the clock. "Oh no! I'd better hurry, or I'll be late for work."

A loud knock shakes the door.

"Who could that be?" Claire peeks through the window. "Oh, good. It's just Laura with a handsome young man."

Claire wipes her hands on a towel. "Thank goodness those reporters are gone. I can't believe how unprofessionally they dress these days. One of them showed up here wearing a wife-beater, of all things. He didn't even bother to cover up the big snake tattoo on his arm."

My hands tremble. Steve and I finally agree on something.

That tattooed guy wasn't looking for a story.
He was looking for me.

CHAPTER THIRTY-NINE

BOOK, BOOK, WHO'S GOT THE BOOK?

told you the Cobras were after you," Steve warns. **"And now** *they know you're here. Send Abby and the baby away. Do it now."*

"Hello, Laura." Claire swings the door wide open. "Come on in. We're having pancakes."

I tense as Laura enters the kitchen. She has my *Book*. I can feel it. And despite Steve's protests, right now it's the most important thing in the world.

Just wait, I tell him. *I need my* Book of Shadows *to fight the Cobras.*

"Hello, Laura," Mom says. "And who's your friend?"

My heart flutters as I meet Jake's meaningful gaze.

"This is... Mike," Laura squeaks an introduction, a fabric tote held tight against her hip. A brown sweater drapes her shoulders even though it's the middle of summer.

Jake frowns at his sister. Why on earth would she choose *that* name?

I stare at Laura's oversized sweater. She catches my eye and tightens her grip on the tote bag.

Why is Laura wearing a sweater? I ask internally. *What does she have to hide... besides my Book?*

"You should know," Steve responds. *"You're the one wearing all the turtlenecks lately."*

I know. That's exactly what I mean.

Mom grins. "Laura, you never mentioned you had such a *handsome* boyfriend."

I groan. I'm going to be sick.

"Oh, no. We're just... friends." Laura swallows the last word.

"I'm Cheryl." Mom extends her hand to Jake. "Now that I think of it, you look familiar. Have we met before?"

"Uh, I don't think so." Jake can't help but glance my way. I cringe, remembering the pictures Mom unknowingly took of him last year at her pre-Christmas costume party. Someone needs to change the subject fast.

"Anyone hungry?" Claire hefts plates of pancake perfection.

"I am." Jake grabs one and sits at the kitchen table.

"Emma, let me take Stevie," Abby says. "I have to nurse him before I go to work. That way you can eat your pancakes before they grow cold."

"Thanks." I choose a plate and dig in, keeping an eagle eye on Laura who sits across from me. I can almost reach her tote bag under the table.

"Here you go." Claire holds a generous serving in front of my mom.

Mom waves her hand. "Thanks, but I'm not hungry. I need to get to the hospital soon." She sounds tired even though she just woke up.

"Nonsense." Claire shoves the warm dish in her hands. "You need your strength."

After everyone's belly is filled, we meander into the living room as Claire tidies the kitchen. Abby and Mom flank me on the nearest couch, pinning me in. Jake and Laura sit close together on the far loveseat, their heads bent together in whispers.

Mom gestures at them and coos. "Aren't they cute together?"

"Sure, Mom." If you enjoy incest.

"Why can't you get a boyfriend like that?" Mom asks.

I sigh. You've got to be kidding me.

Steve laughs with utter abandon. Thank goodness only I can hear him.

"I'd better freshen up before we leave for the hospital." Mom heads for the bathroom as Bernie strolls into the room, tail erect.

As soon as Mom exits, I jump up. Bernie hisses at my sudden movement.

Jake also stands, meeting me halfway across the room. "Emma, we have to talk. This is important."

I rip my eyes away from his earnest gaze. "Just a minute, Jake. I need to ask your sister a question first." My eyes narrow. "Laura, where's my *Book of Shadows*?"

She shrinks into the seat, pulling her sweater tight. "I don't know."

"Give it to me," I order, holding out my empty hand.

Laura's grip tightens on the fabric tote bunched in her lap. "I don't have it."

"I don't believe you," I growl. "And what are you hiding under that sweater?"

"I'm cold," she says through clenched teeth.

"It's 78 degrees out." I step closer. "You're lying."

"Prove it!" she snaps.

"I'd be glad to." I grab her sweater and yank it down, exposing her left upper arm for a mere second before she covers it back up again.

"You have a snake tattoo, too?" Jake yelps.

"Wait a minute," Claire begins. "That's the same tattoo as the guy who came to the door earlier..."

I pull down the shoulder of my own shirt for comparison. "And it's the same tattoo that I have on *my* arm. Claire, you'd better not answer that door anymore—unless you've got a loaded gun with you. And that might not even help. Maybe all of you should relocate for a while."

"I could stay with my sister, or my neighbor, Gertie, down the street," Claire turns to Abby. "We need to get your baby out of here."

Abby's grip tightens on little Stevie, causing him to squirm.

"I know how I got my tattoo." I tower over Laura's cowering form. "What I'd like to know is how you got yours."

Jake grabs my arm. "Hey, what's going on here?"

"This is between me and your sister." I slap his hand away. "It doesn't involve you."

"Anything that involves either of you involves me, too."

"Then tell her to give me back my *Book*," I demand. "And make her explain the tattoo."

Bernie hisses and spits, his eyes dilated and wild.

"Fine." Jake turns to his sister. "Laura, do you have it?"

She hangs her head. "No. I don't."

"Well, there you go." Jake turns to me. "She doesn't have it. Stop acting hostile. You're pissing off the cat."

"That cat has issues." I point my finger at Laura. "And I know that you're lying." I try to use mind-control on her, but my heart's racing and my hands tremble so much I can't focus.

Laura bolts up. "Let's go, Jake. We're not wanted here."

He throws up his hands. "What the Hell's going on? Sit down and let's talk things through."

"I'm not staying here." Laura brushes past him and bolts for the door.

Jake lingers. "Emma, why are you acting like this?"

Ignoring him, I stalk after his sister. At the doorstep, I focus on my target. Laura trips and falls down the three steps leading to the driveway. Her fabric tote soars over the pavement. My *Book of Shadows* flies out in an arc, landing on the driveway with a heavy thud.

My head fills with memories. The first time I saw my *Book* was on Angie's shelf at her home, surrounded by colored candles and pictures of her grandmother. After a nightmare-soaked sleep, I spotted my *Book*, deserted and dusty, tucked in the far corner under my bed. Lit candles trailed along the bridge over the Chippewa River as I cast my spell into the night, calling the water to crash down upon me.

Back in the present, I dash out to grab my *Book of Shadows* off the driveway and hug it close. The tightness in my chest recedes.

I can finally breathe.

The *Book of Shadows* is, and will always be, mine.

CHAPTER FORTY

THE MAN IN BLACK AND HIS DIRTY LAUNDRY

What's this?" **Father Joe sets down a briefcase** in the driveway and offers Laura a hand. "Are you all right? You took quite a fall."

Her face blanches. "I'm fine." As soon as she's back on her feet, she ducks out of his grip and flees for her car. "Jake, let's go."

Jake pauses a moment in the driveway before he follows in his sister's footsteps with a bewildered expression. A stab of pain jolts my heart until the *Book of Shadows* begins to hum in my arms, warm under my cold fingers. My shoulders tense and relax. I break my gaze away from Jake as he backs out of the drive.

"They're leaving already?" Mom asks, appearing in the doorway. "That's too bad. Oh, Father Joe, how good of you to visit. Come inside."

Father Joe trails her into the kitchen. I squeeze into the corner farthest away from the stove, the *Book* vibrating in my hands as I hide it behind my back.

"Now we're back in action," Steve says.

"Are you hungry, Father Joe?" Claire gestures toward the stack of remaining pancakes.

Bernie scampers up to the priest, purring loudly.

"I'm sorry to say I've already eaten." He bends down to pet the cat.

"I just came to check on the Roberts family."

"That's kind of you," Mom says, ducking into the living room. "Could I speak with you for a moment in private?"

"Of course." The priest follows, taking the briefcase and the cat with him. He throws me a knowing look as he slides shut the pocket doors.

Fifteen minutes later, the doors open, but only my mother exits the room.

"Thank you, Father. I feel much better now." Mom eyes me. "Emma, he wants to see you now. In private."

"He does?" My breath catches in my throat.

"Yes." Mom glances at her watch.

"I can drive Emma over to meet you at the hospital later, if you're worried about the time," Claire offers.

"That would be great. Thank you." Mom grabs her purse and leaves.

Bracing myself, I approach the exorcist, the *Book of Shadows* still clenched in my hands. Clouds cover the sun outside, and the living room is shrouded in shadows. The bright glow of the TV illuminates Father Joe's face as he waits on the couch. He clicks past PBS kid shows, old ladies exercising in chairs, and stops on the local news.

"Emma, you need to see this." He gestures with the remote toward the TV.

There's a thrill in the newscaster's voice. "In local news, Officer Charlie Walker was released from prison yesterday after numerous charges against him—including battery, arson, and attempted murder—were dismissed."

Walker's mug shot glares at me from the screen as the announcer prattles on. "There are still numerous unanswered questions regarding the severe injuries sustained by twenty-year-old Emma Roberts, daughter of the millionaire founder of the Roberts Lumber and Hardware store chain."

I groan. "Why do they have to bring that up?"

"Just wait. It gets worse," Father Joe warns. "I watched the earlier newcast."

The reporter narrows her eyes. "Was this a love affair gone wrong?"

"Seriously?" I gawk. "Me and Walker?"

The newscaster continues with glee, "How did Emma Roberts sustain multiple life-threatening injuries? Who is Officer Walker's anonymous source for information used to solve local cold case murders?" Dramatic pause. "So far, Officer Walker has refused to answer any of these questions."

When the news moves on to the weather, Father Joe clicks off the TV.

I pace the room. "This is awful. They don't want the truth. They want scandal. Walker's already been cleared of all charges. Why isn't that enough for them?"

"They're reporters. It's their job to spread gossip." Father Joe sets down the remote. "But I didn't come here just to show you the news."

"You didn't?" Oh, dear. He sounds serious.

"I'm an exorcist." He raises a cross, gripped in his hand. "You're still possessed. I've come to finish the job."

"How did you know?" I back away. "The spirits have been so quiet."

Father Joe pulls a floral blouse out from his briefcase. "Do you know who this belongs to?"

A flashback of the living, festering dead fills my mind. "It's from one of those zombie-ladies who chased me out of the church when I went to you for help."

"What?" His jaw drops. "You saw zombies in *my* church? Are you sure?"

"Didn't you wonder why I wasn't around when you came back?"

"Of course, but—"

I spot a red shirt poking out of his briefcase and rush forward to grab it. "This was Mike's." My hands scatter the remaining items, holding each one up in turn. "This skirt got ripped when Jennifer Pearson was attacked. This is Jake's jacket. And this plaid shirt looks like something Dominic wore."

Father Joe's eyes widen. "Are you telling me these are all dead people's clothes?"

"Yeah." I pause. "Where'd you get them?"

"This probably sounds strange, but I found them in my clothes dryer this morning. As you might expect," Father Joe tugs at his traditional black attire, "I'm used to a more monochromatic wardrobe."

I raise the flowered blouse. "This isn't your color, anyway."

Father Joe's face relaxes into a smile. "But there was more than clothes in the dryer. I heard a rustling, and when I opened the dryer door, a black crow flew out and scared me half to death before it disappeared into a cloud of dust."

"I've seen crows before, too. But not in my laundry. They were in my apartment. And then with God, which sounds wrong, of course."

Bernie rubs on Father Joe's ankles, purring.

"Emma, we need to exorcise your demons." Father Joe removes other things from the briefcase: holy water, a cross, and a prayer book.

"Don't let him!" Steve demands. "He'll cast me out along with the others. We've still got things to do."

"No!" I yell, the volume of my own voice startling me. "They're not all bad. And the worst one is already gone. If God didn't get rid of the others, then I don't think you should, either."

The priest frowns. "If I have to round up the others again to help me, I will. This is for your own good."

"I don't want to hurt you." I raise the Book of Shadows. "Please don't make me."

"If you think that's going to protect you, you're wrong." Father Joe approaches, a cross clasped in his outstretched fist. "It can't save you, but I can."

"Stay away from me!" I warn. My hands tremble then calm.

A strong wind whips through the living room.

Curtains swirl.

Sheets of piano music fly across the room.

My heart pounds and my legs shake so hard I can barely remain standing.

"This is for your own good," Father Joe pleads. "Please let me help you."

"Stay back." I hold out the *Book*. "Just leave us alone."

"I can't." Father Joe raises his arms and chants above the din. "*I cast you out, unclean spirit, along with every Satanic power of the enemy, every specter from Hell—*"

"RREEOOORROOWW!" Bernie flies through the air, yowling. He knocks the *Book of Shadows* out of my arms. His sharp claws rip my shirt and dig into my chest before he races away, his tail whipping madly.

The wind and noise disappear. Wincing, I bend down to retrieve my *Book*.

Father Joe gasps for breath. "Let me help you."

"I can't let you do this. I know you mean well, but not everyone in here is all bad. One of them is a friend—was a friend of mine."

He collapses into the nearest chair. "Why would you want to stay this way?"

"I *have* to, at least for now. Just let me talk to Walker—"

"He doesn't want to see you," Father Joe reminds me, still breathing heavily.

"That's okay. I'll wait until he changes his mind. I need to visit Dad first, anyway. If you really want to help, give me a ride to the hospital and keep Mom busy. I have to ask Dad about a family matter."

CHAPTER FORTY-ONE

GRANDMA BERTHA

Dad is sleeping when I enter his hospital room. There's a hint of pink in his cheeks. I hover near his bed, standing watch over him, examining his every breath. I keep my *Book of Shadows* close in the fabric bag hanging off my shoulder.

"Don't bother him," whispers Mom.

At the sound of her voice, Dad's eyelids flutter. It takes him a few seconds to wake up.

"Emma," he breathes my name. A weak smile flickers on his lips. "You're okay."

"I'm here, Dad." I take his hand, trying not to panic at the lack of strength in his grip.

True to his word, Father Joe invites Mom to the hospital cafeteria for coffee. This time, she seems grateful for the excuse to get away. As soon as Mom leaves the room, Dad adjusts the bed controls. He struggles to get into a sitting position, coughing as he fusses with his necklace.

"Dad, please lie back down." I press ever so gently on his thin shoulders. "You should rest."

He chuckles. "You're one to talk." With a final effort, he unlatches the metal chain. The necklace falls, clinking into a silver puddle in his lap. Breathing hard, he scoops it up and holds it out to me. He pours the chain into my open palm, then closes my fingers over it.

"What are you doing?" I ask.

"Put it on before your mother comes back." He pats his chest. "Hide it under your shirt."

"But it's *your* necklace," I argue. "You always wear it."

"It's time to pass it on," Dad insists. "Take it."

"I don't know, Dad." I study the heavy cross-shaped charm encrusted with pink gemstones. "This looks like old lady jewelry to me."

"Are you calling me old?" He gasps out the words. "And gender-confused?"

I watch his mouth as he breathes. I sense we're both drowning now. And we're running out of time. "No. But I did see an old lady wearing this exact necklace. Maybe it's time you told me about your mother."

Dad grabs my hand. "You saw my mom?"

"Yes." I squeeze his hand. "How come you never told me she was a witch? All you ever said was that she made the best fried chicken in the world and had a house full of African violets."

Sweat beads on his brow. "She did. But you're right—I never told you the truth."

"Do you know anything about a special book Grandma had?" I ask.

He nods, panting hard. "I should've guessed what you were up to earlier. I'm sorry. I wasn't paying close enough attention."

"Don't work yourself up, Dad. I never told you the truth, either."

He laughs, but sounds so sad. "The funny thing is that you *hated* witches as a little girl, do you remember? You'd never dress up as one for Halloween. Cheryl even bought you a witch costume once, but you refused to wear it."

I glance back at the door. "Does Mom know?"

"No. I never told her that witchery runs in my family. I have no gifts, except in the business world, but my mother had talents like you." He coughs so hard his face turns red.

I hand him a glass of water, my hands shaking so that I spill on his bedclothes. I recall old pictures of Grandma wearing long, flowered dresses. She didn't look like a witch, either. Not everyone is as obvious about it as Phoebe.

"Thanks." Dad hands back the glass. "I wish my mother was here to guide you. You need the help. You get yourself into far too much trouble."

I smile. "That's what she said."

"I'm glad you got to meet her." His voice catches.

"But I'm still confused. You always said that Grandma Bertha was a good German Catholic." She certainly looked German. Mom always worried that I'd end up built like her, with massive thighs and hips.

"Somehow, she managed to do both." He points at the necklace. "Look closer."

I study the silver amulet. I run a finger over the cross, formed by rows of miniature pentagrams, each inlaid with rose quartz crystals.

"Let's see how it looks on you." Dad smiles weakly. The pallor of his lips frightens me.

I hang it around my neck. As soon as the metal touches my skin, a flush of warmth soothes my tense shoulders, like an instant massage. A faint humming noise buzzes in my ears.

"Can you hear that?" I finger the necklace, searching for the source of the hum.

He raises a hand to cover another wet cough. "I don't hear anything."

"Then it must just be me. How long have you known I was doing witchcraft?"

He tenses. "I went to the park where you collapsed."

"You mean afterward?" Mom didn't tell me about this.

"The smell of candles brought back many memories." His voice weakens. "I need to rest now. Can you help me?"

"Of course." I readjust the bed and pillows the best I can. "Should I call a nurse?"

"Not yet." He searches my eyes. "Does the necklace make you feel stronger?"

"Yes." My hand flutters against the warm crystals. "Doesn't rose quartz have healing properties? I read something about that, once."

"That's right." He coughs so hard it shakes the bed, making the metal bars clink. "Especially for the heart."

Realization dawns. I tug at the necklace to take it off. "You should be wearing it instead."

"No!" Dad sputters. "It's from your grandmother. It helped me, and now it will help you."

Tears fill my eyes. "But you need it *more.*"

He reaches for my hands again. We hold tight to each other.

"Oh, Emma, I've been living on borrowed time for years." He glances at the closed door, then speaks as fast as his coughing fits allow. "I was born with a weak heart. My mother knew it and made this necklace for me. I would never have lived this long, never have had a wife, or you, without it. But my mother shortened her own life to create it. In using her powers to save me, she gave up part of herself."

"So that's how she cheated Nature." I finally understand. "But, Dad, what are you saying? That you're giving up your life for mine? I don't want that!"

He clenches my hand even harder. "You need its protection. I won't have it any other way."

"Not if it will save you." Tears spill out from my eyes, my chest aching. "Take it back! I want you to live!"

Another vigorous coughing spell silences both of us until Dad recovers enough to speak again. "My time's up. It's *you* who must live, despite your best efforts to do otherwise."

"Dad, listen to me." I want to rip off the necklace and force it back over his head, but his steady gaze keeps me from moving.

"Call the nurse," he wheezes.

"Take it back!"

"Call the nurse *now.*" Dad's eyes roll back in his head. His body jerks, as if he's seizing. Alarms wail around us. I break our grasp and race for the door.

"Help me! Somebody! Help me!" My screams echo down the hospital corridor.

CHAPTER FORTY-TWO

GOOD-BYE

Mom races down the hall, along with Father Joe and the cardiac crash team.

"Wait out here, please," a nurse directs as Dad's room crowds with hospital personnel.

Father Joe ushers us into a cluster of seats in the hallway. "Perhaps we should sit here."

Minutes tick by, an hour in every second.

Mom wrings her hands. "Why aren't they telling us anything?"

Father Joe pats her shoulder. "They need to focus on John right now."

I clutch Dad's necklace, which hangs like guilt. It takes everything I have to respect Dad's wishes and remain seated, and not barrel back into the room to force the charm over his head.

Mom glances at me. "Why are you wearing that?"

"Dad gave it to me."

She stiffens. "I never understood why his mother gave him a pink necklace."

I glance down, my hand fluttering over the necklace. "It's more purple than pink."

"Same difference." She stares at the necklace for a long moment. "It looks good on you," she finally decides.

"No, it doesn't." Guilty tears threaten to fall. "I shouldn't be wearing it."

Mom rolls her eyes. "I can't say anything to you anymore without starting an argument."

"I could say the same about you," I grumble.

Her lips quiver. "I suppose you think it's easy for me to sit around and watch my family fall apart."

I tense. Why is she so overprotective? "Mom, I'm *fine!*"

"What's *wrong* with you?" Her face reddens. She grabs my shoulders and shakes me. "Are you so self-absorbed you can't even see your father is dying?"

"Don't say that," I yell. "Take it back!"

Father Joe steps in. "This is no time for arguing. You need each other."

"I can't sit here anymore. I'm going back in." Mom hurries into Dad's room.

I stand to follow her, but Father Joe grabs my elbow and pushes me into a chair. "Sit here with me. You aren't making things any easier."

"Get out of my way."

He holds me down. "You're acting rude and insensitive—"

"So is she," I snap. "Maybe it's genetic."

"Put yourself in her shoes for once. Have some sympathy for her position."

I cross my arms and slouch in the stiff-backed chair.

"You almost died. Her husband teeters on the edge. Do you have any idea how scared she is right now? Why do you think she wanted to talk to me this morning? She doesn't feel strong enough to face this alone."

"She's not alone," I argue. "I'm here, and everyone else is helping her."

"She *feels* alone. And that's what matters. It's not like she knows the truth about you— although that might make things even worse, I suspect." He pauses. "Speaking of that, you really should allow me to assist with your unwelcome guests. Why are you protecting them when they intend to hurt you?"

I get up and lean against the wall, arms crossed. "I told you—not all of them are bad."

"Don't fool yourself."

The door swings open and a nurse steps out. "Emma Roberts?"

I tense. "How is he?"

Her stiff smile is not reassuring. "He's been stabilized for transport to the ICU."

The door opens again with doctors and nurses spilling out into the hallway. Their voices sound muffled and far away.

"Okay, thanks." I place a shaky hand on the wall to steady myself. "How's my mom?"

"She'll be out soon," the nurse assures me. "Excuse me. I need to make arrangements in ICU."

As she hurries down the hall, Father Joe glances at his watch. "Emma, confessions begin in a half hour, but I can cancel if you need me to stay."

"That's all right." I long for Mom to come out and tell me everything is going to be okay, even if it's a lie. "You can go. We'll be fine. And thanks for everything."

Father Joe pats my shoulder. "Think about what I said. You need my help."

A half hour later, Mom and I still wait outside the ICU. We sit in silence, but Steve, unfortunately, does not.

"You could call Charlie while you're waiting," he says.

Not now, I growl internally.

"It was just a suggestion to help you pass the time," he grumbles. *"We need to do something about that gang before they hurt anyone else."*

You don't fool me, Steve. You only care about yourself.

"I wouldn't be so sure of that if I were you." Then Steve, thankfully, goes silent.

Finally, a nurse walks toward us. "You can see Mr. Roberts now," he says, but he's not smiling.

"Emma, you go on ahead," Mom instructs. "I need to talk to the nurse."

I enter the unit and approach Dad's bed. It's surrounded by more monitors than before. Dad has oxygen tubes in his nostrils and a face the color of cement.

He smiles weakly and speaks in winded bursts. "I... gave you a scare. I'm... sorry."

I grab his hand, tears rolling down my face. My words get stuck in a painful lump in my throat.

"I need... to tell... you something," he wheezes.

"You don't have to say anything." I don't even bother to wipe the tears away.

"Let me... say this."

I shut my mouth and force a smile. I wish Jake was here. He'd be so much better at this, but he doesn't know I need him right now. He doesn't know anything.

Dad struggles to speak. "Every minute with you... has been a miracle... for me. I love you... Emma."

"I love you too, Dad." I choke out the words that need to be said.

Dad drops my hand as Mom and two nurses approach the bedside. "Now... go... away."

"What?" I balk. "No! I want to stay here with you."

Mom puts her hand on my shoulder. "You can come back tomorrow, honey."

I back out of her reach. "You mean you get to stay?"

Dad coughs. "Emma, please..."

"You're upsetting him." Mom's eyes water. She's trying so hard to not lose it. "Just go. You can come back later."

She's lying, even to herself. There is no "later."

Emma, maybe he doesn't want you to see him like this," Steve says.

My legs tremble, knowing he's right.

Mom whips out her phone. "I'll call that nice Phoebe. She'll give you a ride."

"*I'm sorry,*" Steve says. "*Really, I am.*"

I stare into Dad's blue eyes as Mom makes arrangements.

Mom hangs up. "Phoebe's on the way. Meet her out front in

fifteen minutes."

"Fine. I'll go." I hoist the bag on my shoulder and squeeze Dad's hand for what I know will be the last time. In my other hand, I clasp the necklace, which hangs over my heart. "I'll wear it forever."

Dad nods silently.

I bolt out of ICU like an Olympic sprinter, the fabric bag banging against my hip, my vision blinded with tears.

CHAPTER FORTY-THREE

CHEAP SUNGLASSES

I **wait in the parking lot. Hot tears race down my cheeks as I** stare out at the oily summer sky. Insects sing, filling the air with their scratchy violins. I never thought I'd lose Dad. I can't bring him back from this. I can't fix this.

I can't do anything but cry this time. So, for once, I let myself go.

Ten minutes later, after my emotional storm has subsided to the occasional uncontrolled sniffle, Phoebe's Volkswagen van pulls up. She has somewhat unwelcome company. Jake and Laura both ride in the backseat.

Neither looks particularly happy to see me.

"I thought he liked you," Steve says.

He must like his sister more. My heart sinks.

"I call shot gun," I mutter as I open the door and sit down.

Phoebe forces a nervous laugh and pulls away from the curb. No one speaks, and I don't mind.

After a few blocks pass, Phoebe clears her throat. "I suppose you're wondering why Jake and Laura are with me."

"Not really." I stare out the window. "I have more important things to think about right now."

"Like your obsession with witchcraft?" Jake grumbles. Great, now he sounds like Mike.

I spin around to glare at him. "My father's dying of heart failure and he won't let me stay with him. That makes me *not care* why you and your thieving sister are here."

Jake's mouth falls open. Laura has the decency to look away.

Phoebe recovers first. "I'm sorry, Emma."

"Thanks." I turn back to the window.

"Did you know this was coming?" Jake asks.

"What kind of question is that?" I retort.

"I meant... well... you never mentioned he had heart disease and he looked fine at that Christmas party."

"No. I didn't know. And he *was* fine back then." I clutch at the necklace, which begins to quiver.

"Maybe this wasn't the best time to bring Laura around to apologize," mumbles Phoebe.

I barely hear her, because the necklace has taken over. It demands and I obey.

"Turn here," I direct Phoebe.

"Why?" she asks, but obliges.

I pause. "Something tells me we need to—okay, now turn left. Then go straight for a while."

I flip down the make-up mirror so I can see Laura and Jake. Laura glances up and gawks at my double image. Maybe she can see the others, too. I don't know or care. Narrowing my eyes, I hold the bag containing the *Book of Shadows* closer to my chest.

Jake sighs. "Laura didn't mean to take your *Book*. She just found it in the fire pit after they tried to bring you back."

"That would have been fine if she had returned it when I asked," I growl.

"Jake, why do you even like her?" Laura reaches for Jake's hand. "She's *horrible* to me."

Another surge of bright green envy shoots through my veins. She wants to take everything from me!

"It's never easy getting along with the in-laws," Steve jokes in my head.

Jake frowns, his face pained. "I can't understand why you two *hate* each other. It doesn't make any sense. Normally, neither one of you acts like this."

But I'm not listening to him.

I'm listening to the necklace, which brought me where I need to be—Walker's truck is parked at the gas station on the other side of the road.

Steve whoops. *"You've found him! There he is! Let's go!"*

Once again, I agree with him.

"Stop the car!" I shove open my door and barrel toward the station.

"Get back here! You're acting crazy!" screams Phoebe as I race across the busy street, dodging cars.

Horns honk and tires squeal. Somehow I manage not to get hit. Finally I reach the gas station, my heart galloping faster than a winning racehorse. The bell chimes as I push open the glass door and step inside. Breathlessly, I scan the aisles of milk, bananas, and candy.

"He's got to be here!" Steve mutters. *"Where is he?"*

Shut up, Steve! I'm looking, I'm looking.

I spot Walker trying on sunglasses near the ice cream novelty freezer. I come up behind him as he checks out his reflection in the mirror.

He groans. "Emma, don't you know when to leave a guy alone?"

"I guess not."

He removes the sunglasses from his bruised face. "I need some shades to cover this shiner I got because of you."

"I'm *so* sorry," I say. He looks awful. And, like everything else, it's my fault.

He shakes his head. "The weird thing is that it was the cleaning crew who beat me up. Of course, they deny ever touching me. It's like they were possessed or something. They claim they never even saw me."

"Possessed?" I shudder as the door rings again. "Then I guess I'm not the only one."

"You've got that problem, too?" He tries on another pair of sunglasses. "Why am I not surprised? Hey, is that what you were trying to tell me that night?"

I clear my throat. "Yeah. That was it."

Walker chuckles. "Mom told me to stay away from you. She thinks you're trouble."

"I'm afraid she's right." I press further. "But I'm so glad you're speaking to me again. I have to give you something." I dig in my fabric bag. "It's important."

He waves his hands at my bag. "It better not be something creepy, dead, or have anything at all to do with witchcraft. I've had enough of your freakiness."

"That's not fair," I argue. "You asked me to work those spells. You knew it was witchcraft."

"You should have told me what was happening to you. I would have stopped if I'd known." Charlie checks out my double reflection that quivers behind his in the shiny mirror. "Steve's here, too? Now *you're* the host body? This is getting all too weird for me."

The front door bell jangles again. Phoebe, Jake, and Laura spill in, and head in our direction.

I yank out Steve's letter. "Here's the information Steve dug up about Dominic, the gang member who killed him. Dominic's life was sacrificed by the Cobras a few days later. I know this sounds crazy, but somehow in the Afterlife, Steve beat enough info out of Dominic that you should be able to put the Cobras away for good."

I stuff the letter back in the envelope as the front door slams open, ringing the bell repeatedly, like a fake Santa at Christmas time.

The gas station turns ice cold.

The necklace sings a warning and my tattoo itches. I don't even need to turn around. I know who's here.

The Cobras. They found me.

I didn't run fast enough.

My heart sinks.

"The Cobras are here," I whisper. My hands tremble, and my body shudders.

Walker's sunglasses drop to the floor as he orders, "Emma, you get the Hell out of here."

"*No. It can't be. Not now,*" Steve whimpers in my head.

Three thugs cover the entrance, shooting out the lights and cameras. Breaking glass falls from the ceiling.

The cashier drops to the floor.

More gang members burst into the gas station. My arm burns as I stare at their Cobra tattoos. I reach for my bag as a hood charges me. He grabs my arm, twisting it behind my back.

"Let go of me!" I scream.

"Shut up, bitch," a deep voice growls in my ear. "They're over here!" he calls out.

The hoodlums flood our aisle. Walker's eyes bug as he reaches for the gun that isn't there. Two hoods spin him around and pin him over the ice cream freezer. They bind his arms together behind him.

Thugs surround us.

A sneering punk steps in front of me, holding out his hand for my stash of papers. "I'll take that."

"*You can't give it to him!*" Steve begs. "*Not after all I went through. Please, Emma.*"

"You can't have it," I say.

He slaps me. My eyes water, but I don't make a sound. My ears ring and buzz.

"Let's try this again," he growls. "Give me those fuckin' papers, bitch."

He rips them out of my hands. Steve shudders. These creeps already killed him once, and now they're threatening him again, this time trapped inside my body.

"*Help me,*" begs Steve. "*Emma, it's up to you now.*"

I struggle to focus.

I need to get to the beach, control the gang members' minds.

I close my eyes and open my mind.

WHOMP!

A harder blow to the face, and I fall to the floor, gasping.

"Don't try no mind games on me, witch," the thug warns.

I struggle to breathe. What am I going to do? They're going to kidnap me and kill everyone else in this place.

Something large and furious flashes by the front glass door.

An accompanying deep growl whispers, HELL HATH NO FURY LIKE AVENGING ANGELS. I LEFT THOSE SPIRITS WITHIN YOU FOR A REASON. IT'S TIME TO SET THEM FREE.

But how? I almost yell aloud, desperate for the answer.

The necklace crackles and hums like an old radio. *"Emma, can you hear me?"*

Grandma? Is that you? How many voices can be in my head at one time? This is crazy, not that I don't appreciate the help, of course.

"That's right. You better be good at following directions," she warns. *"Now, do everything I say. Let's kick some butt."*

I smile at the thug. "You better watch out. Grandma's pissed."

"You're one crazy bitch." He sneers.

Grandma gasps in my head. *"Nobody calls my granddaughter a bitch."*

The thug flies across the room and smashes against the far wall.

Muffled screams follow.

Wow. Grandma. You rock. I wish I was that strong.

"I've never understood that phrase," Grandma mutters.

Shots ring out across the store, sending another shower of sparks from the ceiling.

I have to keep my friends alive, even if one of them is a *Book* snatcher.

A short Cobra yells out, "He's dead."

"Leave him," another calls back.

"All the security cameras are down," reports another.

A tall thug nods. "We got five minutes. Enough time to take care of Mr. Nosy Cop."

Walker's nose is bleeding. A stocky thug holds him upright.

"We drove by your house that night your girlfriend tried to set the world on fire," the tall Cobra taunts. "Or didn't she tell you? Good thing she didn't succeed in killing herself. Master thinks she'd make a great personal slave."

"Leave her alone!" Jake snarls on my left. Two Cobras struggle to contain him.

"Ooh, I like him!" says Bertha.

But why'd he have to come in here? I fret. *Now I have to worry about protecting him, too.*

"Don't you know anything about love?" asks Bertha.

I hear a whimper and scan the store. Customers slump unconscious against the dairy cooler. Spilled milk streams across the floor.

One Cobra holds a gun to Laura's forehead.

Another presses a knife against Phoebe's throat.

Laura's pale face drips tears, while Phoebe glares defiantly at her captor. Her eyes catch mine and she stiffens.

The guy restraining Phoebe scowls. "You're not thinking of leaving, are you honey? The party's just getting started. I've got *special* plans for you, pretty girl."

One of his buddies laughs. "Better make it quick, T-Jay. You got three minutes, tops. But, knowing you, that's all you'll need."

"Disgusting!" Bertha mutters. *"Now get ready to move. You'll need your Book, even if it is inferior to mine."*

Since I fell on my right arm, my bag remains hidden beneath me. I creep my fingers into the bag. It takes forever to find the fabric cover.

Got it.

"Now stand up," she instructs.

I rise to my feet.

"Haven't had enough?" A Cobra sneers, stepping toward me.

"Aim the Book at him!" Bertha orders.

"Stand back!" I hold out my *Book* with unsteady hands. Blue light flashes from the cover. The approaching Cobra flies across the room instead, smashes into the milk freezer, and drops to the floor dead.

The other Cobras gasp. "What the Hell? What was that? That bitch is crazy!"

I will my shaking legs to still. *Now what?*

"Let the Book show you the way," Grandma directs from inside my head.

I open the cover. The pages flutter to a protection spell. I memorize it.

"Don't try to be a hero." The tall Cobra aims a gun at me. "Sit your ass down."

I smile sweetly. "Did someone say all the cameras are down?"

"Yes," he snaps. "Now sit!"

"That's good." Confidence floods my limbs. "Then no one will see how you're all going to die."

I hold out the *Book of Shadows*. An earthquake of power runs up my arms.

"We can't take her alive—just kill her now!" shrieks one of them. "Master can always bring her back."

I laugh then cough as blood drains into the back of my throat.

The punk's arms shake as he holds the gun. "Aren't you afraid of death, little girl?"

I cock my head to one side. "Been there, done that already."

"*Oh, good,*" says Grandma. "*You're a smart-ass. You did inherit something from me.*"

Blinding light flashes through the entire store. The Cobras raise their hands over their eyes. A thin whine hums in my ears. I raise the *Book of Shadows* and chant:

"Use those murdered to protect my friends

Protect them all until the end

I summon thee.

I summon thee."

I repeat my words until they blur together.

"Use those murdered!

Protect my friends!"

Gunshots ring out. Cigarette boxes crash upon the cash register.

Magazines, drink cups, and napkins fly through the air.

"Protect them all until the end!"

Oil cans swirl over our heads.

Energy surges through every molecule of my body.

"I summon thee!"

Something rips deep inside.

A flash of blond hair races by.

Jennifer, help me.

Long, dark hair fills my sight then dashes away.

Eva, protect my friends.

Cobras hurtle through the air, screaming in agony.

Glass shatters onto the floor.

"I summon thee!"

Another tearing from deep inside.

Blood dances within my veins.

A tattooed arm flashes in front of me.

"Holy shit! Dominic?" A Cobra's voice morphs into a howl of pain.

"I summon thee!"

The ripping inside me intensifies. Arms and legs being pulled out of their sockets.

I gulp air, trying to endure the pain.

"I summon thee!"

"You're all dead meat!" Steve hollers as he leaps away.

Cries of agony bounce off the walls.

With all the spirits gone, I stagger blindly, knocking down a metal rack behind me.

Shadow stands near the entrance, gun raised in the air, pointed directly at me.

The gunshot echoes across the room.

I clench the *Book of Shadows* as a bullet pierces its center.

The air sparks with the energy of a sudden pressure change.

The glass doors of the frozen food section heave and shudder until they blow apart.

The *Book* explodes in a shower of shredded paper.

The whole world turns blood red as a volcano erupts within my head.

I sob, clenching the mangled book with my trembling hands.

Writhing in pain, I scream as the world shifts from red to black.

CHAPTER FORTY-FOUR

THE REAPER

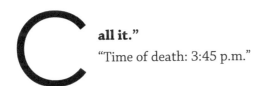 **all it.**"

"Time of death: 3:45 p.m."

CHAPTER FORTY-FIVE

INTO THE WOODS

Sunlight filters through the leafy canopy. Ripe raspberries line the worn dirt path, deep in the woods near my childhood home. Birds sing and leaves rustle. Stepping out from under the heavy shade, I approach the dry, dusty sledding hills that bake in the summer sun.

A man waits at the bottom, wearing a blue short-sleeved shirt.

"Dad? Dad!" I race down the steep decline, a shower of sand cascading before me.

"Emma?" He smiles, his face tanned and healthy, as I reach his side. "Thank goodness I found you. Your mother was worried."

"How did you get so tall?" My head only reaches to his waistline.

"We need to hurry." He grabs my hand and pulls me down the path. "I *know* you didn't practice much this week, but you still have to go to your lessons."

"Dad, what are you talking about? I stopped taking piano back in high school."

His eyes crinkle. "You must face the music, as it were."

Sunlight blinds me. Again I find myself in the woods among the raspberries, long past their season. Trees flash past as I rush toward the sledding hill, zipping up my jacket to block out the crisp breeze. My steps crunch on crunchy, fall leaves until I reach the brink of the sandy hill.

There he is again, huddled in a navy blue windbreaker.

"Dad! I'm here." I race down the hill.

This time he doesn't seem so tall. "Emma, you're too old to fight like this with your mother and then run off into the woods for hours. You're upsetting her."

This is getting weird, but I'll play along this time. "How come *we* never fight, Dad?"

He smiles. "Because we're alike. Mom's different. She's special. You and I, we're peas in a pod, and you don't even like peas."

Sunlight flashes in my eyes and, once again, I'm hiking the wooded trail. Heart pounding, I race to the sledding hill, slipping on the snow and ice. Once I reach the crest, I pause to catch my breath. Dad faces away from me, this time wearing only a hospital robe that swallows his thin form. His hand pats his neck, as if searching for something.

"Dad! I'm here!" I run, almost tumbling down the hill in my hurry to reach him.

He faces me, eyes wide and confused. "Honey, where's my necklace?"

"I'm wearing it." I pull it out from under my T-shirt.

He smiles, but weakly, as if it takes some effort. "Oh, good. I wanted you to have it. It's your grandmother's. You'll need her help."

I place a hand on his icy arm. "You're freezing. We should get inside."

His eyes search the snow-tipped evergreens lining the embankments on both sides of the sledding hill. "No. I'm waiting for someone. Your friend Steve was here earlier, but he got chased off."

"Chased by who?"

His eyes scan the tree line. "I'm not sure. It looked like an enormous dog, but its eyes were human."

"Dad. I think that was God."

His eyes widen. "That's why It winked at me. I always knew God had a sense of humor. Oh, look, there's Steve now."

I spin around to search where he's pointing. A faded, flowered dress flits in between the trees.

"That's not Steve. That's Grandmother. Can't you tell?"

He squints. "Oh. You're right."

As she approaches, Bertha's tangled gray hair lengthens and darkens to black. Her dress flutters in the cold breeze until a deep purple gown takes its place. Over her neck hang two necklaces, both identical to mine.

Dad's face brightens, despite its pallor. "I missed you, Mom."

She lifts one of the necklaces over her head and places it around my father's neck. He takes a deep breath and his face flushes with color. In seconds, a jacket and jeans replace his hospital robe. He gulps deep breaths.

Grandma turns to me. "I'll be seeing you again soon, I'm afraid."

Crows cackle in the distance.

"Why?" I ask her. "Are we still in trouble?"

She laughs. "No. I've been forgiven for saving my son. Now that he's passed on the necklace, the balance of nature has been restored. But that was a small problem, only affecting me. There are much worse things out there to worry about."

The cawing birds swarm closer. A whole flock circles overhead, screaming their jarring song.

Bertha watches the crows swirl and dip in the sky. "The Cobras still want you, my dear. They lust for your *Book* and the power you have when you use it. What you battled at the gas station was only the tip of the iceberg. They'll keep coming back for you. No... Wait a minute..."

Moving as one, the whole group swoops down once more before tearing away, screaming in unison.

"They're leaving." I watch until they're no longer even black dots in the sky.

"Something's changed. They're not after you anymore." Grandma grabs my shoulders and stares deep into my eyes. "You'll have to go after *them* instead."

"What?" I back away. "Why would I do that?"

Grandma points at my necklace. *"Never* take that off. You need all the protection you can get. Your Dad and I have to go now. But I'll be back. I promise. And in the mean time, you should clean out John's study."

She lets go of my arm and walks away, my father at her side.

"Dad's study? But it's locked," I call after them.

"Then find the key." Her words float back to me as both of them disappear.

I'm alone again with only the trees for company.

The necklace warms my neck and chest, glowing pink and purple. Like a burner on an unchecked stove, the heat builds. I claw at the necklace as it sends electric shocks directly into my heart.

My chest fills with explosions.

"CLEAR!"

CHAPTER FORTY-SIX

OBITUARY

P age three of the Leader-Telegram Newspaper:

John Roberts, 58, passed away Friday at Sacred Heart Hospital, in Eau Claire, Wisconsin. At the age of 24, he opened the first Roberts' Lumber and Hardware store, which became a nationwide chain.

Survivors include his wife (Cheryl) and daughter (Emma).

Funeral services will be held at 11 a.m. Wednesday at St. Olaf's parish, with Father Joseph O'Malley presiding. Friends and family may call one hour prior to the service.

In lieu of flowers, please send donations to M.A.G. (Mothers Against Gangs).

CHAPTER FORTY-SEVEN

LOCAL POLICEMAN SAVES TWELVE LIVES

Front page of Leader-Telegram Newspaper:

Eau Claire policeman Officer Charlie Walker has been credited with saving the lives of twelve people Friday afternoon at a gas station shootout. Although unarmed and outnumbered, Walker managed to disarm members of the notorious Chicago Cobra gang, thought to be in the area due to his "Smiley Face" murder investigation. Eight gang members were killed during the confrontation. At least one escaped.

The cashier, name withheld, was shot and killed. Several others suffered concussions and were treated at the hospital. Most were released within 24 hours. Four remained at the hospital overnight before discharge. One remains in critical condition.

Phoebe Swift, one of the survivors, spoke at length of the incident. "Charlie saved us all. He was amazing. He must study karate or maybe kick-boxing. The way he jumped around, it looked just like a Jackie Chan movie."

In response to questions, Charlie Walker claimed that "it was all a blur" and he has "no further comments."

CHAPTER FORTY-EIGHT

MORPHINE HAZE

swirl my hand in the Chippewa River, but my fingers remain dry. I keep plunging my hand in and out, but can't feel the water. "C.S. Lewis, *The Lion, The Witch, and the Wardrobe,* page one..."

I spin around to find Father Joe sitting on Putnam Rock. In his hands rests the children's book I've read more times than any other. Over and over again I disappeared into the wardrobe, wishing I never had to come out.

"Your mother says it's your favorite." Father Joe clears his throat. "I hope she's right and didn't just choose this because it seemed 'church-appropriate.'"

"Father, what are we doing here?" I ask.

His eyes never leave the page. "Emma, I have to tell you how sorry I am. I failed to protect you from the demons. Just look at what they've done to you."

"Don't worry. The spirits are gone." I stand up to show him, but he doesn't seem to notice. "See? I'm fine now."

He looks right through me. "I didn't finish the job I was trained to do."

I step right in front of him but he doesn't react. "Can't you hear me?" I ask, waving my arms.

He sighs, rubbing his forehead. "But I didn't come here to wallow. I came to read. They say that you can hear me. Here we go..."

By the third page, I grow sleepy. I want to sit down and rest my head on his shoulder.

Instead I step into the wardrobe.

The wind whips my hair as I stand on the bridge. The Chippewa River rushes past, always in a hurry.

"Emma, you can't just leave me." Jake leans on the bridge railing, his shoulders slumped.

"Jake!" I run to him.

He never even looks at me. "Not when I'm back, maybe for good. I couldn't bear it if you went on without me."

"Jake, I'm right here—look at me!" I scream.

"And I don't know what to do about Laura. She's missing. She disappeared after the gas station and I can't find her anywhere. I need your help. Please wake up."

I grab at his arm but my hand sails right through him.

Jake sighs. "I'm guessing Steve's gone now because you look like yourself again. That asshole. He deserves whatever he gets."

I jump up and down, hollering. "Why can't anyone *see* me?"

"Did you know that my dog, Nani, died? Compared to everything else, maybe that's not important, but, I swear, she was the best dog ever... Damn it, I wish you'd wake up."

I stamp my foot. "And I wish you'd notice that I'm standing *right* here."

The river glows orange, mirroring the fiery sunset. My mother hovers on the same spot Mike and I entered the river almost one year before

She wrings her hands. "I'm trying to stay positive, but it's not easy. I'm supposed to be your cheerleader, encouraging you to come back, but it's hard for me to pretend that what I say will matter."

I try to touch her shoulder, but my hand slips right through.

"You'll either come back to me or not." Mom lets out a short sob. "It's not up to me to decide. If it were, both you and your father would be on a boat with me sailing somewhere in the Caribbean and we'd never come back."

She stares at the rushing water, tears streaming down her face.

I start to cry, too, and I *hate* crying. "Please stop, Mom. Don't say anymore. I can't take it."

She clears her throat. "I'm sorry you missed your dad's funeral. I know you would've wanted to be there. He loved you so much that he couldn't bear for you to see him at the end. I love you too, honey. I know we argue, but..."

I close my eyes to block out the pain, but my ears still hear every word.

"Your friends helped with the funeral. Officer Walker was a pallbearer. He looks rough, but he's healing. His family's been wonderful ever since you got hurt. His mother's a fabulous cook. I'm afraid it's bad for my figure."

My jaw drops. "Mother Walker invited you to dinner? I hope you finished your peas." I know she doesn't hear me, but that doesn't stop me from trying.

"We had the funeral here in town so I could stay close to you. My friend Susan sang *Nothing Compares to You*. You know how Dad always liked that song."

"I hope she didn't dress like Madonna."

"I'm sure some people thought it inappropriate, you know, a Sinead O'Connor song in a Catholic funeral, but Father Joe said he'd allow it. He's such a nice priest." She delicately blows her nose into a tissue. "Oh, Emma, why won't you wake up? Things are too hard here without you."

Mom steps into the river.

"Don't go in there!" I holler, my feet sinking into the mud. I'm stuck. I can't move. I struggle until a giant wave washes ashore and drags me out into the rushing river. I thrash and claw for the surface, growing ever more tired.

Finally, I quit fighting and let the river have what it has always wanted. Me.

CHAPTER FORTY-NINE

CHARLIE WALKER RETURNS

Through half-open eyelids, I watch dust particles sparkle in the sunlight. I can't see Walker but I can hear him.

"Cheryl, you look exhausted," he says. "How're you holding up?"

Mom sighs. "I'm so sick of this hospital."

What hospital? I turn toward the sound of my mom's voice. Sunlight blinds me.

Mom's voice sounds hopeful, but forced. "As you can see, she's finally showing some signs of life."

Am I dead again? Ooh, look at those pretty sparkles.

Walker's footsteps come closer. "Has she said anything yet?"

"Not really." Mom sighs. "She mumbles sometimes. I can't make out a word she says."

"She'll snap out of it. Emma's a fighter."

"I hope you're right." Her chair squeaks. "Now that you're here, I think I'll take a short break, if you don't mind. I need some air."

"Take as much time as you need," he offers. "I'll sit with her."

The door clicks shut. A chair scrapes across the floor.

"Hey, Emma. It's Walker, recently hired as your mama's bodyguard. You'll be happy to know I make twice as much money as before, and even though I didn't move home my mom's thrilled with the raise. She likes your mother, actually. And she's worried about you. Everyone is."

Sparkles. Pretty sparkles of light. There's magic in the air.

"Listen. You better wake up soon. If I have to hear that crazy friend of your mother's sing *Wind Beneath My Wings* at your bedside one more time, I'll have to shoot either myself or her. Which one do you suggest?"

So many pretty colors. Just beautiful.

"I'm sure you don't want to wake up. This is probably the most peace you've had all year. But you're taking too long. Getting lazy. Father Joe thinks you don't have a good enough reason to wake up."

"Why don't we see if he's right?" The chair scrapes closer. "I was going to wait until you came around to tell you this, but..."

Machines beep. The smell of sanitizer. My arm brushes against cool steel.

But what?

"I hope you're ready for this..."

For what?

Walker's breath warms my cheek as he whispers in my ear, "Laura has your *Book* again."

My legs are stuck, entwined in the rough sheets. I struggle to escape. The beeping gets faster.

"Emma, can you hear me?" Walker's voice gets louder. "Laura has your *Book of Shadows*. It's hers now."

My Book. Mine. I kick my feet to loosen the sheets. Blindly, I tug at the tubes in my arms.

Something blocks the pretty sparkles. A shadow.

His shadow.

"Walker?" I whisper.

"Emma?" He squeezes my hand. "Do you want me to get your mom? She left a second ago."

"No." The room spins. What's real? What's a dream? Where's my *Book?*

Wait a minute. I've been here before. In this room. With him.

I tremble. "Are you here to tell me that Mike drowned?"

"No." He pats my arm. "That was a long time ago. Do you remember what happened *afterwards?*"

Waves roar in my head. Bodies float down the river. Sam and Jake and Mike and Bernard and Steve. That horrible Smiley Face staring down at me from the oak tree. The creepy church ladies and the black crows.

My voice croaks. "It was bad, wasn't it?"

"Yeah, I'm afraid so."

Where is it? I search under the sheets with my free hand, not entirely sure what I'm looking for. My vision blurs every time I move.

"Emma, are you looking for your *Book?*" he asks.

"Yes." I force myself to focus on his face. "Where is it?"

Walker holds my gaze. "Laura Cunningham, Jake's sister, took it again."

"Wait!" Memories of the gas station come roaring back. "That can't be true. It was destroyed. This time for real. I saw it. Shadow shot it."

"Listen to me closely. After you passed out, pages swirled around the room and came flapping toward you like a flock of crows. Somehow the *Book* melded back together. It was freaky. And I've seen freaky before. I know *you*, remember?"

I slowly nod.

"That's when Laura snatched it from under your arm and raced out of the store." Walker clears his throat. "Shadow escaped, too, unfortunately."

I struggle to sit up straight. "Why didn't you stop them?"

"Emma, what do you expect? I had a concussion, two broken ribs, and my arms tied behind me. There wasn't much I could do. Thank God Jake undid the bindings before the other cops arrived, or I would've been a laughingstock. Instead I'm some freakin' hero because of that crazy Phoebe."

"Phoebe?" My vision goes wonky again. "Is she okay?"

The sparkling lights take over again then vanish, leaving me alone on the dirt road leading up to the Smiley Face tree. Except now there are hundreds of evil faces painted on the tree trunks, all sneering at me.

Laura crouches near the base of a tree, encircled with red candles. Her tattooed arm glows in the candlelight. Dirty tears streak down her pale face. She clenches the *Book of Shadows* to her chest.

My *Book*. Mine.

My stomach drops as Shadow approaches. He grabs Laura's arm and drags her away, her legs splayed out across the dirt behind her.

Her screams float back to me on the night wind, "No! Somebody help me!"

The trees slip out of view.

My heart races and I want to scream.

This isn't over. It will never be over.

The hospital room comes back into view. I need to focus. Taking deep breaths, my gaze catches on the sparkles in the sunlight. I fight against the fuzziness trying to take over my brain. Don't let the drugs win. Ignore the sparkles. The sparkles don't matter. So many things don't matter.

But some do.

Metal clangs as the bed begins to shake.

My voice trembles. "I did everything I could, and they still won."

"Emma, can you hear me?" Walker's blurry face hovers nearby. "You're okay now. There's nothing to fear. We'll help Jake find Laura and get your *Book* back. And the Cobras didn't win—you did. The battle's over."

I sit up. My vision clears.

I turn to Walker. "Trust me. The battle has only just begun."

ACKNOWLEDGMENTS

As a responsible author, this is where I should go on for approximately two pages thanking all the other writers, cover artists, beta readers, etc. who helped this book come to life.

I'm not going to do that. Not that I don't appreciate everyone, but my Mom died the day after Christmas and I'd like to acknowledge all she did for me instead. She read Laura Ingalls Wilder books to me at bedtime. She brought me to the library so often I ran out of new books to read (at least age appropriate ones, but that's another story). I miss arguing with her about how I should stop wearing black all the time and should wear a nice, collared, buttoned-down white shirt instead. I wonder at her ability to frost cookies so flawlessly, get just the right crispness to chicken, and wrap presents without fighting with the tape. I miss watching *Little Women* together, shopping at the mall as a team, and watching Mom hug my children so tight they squirmed to get away.

I've been missing her for five years, but only now am I allowed to officially grieve.

I'd also like to thank all those (both in the writing community and my family and friends) who have listened to my lamentations all these years. Thanks for easing my pain. You have no idea how very much your kind words have helped me stay afloat.

My advice: love your family while you can, because once they're gone it's hard to know if they can really hear you anymore.

ABOUT THE AUTHOR

My to-do list dictates that I attempt to cram forty-eight hours of living into a day instead of the usual twenty-four. I've chosen a life filled with animals. I train for ultra-marathons with my dog, then go to work as a small animal veterinarian, and finish the day by tripping over my pets as I attempt to convince my two unruly children that YES, it really IS time for bed. But I can't wait until the house is quiet to write; I have to steal moments throughout the day.

Like all busy American mothers, I multi-task. I work out plot holes during runs. Instead of meditating, I type madly during yoga stretches. I find inspiration in everyday things: a beautiful smile, a heartbreaking song, or a newspaper article on a political theory. For example, a long drive in the dark listening to an NPR program on the Smiley Face Murder Theory made me ask so many questions that I wrote *HOW TO DATE DEAD GUYS* to answer them to my satisfaction.

I'd love to have more time to write (and run, read, and sleep), but until I find Hermione Granger's time turner, I will juggle real life with the half-written stories in my head. Main characters and plot lines intertwine in my cranium, and I need to let my writing weave the tales on paper so I can find out what happens next.

THANK YOU FOR READING

Please visit http://curiosityquills.com/reader-survey to share your reading experience with the author of this book!

Of Scions and Men, by Courtney Sloan

Scion Rowan Brady has sold her life, her career and her very blood to the controlling paranormal ruling class of America, all to make sure her kid brother can eat. But juggling her job and duties becomes even tougher when tasked with keeping a contingency of diplomats from getting gnawed on. However, geopolitical babysitting is interrupted by a supernatural serial killer. Now Rowan must rely on her talent and wit to defend the society she despises. As she stumbles into the truth, she becomes the target of not only the killers, but of her own government.

The Dead Detective, by J.R. Rain & Rod Kierkegaard, Jr.

Medical-school-dropout police detective Richelle Dadd is... well, dead. But that won't stop her from trying to hold on to her house in a divorce battle with a bitter husband. Or keep her from digging into her own murder, to discover who put the bullet into her heart. And it certainly won't stand in the way of finding out the reason she's been reanimated as a zombie assassin. Richelle will face off against Gypsy shamans, double-crossing ghosts, a partner she can't trust, and her own undead nature in a journey into the depths of the occult world.

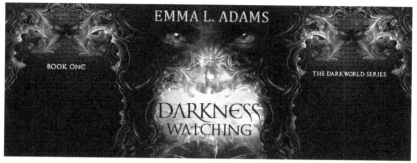

Darkness Watching, by Emma Adams

Eighteen-year-old Ashlyn is one interview away from her future when she first sees the demons. She thinks she's losing her mind, but the truth is far more frightening: she can see into the Darkworld, the home of spirits– and the darkness is staring back. At her new university in the small English village of Blackstone, she meets a hidden group of sorcerers and, for the first time, finds a place where she belongs. But her new life turns dark when she's targeted by a killer. The demons want something from her, and not everyone is what they appear to be…

Fade, by A.K. Morgen

When Arionna Jacobs and Dace Matthews meet, everything they thought they knew about life begins to unravel. Neither understands the frightening things occurring around them, and they're running out of time to figure out what it all means. An ancient Norse prophesy of destruction has been set in motion, and what destiny has in store for them is bigger than either could have ever imagined.

CPSIA information can be obtained
at www.ICGtesting.com
Printed in the USA
BVHW04s2019290518
517560BV00034B/643/P